ALSO BY KRIS MICHAELS

THE KINGS OF GUARDIAN:

Jacob

Joseph

Adam

Jason

Jared

Jasmine

Chief

Jewell

EVERLIGHT SERIES:

An Evidence of Magic

An Incident of Magic

STAND ALONE:

A Heart's Desire

JOSEPH

KINGS OF GUARDIAN

BOOK TWO

Copyright © 2015 Kris Michaels

Cover Art: Digitally Imagined

www.digitallyimagined.com

Formatting by: Digitally Imagined

www.digitallyimagined.com

978-1-947178-12-0

JOSEPH

KINGS OF GUARDIAN SERIES
BY
KRIS MICHAELS

PRINT EDITION 2017

Ember Harris has sworn to save lives. Joseph King is an assassin. Death is their common ground, only they stand on opposing sides.

Thrown together they find that in life, like death, everyone needs a Guardian.

A dead man's plea pushes Dr. Ember Harris headfirst into a swirling mire of drugs, death and political corruption. The Cartel boss who murdered Ember's friend will stop at nothing to get the information entrusted to her. After all, finding and killing a mere woman in order to claim the evidence should be easy. A matter of a contract, time and money. Terrified, alone and on the run, Ember reaches out to the only person she knows she can trust.

Joseph King is an assassin. He'd just unpacked his bag from an assignment he probably shouldn't have survived. A life such as his comes with an expiration date. Sooner or later your competition or your target will get lucky. Out of spare lives, Joseph knows it is time to hang it up and walk away while he still can. Best laid plans, right? One phone call from the only woman he'd ever cared about successfully sidelines his disappearing act. Protecting Em will be his last mission. This time he'll risk anything, including his life, to keep her safe. For her, he'd stroll through the sin-stoked fires of hell and gut the devil himself.

CHAPTER ONE

JOSEPH'S MUSCLES CLENCHED, CONVULSING AGAINST THE RELENTLESS ATTACK. He couldn't take much more. The searing agony following the whip's sickening snap burned white-hot against his back, shoulders and ribs. Its unrelenting tentacles wrapped around his ribcage, wire barbs viciously rupturing skin from muscle. Blood ran down his body in small streams merging into tributaries of crimson. A pool of his own blood formed at his feet.

From the damage inflicted, he knew his window for escape had narrowed, but he still had a chance. The extremist group had made a mistake. They'd underestimated him; carried into the underground room unconscious, his captors had only secured his hands around the post. His legs remained free. Fools. There were no less than five weapons within reach if he could just manage to free one hand. However, time moved in the enemy's favor, no longer his asset.

Soon he would be too weak to fight, too weak to escape, too weak to kill the slimy bastard behind him with a whip. Blood traveled down his arms soaking the ropes that held him to the post. Every time the whip ripped through his flesh, he pulled with all his strength working the lines to loosen and stretch the hemp, sliding his hand ever closer to release.

The man wielding the whip paused before he growled, "Filthy Assassin! I would kill you now, but you're to be alive when you're beheaded in public tonight. They did not say you had to be in one piece!" The vicious taunt echoed around the small cell.

Joseph hunched against the post for support drawing hot, putrid air into his lungs. He fought the pain and stench induced nausea. The ropes biting into his hands had moved more readily the last time he pulled. He leaned into the wooden stake. His eyes focused on his sweat and blood as it co-mingled, saturating his bonds. The distinct sound of the whip slapping the ground brought Joseph's attention back to his sole enemy in the room. His left hand would pull free on the next lash. He swept a covert glance to the weapons he could reach. A hammer and thin wood shims lay on the table at his ten o'clock position. A sneer ghosted across his face. God he would love to pound those slivers of wood under the bastard's nail beds. To the left of the hammer on the same tray lay a surgical knife and a metal spreader. Castration. Not today you bastard. Seize the scalpel first, then the hammer.

A deafening crack split across the room at the same time as the skin covering his shoulder and ribs seemed to be torn from his body. He couldn't prevent his wrenching scream. His body convulsed in pain and his hand erupted from the binding. In one short lunge, he grasped blindly for the scalpel. His hand was numb, his body on fire. Instinct and training took over. Pivot! Aim—throw.

The man holding the whip froze in mid-swing, stopping with the cat o' nine tails over his shoulder. Joseph dropped to a crouch to catch the blood-soaked strands should they strike at him again. The man fell heavily to his knees. The scalpel had missed its mark. Instead of lodging in the man's eye, the metal had somehow flattened in flight, spinning into the man's neck.

Blood spurted in hematic spews from the severed carotid artery. The man was dead. Physiology 101: Six seconds without blood killed the brain. The asshole's body just hadn't gotten the message yet. Crimson foam bubbled from his mouth as it opened and closed gaping like a fish out of water, and then he fell to the ground. Joseph stretched out and grabbed the hammer. Using the claw, he pried his right hand free from the rope.

He had to get out. Clothes. The filthy robes of his tormentor hung on the wall, abandoned when the bastard got too hot. The layers of coarse material would prevent the blood from showing too quickly. Using the man's keffiyeh, he wrapped his head, hiding his face, and ducked out of the cell.

There was no one in the hall. His body moved awkwardly as he pushed through the pain of his escape. Adrenaline surged through his system giving him the ability to propel himself across the basement and up the stairway. Hitting the door at the end of the passage, he ran through the narrow hallway into the kitchen.

An elderly woman lifted from her task of flattening disks of dough to look at him. The keffiyeh slipped showing his face. Shouts from behind him seemed to push the woman into action. She gestured wildly with her hands for Joseph to follow and God only knows why, but he did. Opening a pantry curtain, she kicked a camel hair mat to the side and pointed to the floor. A small trap door underneath the mat was exposed. The woman darted back out of the pantry and pulled the draped material closed behind her.

Every movement pushed unfathomable pain through his body, yet he moved. If he didn't, he would die. He lifted the trap door and with numb hands clumsily attempted to position the mat over the top. When the door closed, the rug would conceal the small door. He hoped. The crawl space below was barely big enough for him to curl up and lie down in. The darkness smelled of mildew and earth, but it was cool and dark and, for a moment, safe. Minutes passed or perhaps hours, the complete darkness disrupted his sense of time. Vaguely, Joseph heard the angry shouts of men and the sounds of people moving above.

How much time had elapsed? The room above was quiet now. Slow steps and the smell of cooking food settled around him. The delicious aroma pulled wildly at his memories. Memories of home and of comfort. His body shook violently, so much so his teeth chattered. The pain and blood loss forced his body to do what his mind desperately needed to prevent. Oblivion consumed him.

EXHAUSTION SPREAD THROUGH EVERY FIBER OF DR. EMBER Harris's body as she drove around the block for the third time looking for a parking spot. And once again, she was late for her date with Dale. That seemed to be the story of her life. Small wonder their relationship hadn't prospered.

Her twelve-hour shift turned into fifteen because of a multi-vehicle accident on the New Orleans I-10. The ambulances arrived at the trauma center just before shift change. The last three hours drained her physically and emotionally. Despite her team's best efforts, the two children mangled in the collision died. The parents, rushed by her staff into surgery, probably wouldn't make it. Ember was the one to make the trek to find the grandparents and tell them the grim news.

She pulled the grief-stricken couple from the emergency room waiting area into a side room. You learned as a doctor to give the news directly and as compassionately as possible. Never tell a patient's family they're gone, had left or passed. Confusion, hope, and denial played cruel and bitter tricks with a desperate person's mind.

"Mr. and Mrs. Murphy, I'm sorry to tell you both Kyle and Mandy died as a result of the injuries they received during the accident." The grandmother's shattered wail and the old man's tears tore at her heart.

Ember continued as she gently touched the thin hunched shoulder of the grandfather. Looking into his eyes, she said the same thing she always said when delivering the worst imaginable news. "My staff and I did absolutely everything humanly possible to save them. Their injuries were just too severe."

The old man held his small fragile wife tenderly. "Did they suffer?" The grief in his voice begged her to answer the question in a way he could accept. Ember closed her eyes and shook her head.

"No and they're at peace now." As a doctor, she didn't condone lies and deception but what good would it do for them to know? Of course, she wouldn't tell them the little girl remained conscious during the excruciating extraction from the vehicle. Nor would she say the terrified little boy had begged for his parents as they triaged him before his heart stopped for a second and last time. No, some things are best unknown. Ember arranged to have a ward nurse take them to the surgical waiting area and prayed the parents would be strong enough to pull through.

The tragic accident and her conversation with the grandparents would be a bitter memory that would forever define her parting recollection of three long years at the hospital. In a cruel twist, the drunk who crossed the median and drove into the family at ninety miles an hour would be fine. Ember personally oversaw the collection and processing of his blood sample.

"Pull the check sheet on this one Tammy. We're doing it by the numbers. There's no way I'm letting some bloodsucking lawyer get this guy off because of a collection error on the part of the hospital staff."

"I understand Dr. Harris. It's so tragic. The entire family... I've established the chain of custody and believe me this is one sample that is going to be pristine when it goes to court." The lab tech's pen inked her initials, date and time onto the evidence tag after she sealed it.

Ember shook her head as if the physical act would clear the memories. She fell into stride with the trauma room's head nurse and started the normal rundown. "Gloria, make sure Dr. Rawlings gets the neuro consult on bed three. Dr. Sebastian needs to ensure the elderly woman in exam five is tested for Lewy Body Dementia. The tactile hallucinations indicate more than Parkinson's."

"You know, I do have a medical degree. You don't need to ensure I do anything," a deep voice boomed from behind the two women.

Ember jumped and pivoted. Dr. Sebastian glared down his rather large nose at her. Intimidation was his first line of defense and he had his doctorate degree in that skill.

"Really? Forgive me for ensuring my patients are looked after." Ember responded.

"You're here to triage and push them through to the specialties, not be the whole damn hospital. If I had a dime for every time you intentionally showed me up with your superhuman medical knowledge, I could retire and leave them all to you."

"Well, it's a damn good thing I'm leaving, isn't it? Wouldn't want my habit of being right to interfere with your career."

"It's a personality flaw, you know." He fell in beside her when she attempted to storm away. His longer legs easily kept up with her smaller strides.

"What? That I'm right or that you're an ass?"

His surprised bark of laughter turned several heads. "When you've had a stressful shift you revert to what you know and start rattling off volumes of medical terminology. That's how you isolate yourself from the pain that surrounds you. We all have our coping mechanisms. That's yours."

"Well, this is the last time you get to see it. I was done as of three hours ago."

"We're going to miss you around here. Even the medical lessons."

"You'll live. Hopefully, your patients will too." She slung her bag over her shoulder and hit the crash bar on the door.

Those memories faded as Em whipped her SUV into an opening slot on the street near the busy French Quarter restaurant. She took a moment to gather herself. A deep breath filled her lungs in a seemingly futile attempt to calm the shaking of her hands. Undoubtedly, the shakes were her system's way of revolting against her steady diet of black coffee, Red Bull, and vending machine food. She'd been living on nothing but caffeine and stress for the last week.

Ember's head dropped back against the head rest and she looked at the restaurant. Dale Landis, a lawyer she had occasionally dated, waited for her inside. Pulling her thick sweater tighter around her scrubs, she tried to compose herself. She patted a stray hair back checking to make sure her abundance of red curls were still tightly wrapped in the braided bun she'd forced her hair into for work. With a resigned sigh, she left her vehicle and walked to the entrance.

Ember waited just inside the door until her eyes adjusted to the dim light of the bar and grill. The hostess led her to a corner table where Dale waited.

"Well, if it isn't God's gift to medicine! So glad you could grace me with your omnipotent presence!"

Ember sat down and looked at the handsome man across the table. "Shit. You're drunk and yes, I'm late…again."

He chuckled and toasted her with his glass before downing the drink. "Damn straight I'm drunk."

"Yeah and what are you celebrating tonight?"

He leaned forward slightly in the chair. "This is not a celebratory binge, sweetheart."

Ember flagged down the waitress and asked for the menu. "Why did you want to meet me tonight? I'm leaving in a couple days. I told you that." The waitress hovered near the table, and Ember waved her over. She ordered as Dale waved his glass for another drink. The day after tomorrow she was leaving New Orleans, probably for good. When her contract with the hospital came up for renegotiation two months ago, Ember decided not to renew. She wanted more, more than the ever present adrenaline rush, more than the constant work. She wanted a life, a relationship and maybe someday a family. She hadn't had any time off since she started college. Four years of undergraduate work with a double major in Chemistry and Biology set the pace early. A follow on to medical school and her emergency medicine residency in Los Angeles all flowed seamlessly into her accepting a job at New Orleans' premier trauma center. She had plenty of money. Her mom's life insurance had paid for medical school, and scholarships paid for her undergraduate.

Dale leaned across the table taking her hand in his. He palmed a small object into her hand but gripped it to stop her from looking at it. He whispered without a trace of slurred speech, "This is why I had to see you. I need you to hold onto this for me. Take it with you when you go. Nobody can know you have it."

"Why? What is it?" Ember's tired body tensed.

He grinned and laughed drunkenly waiting until the approaching waitress delivered his whiskey. When the server left, his face grew grave again. Tapping her closed hand lightly, he lowered his voice, his demeanor completely serious and sober. "Ember take this with you to wherever you're going. The information on that thumb drive is evidence. I'm in some pretty deep shit at work. I don't want to involve you, but you were the only person I knew I could trust and the only one who was leaving the area legitimately. No red flags when you drive away."

"Dale, what are you talking about? Are you in danger? Have you gone to the police?"

He scanned the room. "I can't go to the police or the courts. They're involved and this situation is significant. My law firm had me doing forensics accounting research. One thing led to another and after months of digging and a lot of clandestine and unauthorized investigations I ended up with the information on that drive. I may just be overly cautious, Emmy, but if something happens to me, if I suddenly end up missing or dead? Get that information to someone out of this state. Find someone who has the power to make people listen. You can't give it to anyone in the state of Louisiana. Take it national. A major network reporter or maybe the FBI."

"Wait... what? Dale, you're scaring me. What are you mixed up in?"

His eyes warmed and he smiled softly. "Hopefully nothing, probably enough to get me disbarred and maybe, just maybe, enough to piss off some really powerful people. But now you need to do me one last favor."

Ember put her hand in her sweater pocket and dropped the thumb drive. "Really? All this drama and a favor too?" Could the day get any worse?

"Yeah, honey. I need you to stand up, slap my face and call me a bastard. Anyone who's in here has to infer that we are not parting as friends. I don't want anyone to get the idea I would give you anything to hold onto. Get out of here and don't contact me. I'll find you if I need that drive or if things turn out to be nothing."

"Dale, you know I won't do that and I don't like this. Seriously, you're scaring me. Let's just go and find someone to help."

He shook his head and leaned back in the chair, slipping into his drunken act once again. "Nope!" He chugged his drink as she watched.

With the gusto of a drunkard declaring a known fact to the world, he shouted, "What? You're leaving me? Woman, how in the hell do you think you can do better than me? Is he all that? Can your new man even afford you? Shit, just get the fuck away from me and stay away. Why are you still here? Are you deaf?"

Ember's narrowed her eyes at him before she whispered, "Dale, don't do this, please."

He laughed viciously. "Get lost, I don't need or want your pity. Go screw your new man."

Ember stood, her body shaking, whether from the gravity of Dale's situation or the physical demands of the last week, she didn't know and didn't care. "Dale, please. Stop this now."

"Get out of here! If I never see you again, it will be too soon! Fucking bitch…"

Ember shook her head slowly as he motioned to the waitress for another drink. That he was trying to protect her from his unseen menaces was obvious. "Alright if that is the way you want it, goodbye Dale." She turned and walked out of the restaurant while everyone in the crowded establishment watched her.

On autopilot, Ember drove to her apartment complex and waved at the night security guard. She walked through the foyer into the elevator heading to the fourth floor and her second to last night in her apartment. The living room was vacant except for a few boxes. Each had been labeled, packed, taped and were ready for the storage company to come get them in preparation of her upcoming hiatus.

Hiatus, experience, vacation. Whatever she called it, the goal—no stress. Lost in rebellious desire, she longed to drive leisurely across the country and see everything. Stand on the edge of the Grand Canyon, climb the Rockies, drive over Hoover Dam, swim in the Florida Keys, and travel to the Northeast in the Fall to see the leaves turning.

However, all of her plans of fun and adventure seemed to crash and shatter around her feet tonight when Dale had given her this stupid thumb drive. She stood in the living room and looked at the small object in her hand. The callous seriousness of life seemed to intrude rudely into her headlong attempt to run away from it.

"Damn it, Dale, what have you gotten yourself into?" Her voice echoed in the darkness of the nearly empty room. Ember closed her eyes and said a silent prayer for him. Walking into the bedroom, she dropped the drive onto her nightstand, pulled off her clothes and let her hair down as she walked toward the shower.

Dale loved the drama in his job and seemed to be drawn to intense situations and activities, which is one of the many reasons they never really clicked. Ember dealt with enough tension at work as a trauma doctor. Any additional stress away from the hospital was the last thing she wanted. What she wanted she'd probably never find. She wanted someone to hold her when she came home feeling like a shell, void of emotion and decimated because a patient didn't make it. Silent strength, a loving touch, knowing deep inside that he would love her no matter what else happened in the world—she longed for that kind of connection. Ember sighed and fought back tears. She had it once when she was too young to know what it was. A sniff and huff of laughter buoyed her thoughts. Depend on Dad? Hell, he was never there. And Mom? Mom died way too young. Oh and the boyfriend you trusted who cheated? Yeah, you've got trust issues girl. She knew the psychobabble and could recite the textbook language… just like Dr. Sebastian taunted. Em knew she wanted someone to lift the smothering sense of responsibility off her shoulders—just for a while. She knew why. What she didn't know was who. Now wasn't that a conundrum. Conundrum? Do people actually talk that way?

"So I'm smart. Sue me." Ember tried to shrug off the thoughts, but the echo of her voice reinforced the loneliness in her heart. The room where she stood had never been a home. It was a place to sleep and shower. She'd never had friends over, never decorated it or even painted. The white walls stood as unadorned as the day she'd moved in. Whatever, she was leaving. Making a change. Em stared at the wall for a minute and decided the next place she lived she would paint. She turned on her heel and headed to the bathroom. Stopping after three strides, she looked back over her shoulder. What color? A soft green of new life and growing things. I like green.

Once in the shower, the hot water flattened her waist-long auburn hair over her shoulders and down her back. She washed quickly, a habit derived from always being late getting home or being in a hurry to get back to work. With efficiency long ago ingrained, she finished her shower and padded out of the bathroom.

She stood wrapped in a towel at the door to the bedroom and looked once again at the small silver drive that Dale had given her. Damn him for getting mixed up with something that could be dangerous. Ember went back into the bathroom and dried her hair, careful to straighten the curls that were the bane of her youth. She turned off the light and tried to sleep, but the conversation with Dale replayed in a loop through her mind. That mental film coupled with the stress of her pending transition cooked up a perfect recipe for insomnia. The sun was starting to rise when she finally fell into a fitful rest.

Ember woke, looked at the clock and then bolted from the bed. Her restless night had cost her the majority of the morning. Too much to do to sleep until noon, girl! Quickly dressing she headed out, running her final errands before she loaded up and left the Big Easy. She gave a quick wave to the security guard after once again confirming her forwarding address for mail had been given to the apartment complex office. The storage company was being let into her apartment next week by her apartment manager.

She drove to the bank and emptied her savings and checking accounts starting the process to close both. The weight of the cash in her purse made her smile. Her money manager had strict instructions for handling her investments. She only needed to load her suitcases tomorrow morning and she would leave New Orleans in her wake. The drama from last night slipped away as she scratched off the last item on her to-do list and headed back to her apartment.

Ember was relieved to be finished with all the running around that needed to be done in order to finally leave. After a quick meal, she took the trash to the outside dumpster while her computer booted up. She needed to check the weather, her emails and waste some time reading the news before she finished her last minute packing. Returning to her apartment she read the headlines of the Times-Picayune.

Her breath caught as the local headline appeared. Belle Chase Lawyer Found Dead in Apparent Suicide. Her hand hovered over the mouse and it literally shook as she clicked the link. Dale's picture filled the screen. The short article indicated coworkers had gone to his house when he did not show up for a court appearance and found him dead of an apparent self-inflicted gunshot wound to the head.

Oh my God! Oh my God! Oh my God! Dale murdered! If he had told the people who had killed him where the evidence could be found, she might be next. Intense, overwhelming fear stood every hair on the back of her neck erect as if some ingrained instinct signaled imminent attack. Ember bolted up and turned off and unplugged her computer. She raced into her bedroom and threw the remaining toiletries from her bathroom into her suitcase and zipped the bag closed. She checked her jeans pocket for holes, and then pocketed the silver capsule. Stuffing her computer and charger into its case, she gave her apartment one fleeting glance before she shut and locked her door. Walking out of the building for the last time, she loaded her luggage, waved robotically to the security guard and drove out the gate. The calm shell she portrayed was fast separating from the freaked out woman underneath. Fuck, what do I do now? Who in the hell am I going to call?

Think, damn it! Oh God, who can I get this to? Holy shit, where do I go?

Pulling onto the interstate a thought struck her. Could she? Would he even remember her? Ember's mind settled on the one person she could contact to help her although reaching him could prove difficult. Difficult? If you don't do it, you could be dead. How's that for difficult, you idiot?

Okay, so how do I do this? I'm in danger. What do I do?

She'd watched enough crime TV to know to stay away from any form of electronic monitoring. Ember put the SUV on cruise control as she fished around in her purse for her cell phone. Opening the window she tossed the phone out and watched it shatter in a thousand pieces behind her.

GPS tracking on her vehicle was a possibility. She veered off the interstate and worked her way to a mall and parked. Ember walked into the shopping center and located a kiosk that sold prepaid cell phones. She bought three with cash and called a local cab company with one. Walking to her SUV, she retrieved her computer bag, deposited the cell phones, and crammed the contents of the smaller suitcase into the larger one. Taking one suitcase and her computer bag she walked to the far side of the mall and got into the waiting cab. He drove her to the bus station where she paid cash for a ticket on the first bus out of town.

At the bus station, Ember scanned the loading area carefully. There were cameras in the lobby, but not under the overhang. She moved out of the lobby keeping her face averted and waited. When her bus pulled in, she got on and sat in the very back seat. Once the vehicle lumbered out of the depot, she dialed a number she knew by heart.

CHAPTER TWO

"HI, MRS. KING, THIS IS EMBER HARRIS. I know this must be a surprise, but I was wondering if you could give me Joseph's telephone number. I'm in the process of moving and I seem to have misplaced it."

"Ember! Honey, how have you been? It has been forever since you called. Tell me how are you doing? You said you are moving? Where are you going?"

Ember responded politely to the matriarch of the King family. "Yes ma'am, I'm sorry for not calling sooner, but working sixty to seventy hours a week at the trauma center didn't leave me much time to visit."

"Well, you're forgiven since you called now, dear. Where are you moving to?" Amanda King had evidently settled in to catch up. Ember mentally groaned.

"Ummm… I don't know yet? I'm taking an extended vacation and I'm going to do some traveling. I went from high school to college to med school and then straight to work. I never took any time for myself so…"

"So now you're taking care of yourself. I'm so happy for you, dear. Can I expect to see you while you're on vacation?"

Ember shivered at the thought of Amanda King being in trouble because of the drama that surrounded her. "Ah, you know Mississippi isn't on my list but who knows, I may just show up one day."

"I'd love that, dear. You know you're always welcome here. You're practically a member of the family." Ember loved Mrs. King. She was an amazing woman who raised a family of five boys and three girls single-handedly after her husband was murdered. Ember had always felt welcome at the King home. The house seemed to burst at the seams with people and love.

Ember not only felt that love from the gentle woman who led the family, but from Joseph, her oldest son. The one time in her life she felt safe, wanted and loved was when she dated Joseph. Could she reach out to him after all this time? Should she involve this wonderful woman and her family in the torrent of events swirling around her?

Amanda King was a saint and helped her bury her aunt four years ago. The older woman walked her through the multitude of funeral arrangements and stood beside her at the grave site. She made Ember dinners and caught her up on her children's exploits, travels, and occupational choices. Mrs. King spent a particularly skewed amount of time talking about Joseph, Ember's first love, ensuring she knew he was still single and worked for an international security firm. That was the reason she was calling now.

"Yes ma'am, thank you. Ahh… Mrs. King, I can't find Joey's telephone number. Would you happen to have a way I can get in touch with him? It's kind of important that I talk to him right away."

The pause at the other end of the line was pregnant. Finally, Mrs. King asked, "Ember, honey, are you in trouble?"

Ember didn't respond. A long pause followed and in the end she couldn't say anything.

Mrs. King sighed. "Okay, sweetheart, I'm giving you his emergency contact number. Leave a message and give him a number to call you back. I don't know if he is in the country or overseas, but he will call you as soon as he gets your message. It could take a couple days or longer. Maybe you should call Jacob or Jared? They're in the states and they could help you if you're in trouble. If you need a lawyer Jason has an office here in town."

"No ma'am, I don't need a lawyer. I really just need to talk to Joey. If he doesn't call me back soon, maybe I'll ask for Jared's number. Okay?"

"Alright, dear. I won't pry. Lord knows I want to, but I won't. Here is the number."

Ember ended the call after she scribbled the overseas number down. Forcing a deep breath to steady her shot nerves, she called the number. The ringing stopped abruptly and a computer beep sounded. She drew a shaky breath, "Joey, it's Em. Ember Harris. I think I'm in trouble. Please call me back. Ah… Joey… I'm… I think… please would you give me a call. I need help." She left the number of her third phone, powered down the second phone, took out the battery and the SIM card. She broke the card and threw it on the floor. The phone ended up dropped in the toilet of the bus. A flush ensured it went down into the septic tank.

Joseph King, the boy she knew years ago had been her hero. Her mom had raised her alone. Ember's dad was a drunken leech who drifted in and out of her childhood, but was never a constant. When her mom died of cancer, her Aunt Caroline took her in. Ember transferred from a huge Ohio high school with over two thousand students to a small Mississippi school with less than one hundred in her class. Most of the people in the school had been friends since they were in kindergarten and their social circles and cliques were formidable. As a quiet and introspective teen, the death of her mother forced her even further into herself. Tagged as the new 'city girl,' she was circled by the hormone-crazed boys at the country school. All the attention she received from the young men garnered her spite and ridicule from the local girls who desperately tried to attract the boy's attention.

She did her best to avoid talking with anyone, but one afternoon about a week after starting school four boys surrounded her at a lunchroom table. She tried to get up and move, but one pulled her back down. The other three laughed at her surprise.

"Where you going so fast, princess? What? Is the city girl too stuck up to be around us? Do you think you're too good for us, honey?" The blond's sarcastic southern drawl taunted her.

Ember glared at him. "I'm done with lunch and I don't want to talk with you. Go talk to those girls over there and let go of my arm now."

The crowd of boys laughed as the tanned blond continued, "Hey, who said we just want to talk with you, sweetheart? Those girls don't know things like you city girls do. How about you teach us what you know?"

A loaded lunch tray thudded on the table and a deep voice rumbled, "Get your hand off her arm, Kirby, or I'll break it."

Em looked up at her savior. He was taller and broader than any of the boys at the table and appeared older.

"Fuck off, King. This is none of your business. We were just introducing ourselves to the new girl." The blond boy's voice held bravado, but Ember could tell he was afraid of the young man at the head of the table. The three other boys slid down the bench moving away from the angry newcomer.

"If I have to tell you again, you'll be picking your teeth up off the floor." As he growled out his response, four more young men walked up behind him, all with similar looks of short cut black hair and chiseled features. All were exceptionally tall, but none had the intensity of the boy standing over her.

"Hey, we didn't know she was your girl, King. We don't want no trouble with you or your brothers." One of the boys that backed away from the table spoke trying to calm the situation.

"My brothers are the least of your concern, Caleb. Y'all get away from her and stay away. If I see you or anyone else near her again, I'll beat the shit out of you for pure enjoyment."

The blond let go of her arm and the boys moved away from her table. Ember raised her eyes up to him and smiled nervously. "Thank you. I'm Ember Harris."

The young man sat down across from her and his brothers walked away following the offending boys as they retreated. He was wearing a letterman's jacket and the letter was covered in pins from track, football, basketball and baseball.

"I'm Joseph. Joseph King. I couldn't help notice you had a little difficulty. Not a lot of friends around today to hang with?"

Ember shook her head. "Ah… no. The girls here don't like me because the boys do. If I don't talk to the boys, they think I'm stuck up, but at least I don't get harassed by the girls. The head cheerleader wanted to fight me because I talked to her boyfriend. Like I knew the guy was dating her? I asked him one question. I guess 'where's the office?' is a come on. Anyway it's not a good way to make friends or to start at a new school."

He looked at her and sucked his teeth thoughtfully finally declaring. "No, I guess not."

Ember looked at him and drew a deep breath. She straightened her back in a show of bravado she really didn't feel. "Would you please do me the favor of pointing out which girl is going to try and pick a fight with me because you're talking to me?"

Joseph huffed out a sound almost resembling a laugh and shook his head. "None, I don't have a girlfriend and the last time I checked half of the school was afraid of me. The other half is too stupid to be afraid of me."

JOSEPH · 21

Ember laughed at the absurdity of his statement. "Afraid of you? Why? I think you're kinda nice."

His blue-green eyes seemed to search her face almost as if he was looking for a way to tell if she was lying. "You really aren't afraid of me are you?"

"Umm… no. Perhaps I'm one of the stupid ones?" She crossed her eyes at him pulling her lips in a pucker. He choked on the milk he was drinking. The liquid flew from his mouth and she shrieked with laughter. His laughter echoed on the ceramic tile walls of the lunch room, drawing the attention of just about everyone, especially his brothers who looked at each other and smiled.

He wiped his mouth while still laughing, "No, Ember, I don't think you're one of the stupid ones. What's your next class? I'll walk you."

From that day, they'd been inseparable. Ember noticed the wide birth everyone gave him and because she was his friend, they left her alone, which suited her just fine. She eventually heard the rumors about him, how he left school, tracked down and killed the man who had murdered his dad. Some of the girls even went so far as to tell her Joseph was dangerous and violent—that he would hurt her. She knew he wouldn't. He was always gentle with her. Too gentle. His devastating aggression fascinated her—excited her. If he ever, even once, had taken control of those make out sessions, she would have melted. But he didn't. His restraint frustrated her to no end, but how does a seventeen-year-old girl tell her boyfriend that? No, Joey was a master of discipline. He never lost control during a fight and always stopped when he knew he had won. He was always victorious. It did seem that everyone in town feared her Joey. She laughed to herself. Nobody else called him Joey, not even his family.

The two spent their senior year together talking, dreaming, planning their lives or just enjoying the peaceful silence of being together. Both knew that the relationship would end after graduation. With a maturity beyond their years, they accepted it. He wanted to join the Marine Corps and travel the world. She wanted to go to college and dreamed of being a doctor. They were best friends.

Ember compared every man she had ever dated in college and after to him. None ever came close to meeting the thrill Joseph's commanding presence gave her. If only he used that power in other ways. If she had only known then what she knew now? Would she have begged Joey to stay? Would she have become a military wife? More times than not it seemed her life-long drive to become a doctor had cost her more than she wanted to pay. She'd learned too many hard, unrelenting lessons, felt bitter disappointment, survived a mentally abusive boyfriend, a cheating fiancé and suffered through too many disappointing dates to count. If she had known? She would have followed him to the ends of the earth.

When the phone rang two hours later, the shrill noise jarred her frayed nerves. She struggled to answer the unfamiliar phone, the shaking of her hands making the effort even more arduous. How the hell do I answer this thing? Ember hit a button hoping it was the right one to connect her to the caller. "Joey?"

"Yeah, Em it's me. Explain why you think you're in trouble?" The sound of his voice crumbled all her stoic defenses. She swiped at a tear and spoke softly into the phone. The closest person was five rows up, but she whispered anyway. "Oh, thank God, Joey! A friend gave me a computer thumb drive for safekeeping last night. He said if something happened to him to get it to a person I could trust—someone at a national level. I didn't know who else to call. Oh, my God." Ember drew a shaking breath willing herself not to dissolve into tears. "Joey, he was found dead this morning. The paper said it was a suicide, but… he would never kill himself."

"Where are you and do you still have the drive?" His deep rich voice melted her to the core, similar to the voice of the young man she once knew but now deeper with a terse, clipped edge. His voice held a distinct chill, a distance. Ember's mind raced. Perhaps he wouldn't help? How much had he changed over the years? Was she wrong to reach out to him? Well, hell, it had been fifteen—no sixteen years…

"Joey, maybe I freaked a little bit. I don't know. I didn't really know what to do so… I think I may have overreacted? Hell, I threw my cell phone out on the interstate and left my truck in a mall parking lot. Maybe I watch too much TV, but I didn't want to be tracked so I bought prepaid cell phones and I'm on a bus heading to Kansas City. All with cash—of course."

"Being careful keeps people alive. I need information. Now. The man's name? Where did this happen and do you still have the drive?"

"Dale Landis, he is… was a lawyer in New Orleans. I have the damned thing in my pocket." He didn't respond. Nothing. No words, no indication he heard her. Ember looked at the face of the phone to ensure they were still connected. Finally, he responded.

"Turn off the phone and take out the SIM card if it has one and the battery. Put the phone back together in two hours. I'll contact you."

"Alright, I will Joey." She couldn't hide the tremor of fear in her voice.

"I will call you back Em."

"Okay." She sighed and said softly, "Joey, I…"

"Yeah. Do as I told you. Hang up now." Was it her imagination or had the steel edge of his voice softened?

CHAPTER THREE

JOSEPH HUNG UP THE PHONE AND DROPPED HIS head into his hands. Ember Harris. His first and only long-term relationship. He would do anything for that woman. Hell, he had planned on asking her to marry him when he got back from Paris Island. But boot camp transitioned into his specialty training and then he shipped out to the Middle East and the war that changed him forever. He shook his head and punched familiar digits into his satellite phone. He called the only support system he ever needed, his family. Three of his four brothers and all of his sisters worked at Guardian Security. A subsidiary of Guardian International, Guardian Security was the best at what they did. No single nation or governmental agency sanctioned Guardian's actions, but every last one of the bastards used Guardian to resolve what diplomacy couldn't. Joseph and his brothers and sisters had worked their way to the top of their respective specialties. Two of his brothers ran Guardian Security's overseas and stateside black-ops, his sisters worked personal and computer security issues and Joseph, well, he eliminated threats.

As soon as Joseph heard his brother's voice he demanded, "Jacob, I need immediate access to a company jet and tell Jared I need all the information you can get me on the suicide of an attorney named Dale Landis in New Orleans."

"Well, hello to you, too, brother-mine. I received the sit-rep on the Afghani fiasco. We can verify the target you were assigned was neutralized."

"Well, no shit, little man. I fucking slit his throat. I'm in D.C. and I need to get to Kansas City, stat."

"Yeah? Thank God this is a secure line. What the fuck are you doing in the States? You've been off the grid forever and you suddenly appear in D.C? You don't operate stateside. What the hell is the rush to get to Kansas?" Jacob paused and then added with a growl, "Were you compromised during your last assignment?"

"No asshole, I haven't been compromised. Have I ever been compromised? Do you honestly think I'd contact you if I were and lead whoever targeted me straight to you? No fucking way. Shit, boy, get a grip on reality. Now, get me a damn plane and get Jared's ass working on my information."

"Calm down. If your cover hasn't been blown or you aren't being targeted, why the urgent need for a jet? Two, who is Dale Landis? Three, why Kansas City?"

Joseph took a breath in order to reply with a semblance of control. "Do you remember Ember Harris?"

"What from back in the day? Hell yeah. Tall, sexy, red hair, tight ass, great—"

Joseph snarled. "Say one more word and swear I'll beat your face in."

Jacob snorted. "I was going to say personality. Yeah, I remember Ember. Why?"

"Last night this Dale Landis gave Ember a thumb drive and told her if anything should happen to him to get it to someone out of the state that she trusts. He was found in an apparent suicide this morning. She freaked and bolted out of New Orleans. She's on a bus heading to Kansas City."

"So, what's on the drive?"

"Fuck if I know."

"And yet you're going to race to Kansas City to rescue her? Huh."

"Really? You're busting my balls now? Just get me the information and find me a way to Kansas."

"Yeah, how often do I get a chance to mess with you, dude? Never. Believe me, I'll take any opportunity I get." Joseph heard the clicking of a computer keyboard. "Alright I sent over a request for information. It was coded as an Alpha priority."

"Thanks."

"No issues, dude. But ah… Ember, huh? Did you guys ever hook up after you left for the Corps?"

Joseph closed his eyes and shook his head even though his brother couldn't see him. "Nah, I went back after I got out… before I joined Guardian. Wanted to see if she was still interested. Saw her with a guy. She wasn't missing me."

"Damn. Didn't know. You had it bad for that one."

"Still do, man."

"Fuck." The whispered word conveyed one hell of a punch.

"Yeah, you said it." Joseph cleared his throat. "What about that info?"

"Jared should be pulling it up soon… yeah, just got confirmation that he received it and is processing the request."

"Jacob… get me on a damn plane."

"All right, yeah, I'm working it. It's good to have you back in the States. Stop by and see us before you disappear again. Your nephew is getting big."

"Not back here for long. Depends on how this mess with Ember pans out. I will say goodbye before I leave."

Jacob's pause lingered before he cleared his voice and spoke. "You never say goodbye. Why are you back in the States? What's going on?"

"Same shit, different day, little man." Joseph hung up the phone and lay back on the hotel bed closing his eyes. Ember Harris. He remembered her curly dark red hair, huge green eyes, beautiful smile and hot, tight body. That girl did it for him then. Hell, she did it for him, period.

He recalled the make out sessions they had stumbled their way through, learning how to be with her. What to touch, kiss, lick or nip to light her fire. Damn, it got him hot now. He'd taken thousands of cold showers thanks to his raging teenage hormones. Joseph palmed his cock and adjusted himself. Getting up slowly, he groaned and stooped over. Pain hit him in hard rolling waves only slightly dulled by the effects of his second to last oxycodone. He unbuttoned his shirt and winced. Seeping wounds stuck to the fabric of his shirt. The pull of the adhered material killed the reaction certain parts of his body had from his trot down memory lane with Ember Harris.

He picked up his empty bag and repacked it with changes of clothes and ammunition. He'd returned Ember's call as soon as he'd checked in. Joseph glanced at his watch. In the country for less than two hours before he was on the move again. That had to be a record—even for him. He'd just placed his backpack in the closet, only to draw it out once again. His knife, usually idle while in the States, lay sharpened and stowed in its leg sheath next to the backpack. He checked his Desert Eagle .50 automatic and secured it in his shoulder holster dropping it onto the bed. Joseph drew another deep breath and walked to the bathroom. A hot shower might help to loosen his muscles and ease the pain.

The wounds on his ribs pulled open and the pain slashed through his shattered nerve endings. The agony forced him to grab the sink for support. His immediate punch of the bathroom vanity proved utterly fucking stupid. Torrents of misery from his side and now his abused hand cut through him again. Damn.

This wasn't a good time to renew his acquaintance with anyone, especially someone in trouble.

His life had taken so many radical turns since he'd last seen her. The isolation and secrecy that surrounded him now prevented all but the most impersonal of contact. The women in his life weren't relationships. He used them for physical relief of his fucked up needs. He'd changed. The person she once knew no longer existed. For too many years the job was his only focus. He shrugged his shoulders under the hot water of the shower and winced as thousands of lightning bolts blazed through his torso.

Once again, his job had nearly killed him. The recent flaying of the skin across his chest, back and ribs stood in stark testimony to the life he lived. Oh yes, the delightful rami-fucking-cations of misjudging just one glance. One look meant the difference between escaping his enemy and being caught. And he had missed it. How had he fucking missed it?

He'd been over it a million times and still couldn't find the exact second his cover had become compromised. Joseph sighed in resignation. Now he needed to disregard the injuries and pain in order to help Ember. He drew a deep breath and closed his eyes. He had gone through hell many times before. This wouldn't be a new experience. The water ran cool before he left the shower. Exhausted, he carefully stretched out on top of the bed on his stomach. He'd bandage his wounds after he let them air dry. Maybe catch a couple minutes of rest. Just as he hung in the void between sleep and consciousness, the phone chirped beside him. He picked it up and barked, "What."

"I have a company G6 at Dulles. It's being fueled as we speak and can take off as soon as you get there. Jared has made initial inquiries through the stateside agencies and intelligence communities. The word is that Ember is a person of interest in the investigation surrounding the death of Dale Landis."

Joseph lifted up on the bed and sucked in a great draw of air in response to the shooting pain. He grabbed a pillow crushing it in his fist before he growled, "How in the hell is she a person of interest?"

"The local cops wanted to place her as a suspect. Seems she and this Landis had a fight at a local restaurant last night. Evidently they have too many people who can verify her whereabouts, video cameras showing her leaving work, entering her complex, her apartment building and also her exit the next morning. New Orleans PD is calling her departure and abandoned vehicle in a mall parking lot suspicious."

"Alright. I'm heading to the airport."

"Wait, Joseph…there's more." His brother's growl froze him.

"Our office in New Orleans has received intelligence that Lang was attempting to publish information which would connect local cops, attorneys, judges and even a senator to the Morales Drug Cartel. Word on the street is he was going to release documents that showed payoffs, account numbers, dates, names, and amounts. If Ember has the information, she's not safe. Taking down the network in one state could start a domino effect. This is huge. If Landis talked before they killed him, it wouldn't take long for someone to track her to the bus station."

"Fuck man, she has the thumb drive on her person. For all we know they could be following the bus. I need to get her off it at the next stop. Have a vehicle waiting for me at the airport in Kansas City. Use my shadow account to feed me any information you receive. As soon as I can secure the information, I'll upload it to the Guardian server."

"Good. Jared contacted the Attorney General and the heads of the Department of Justice, Homeland Security and the Director of the FBI. They're aware we intend on taking

Ember into protective custody. Any requests for interviews or depositions will be routed through Guardian. The dirty politicos in Louisiana and anyone else they're tied to can't legally touch her once you have her, but the Morales' underground cartel system is deadly. The rumor on the street is that not only has Morales activated his network to search for her, he has also put out feelers for a professional."

"Jesus fucking Christ! A contract hit?"

"Yeah."

"Fine. I got this. I'm taking her to my place in Wyoming. It's isolated, off the grid and if anyone comes after us, I'll know it."

"You have a place in Wyoming? Since when? Fuck man, never mind, just send me the damn coordinates. Christ, Joseph, be careful and let me know if you need assistance. I can launch a team at any time. Or hell, I'll put Jared on it. Stateside operations are his, not ours. We aren't supposed to operate on American soil remember?"

"I have eight safe houses around the world and five more in the states. I can't let anyone know where they are because if I'm being hunted, you're all in danger. I don't give a flying fuck if the lines are crossed. This one's personal. If they go after Ember, they'll have to come through me."

Jacob's voice became professional, transforming from a concerned younger brother to the chief operations officer of a billion dollar security firm. "You're not overseas. These people have not been identified or coded as threats or cleared for termination."

Joseph's evil laugh hung in the air. "If they try to take her out, they'll die."

"You're an asset who works overseas."

Joseph scrubbed his hand over his face and exhaled loudly. "Thanks for the 411, like I didn't fucking know that. I'm going after Ember. I'll protect her, no matter what it takes."

"I understand but any link between Joseph King and your actual function in this organization would constitute a death sentence for both her and for you. A hit would be put out on her simply as retribution for your previous work."

"I'm well aware of that fact. I don't need you or anyone else to remind me. I live this fucking solitary life every God-forsaken day. Make no mistake—I'll do what I need to do in order to take care of her." If push comes to shove, I'll gut the sorry son of a bitch like a fish.

"Understood. Check in when you can."

"Yeah, right." Joseph pulled the phone away from his ear.

"Hey, Joseph?"

"What?"

"You don't have to work this alone. All our resources are at your disposal."

"Got it. Thanks, little man."

Joseph hung up the secure phone and looked at his watch. He dressed methodically. He swallowed back the last pain pill, and the empty bottle of oxycodone rang as it hit the trash can. Pulling his pack off the bed, he tucked the phone in the outside pocket and carefully shouldered it, wincing. This is going to be an interesting week. Exiting the hotel, he took a taxi to Dulles Airport and boarded one of Guardian's many jets. As the plane waited on the tarmac for clearance to take off, he called Ember.

She answered the phone quietly and he could hear the stress in her voice. "Ember, I'm on my way to you."

"Thank you, Joey." Oh, wonderful, she sounded like she was crying. Just what he needed.

"Where's the next stop for the bus?"

He heard Ember pull a ragged breath in before she spoke. "Joey I'm so sorry for being such a wuss. I'm a lot stronger than this. The entire situation is just so bizarre. I feel like I'm an unwilling participant in an episode of the Twilight Zone."

He understood the feeling all too well. She probably needed to be reassured. Like he had any experience with that. What the hell, he'd try. "Yeah, Emmy, I can see why you would feel that way. Don't worry. We'll work through this. Now, do you know where the next stop is?"

She laughed. Not the sweet sexy sound he remembered, rather a stress filled attempt at laughter. "In other words, answer my question, you sniveling woman. Yes, I do know the next stop. According to the schedule, it's Springfield, Missouri, in about five hours."

What the fuck? Like he had ever spoken to her like that. "Sniveling isn't a word I'd use. Listen, when the bus stops, take only what you carried on with you and get off. Leave your suitcase in the luggage compartment under the bus. Don't advertise the fact you're not getting back on. Walk if you can or take a cab to the nearest hotel with outdoor entrances to the rooms. Normally, these types of hotels don't install outdoor surveillance. Check in using cash if at all possible. Go to a local drug store and buy whatever it is that you women buy to change the color of your hair. Hit a clothing store and buy new clothes, clothes that you normally wouldn't wear. Cut your hair if it is still long, color it, and change your clothes. Once you have changed your appearance, try to leave that hotel without anyone seeing you and don't go back."

He waited for her to question him or respond. When she did neither, he asked, "Em are you there?"

"Yeah, I'm here. They're coming after me, aren't they? They're going to kill me." Her voice was emotionless and for that he was glad. She was past the point of being an emotional liability. Now, she focused on survival.

"Do exactly what I tell you to do and everything will be okay. Once you leave the hotel, I need you to go to a public place. Stay there and blend in if you can. By the time you get to Springfield, I'll be driving down from Kansas City. When you find a place, you're going to wait for me there. Text me the address. Wait for me to acknowledge I have received the address and then throw away the phone. I'll find you, Ember. Don't leave that place for any reason. Don't purposely engage in conversation with anyone or get into a secluded area. Do you understand?"

A whisper thin response drifted back to him. "I understand."

"Em, you have to trust me. I may be going overboard on this, but I won't take any chances, okay?"

"That is eerily similar to what Dale said last night."

Joseph leaned forward in the plush leather seat and almost groaned from the thrumming of pain through his back. "Ember, I'm not Dale. Listen, I'm sorry your boyfriend is gone. I can't change that. I assure you that none of the people following you can take me out. I'm not going to let anything happen to you. Please do exactly as I say. I'm on my way. Remember, just take one thing at a time, alright?"

Her pause was lengthy. "Joey? Dale…he wasn't my boyfriend. I'm not involved with anyone. We were just friends and damn it, you better come get me, or I'm going to be really pissed."

"That's the spitfire I used to know. Hang up the phone now and take the battery and SIM card out. Put them back together only to text me the address when you know it."

So, she's still single. That small piece of information packed a hell of a punch and made him feel pretty damned good. Her not being involved with anyone worked for him.

CHAPTER FOUR

EMBER GAZED OUT AT THE HORIZON AS IT sped by. The tinted bus window shaded the world grey. Appropriate. Her entire life right now was muddled. Grey. Confusing, and if she was honest—terrifying. Two days ago, she was the lead emergency room physician at a major trauma center. Today, a friend was dead, probably murdered. A man she hadn't spoken to in sixteen years was flying in to rescue her from the people who killed Dale. The reason? The small thumb drive in her pocket. She shook her head and smirked as she looked out the window. Riiiight, so much for life without additional stress.

When the bus stopped in Springfield, the driver announced a thirty-minute comfort stop. Ember casually exited the bus with the other riders and strolled across the street looking disinterestedly in shop windows. Turning the corner, she hurriedly walked away from the bus terminal and hailed a cab. The driver suggested a hotel nearby and she gratefully accepted his suggestion. Giving him a sizable tip, she exited the cab and entered the lobby of the hotel.

Paying for a room with cash wasn't a problem as long as she put down a deposit for any damages. The desk clerk pulled out a map of the downtown area and circled two drug stores within walking distance and a strip mall two blocks away that had several clothing stores. Ember flipped back her thick red hair that had spilled over her shoulders and smiled at the man. She watched as his eyes lingered on her breasts before he commented. "If there is anything else you need, please don't hesitate to let me know."

Ember walked to the drug store and bought black hair rinse. Off-the-shelf bleaching kits for red hair were not an option. Unless you want to look like a flaming orange sunset or a cartoon character. She'd learned that lesson in college when her roommate tried to bleach a sorority sister's red hair. A shudder ran through her at the memory. She settled on a rinse instead of a permanent dye in raven black with dark red tones and bought makeup to match her new hair color.

The clothing store's stereo system pounded out nauseating heavy metal music. Cringing against the sound of screaming voices and wrenching sounds that in no way resembled a melody, she looked at the clothes offered with trepidation.

"Can I help you find something ma'am?" A male's voice drifted over the abomination someone called music.

Ember glanced at the waif thin salesman. Blue hair stood in four inch spikes over the crown of his head. His cheekbones rose in a prominent lift and his nose hooked radically. Only the piercings in his eyebrows and gauges in his ears kept him from looking like the parakeet she'd had as a child. Barely.

Deciding to take the plunge and buy something like Joey had instructed, she smiled before she nodded. "Actually, I'm looking for something to wear to a club tonight."

"Yeah? So… you're buying clothes… like… for you?" The shocked comment shouldn't have upset her. But it did.

"Yeah, for me. I'm looking to change things up, be a little wild."

"Well, sister I should hope so. You could pass for like… thirty! Let me help you. First you need…" he lifted a hand and spread out his fingers as he made a circling motion in front of her, "style. This thing you have going on here? So last decade. Where do you shop? Like, seriously? You raided your mom's closet, right?"

"Um, no. These are the type of clothes I typically wear."

"Oh sister…" A sucked, "Tsk, tsk." from his black lined lips condemned her as a hopeless case. "This?" His long thin index finger flitted from a limp wrist towards her clothes. "This is not anything anyone should ever wear." With his other hand, he tapped his long fingers against his hipbone that protruded above his tight low cut jeans and below his tighter black t-shirt.

"Well, sweet-cheeks, I didn't anticipate reforming the last refugee of the late nineties today." He extended his limp hand for a handshake. "You're lucky we're slow. I'm Sledge, and you are?"

"I'm Em." An hour later in some worm-holed alternate reality, she paid Sledge a ridiculous amount of money and thanked him for his help. She mentally chastised herself for spending almost six hundred dollars on a few items, but Joseph told her to look different. God knows with Sledge's help she would. He'd picked out a black spandex mini skirt, a pair of faded blue skinny jeans, and black knee high leather boots with three inch heels. A black halter top with silver studs and about two dozen silver and black leather bracelets for her arms were added to the growing stack. Huge silver drop earrings and a silver studded leather choker completed her new look. What the hell that look was she had no idea. Yeah, she would never wear any of the clothes she bought after this fiasco was over. The boots? They were keepers. She loved them.

Em stopped at a second drug store and bought a pair of scissors, more makeup based on Sledge's recommendations, and a few toiletries since her suitcase was presumably on its way to Kansas City. She entered her hotel room and poured her purchases onto the bed. With a resigned sigh, she cut her hair at shoulder level and held up the severed mass of thick auburn tresses at least two feet long. No turning back now, girl.

Forty-five minutes later Ember towel dried her hair and looked at the mass of dark curls in the mirror. The loss of the weight allowed the quirky coils in her thick hair to become riotous. She shook her head and laughed at the jumble of black spirals that circled her face and fell just past the nape of her neck. She used a small hair dryer anchored to the bathroom wall to dry her hair allowing the curls to run amuck. The new make-up was up next. She applied a smoky green shadow heavily to her eyes and liberally used black mascara and eyeliner. The dark red lip stain and dusky rose blush completed the transformation. If she hadn't watched the metamorphosis, she wouldn't have believed the woman in the mirror was the same one that rented the room earlier.

The miniskirt, boots, and halter top took no time to pull on. The addition of the leather and silver jewelry completed her look. She rummaged for the phonebook and finally found it in the bedside drawer. Without her smart phone, she had to find her location on the city map and then find the club Sledge recommended. She found it on Park Central East. Four blocks away. Putting the prepaid phone together, she sent a text with the address to Joseph. Almost immediately, she received a reply.

Got it. Forty miles away.

Her heart skipped a beat as she destroyed the SIM card, pulled out the battery and put all the pieces in the garbage she was taking to the dumpster. She stuffed the clothing indicating her change of looks into the shopping bags. She walked out of the hotel room a different woman.

She put the trash in a large trash bin at the front of the hotel near the reception desk. She had just turned the corner when she heard the desk clerk speaking on a wireless phone as he paced in the parking area adjacent to the hotel.

"Yes, we had a customer who matches that description check in today. I was surprised at her request to pay in cash. Yes, I watched her walk back to her room about an hour ago. Sure, I can stay until you get here. No problem officer, I'm always glad to help law enforcement."

Ember walked down the outside corridor on the other side of the building and across the street terrified she would be recognized, each step taking her further away from the menace that followed. She swung her new black leather satchel containing all her earthly possessions over her shoulder and forced a slow pace along the four city blocks to the nightclub. The line to enter trailed down the block. A bouncer surveyed the crowd and opened the velvet ropes inviting several ladies to move to the front of the line. Ember smiled at him as he motioned for her to come forward. Thank you Sledge.

Once inside she found a small table that faced the door, far away from the bar. Since there was a two drink minimum, she ordered a drink when the barmaid came by. A rough crowd filled the night club. Chains, leather, black clothing and a lot of bare skin seemed to be the unspoken dress code. Heavy metal music inundated the entire building as the bass reverberated from the massive sound system. When the waitress returned, she brought two glasses of wine.

Ember shook her head and yelled over the music, "I only ordered one."

The waitress pointed across the room to a large Hispanic-looking man dressed in black leather leaning against the bar. "Hector bought you a drink."

She watched as the man lifted his drink to her. Ember shook her head and asked the waitress. "Please tell him no thanks. My boyfriend would not appreciate the gesture."

The waitress shrugged her shoulders and walked back through the crowd towards the bar. Ember sipped the wine she had ordered and continued to anxiously scan the crowd. She watched out of the corner of her eye as the man, Hector, listened to the waitress. His hostile glare towards her was unexpected. She lowered her eyes immediately not wanting a confrontation.

Ember breathed slowly trying to control her swelling fear. This isn't a logical fear; you've handled plenty of men who tried to pick you up over the years. He's just looking to get laid. She needed to let him know there was no chance. Ember took a deep cleansing breath. If he built up enough nerve to come over she'd handle it. She watched from the corner of her eye as the man drifted away from the bar and walked casually towards the crowded dance floor. Ember glanced towards the door and swallowed a sob of relief.

The boy had grown into a man. Joseph loomed hugely and marginalized the grand size of the doorway. His demeanor emitted tangible waves of aggression that reached her across the crowded room. Instinctively people moved out of his way. She waited to catch his eye as he scanned the bar and dance floor. My God, he was huge. His six-foot-six-inch frame had filled with more muscle than Ember thought physically possible. Okay, as a doctor you know it's possible… but damn. Phenomenal and just as handsome as she remembered but a harder and more intense man-sized version of the boy she once knew. His body moved with the caged energy she remembered so well. She slid out of her seat and started towards him.

The man from the bar appeared from nowhere, grasping her arm tightly, blocking her way. "Sorry, bonita, you're not going anywhere. He flicked his fingers under her chin, and the ring on her choker tinkled. "Your master's foolish. Can't have a little pet running around unleashed. You and me? We're going to party tonight."

She wrenched her arm trying to free it, but his hold was viciously tight.

"Ah, feisty pequeñs? Don't worry, I'll take care of you. You like it rough, eh?"

"What? Let go of me you sick bastard!" Ember pulled her arm again. The man yanked her against him tightly, forcing his hard cock against her hip.

"That collar. Your foolish master allows you out without his protection? I'll give you some, my little slut."

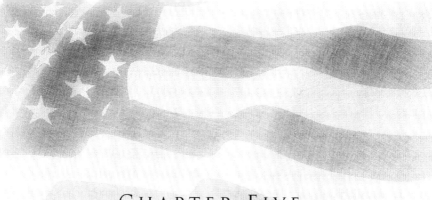

CHAPTER FIVE

A TALL BLACK HAIRED WOMAN STOOD, DRAWING HIS eyes her way. He did a double take. The beautiful vision walking towards him resembled the young girl he remembered, but her body was fuller, softer, her curves more sensuous. She was far more than the girl he used to know. This woman radiated a sultry sexuality and had every male's attention. And holy shit! The outfit she was almost wearing? Hotter than the sin-stoked fires of hell.

A nasty looking motherfucker covered in tats stopped her forward progress. Joseph worked to cross the crowded club, keeping an eye on her as he sent masses of bodies careening across the crowded dance floor. She tensed and tried to shake off the man's grip. Fucking bastard. The animal pulled her close to him and ground his cock against her. Rage seethed through his veins as he stepped behind the man. "That collar. Your foolish master allows you out without his protection? I'll give you some, my little slut."

Joseph clutched the tattooed wrist and squeezed. The man spun and tried to strike out. Joseph blocked the wide swing and with a quick jerk, he snapped the wrist in his grasp. The sickening crack of bone breaking was distinct over the thrum of bass beats. Blood drained from the man's face. Joseph lifted him closer and spoke savagely. "I'm no fool. I protect what is mine. Never touch what you don't own, amigo."

He pushed the man into several dancers. A shoving match started on the crowded floor and quickly escalated into a melee. Ember's shocked expression froze on her face. Her wide-eyed stare held until she blinked and exclaimed, "You broke his wrist!"

"He's lucky that's all I did." Joseph grabbed her and half pushed, half pulled her through the crowd towards the door. The crowd swallowed them providing distance from the growing brawl on the dance floor. Finally, finding space outside the crowded bar, he stopped and pulled her into his arms.

She trembled. He should have hurt the bastard more. "Did he hurt you? Are you alright?"

Collapsing against him, she buried her face in his neck. "No, I'm… he didn't…"

"I got you, Em. Come on, we have to go."

She nodded but didn't move, her shaking more noticeable as her hands clenched the front of his shirt in a death grip. Joseph put his finger under her chin and lifted her face. "Ember?"

Slowly she let go of his shirt and lifted her eyes to his. She moved her hands up his shoulders. He saw her hunger and knew his own. The woman he held lit him up six ways to Sunday. Shit, there was no time for this now. He needed to get them out of the area.

"Come on. Being here is dangerous. We need to go. Now." He put his arm around her waist and almost carried her away from the nightclub. They hot-footed it across the street to his black BMW and he opened the door for her. He slung her bag into the back seat with his pack. His body revolted in pain against the movement when he once again folded into the confined driver's seat. He pulled the vehicle into traffic and looked over at the woman next to him. She had turned in her seat and was giving him the once over. "We're heading north to Wyoming. I have a safe place there."

Ember jumped in her seat. Her muffled exclamation just before she grabbed his arm revealed just how much the incident at the nightclub had shaken her. She put her shaking hand on his arm. "Joey, I overheard the hotel clerk talk about me to the police. Someone knows I'm here."

He glanced at her as he accelerated onto the interstate on-ramp. Joseph fought the desire to floor the accelerator and send the car flying down the road. Being stopped by authorities, who may or may not be on the Morales payroll, wasn't in the plans tonight. "Did anyone see you with your new look?"

She shook her head and ran her hands through her hair. "No, I don't think so and I put all the garbage in the trash bin at the front of the hotel. I didn't leave it in the room. They won't know I changed the color or the length of my hair. Joey? Who's chasing me?"

Laying her head back against the headrest of the car, she reached over and caressed his hand. A thousand needles of electricity shifted through his body. He felt the resurrection of the intense physical reaction he felt in the club. He grabbed her hand and held it not wanting her to become any more of a distraction than she already was. Yeah right, like that had a snowball's chance in hell of succeeding.

"From what we can gather, your man Dale put evidence on that thumb drive tying prominent, politically connected people to the Morales Drug Cartel. If what's rumored to be on that drive is substantiated, the implications will devastate Morales' operation. It could cost him millions of dollars and take down some pretty influential people on his payroll. Guardian Security has placed you in protective custody. The primary concern right now is the underground network of the cartel. Wherever the drugs go, Morales has minions. Wherever he has minions, he has eyes, ears, and people willing to do his bidding, a thousand eyes look for you. Needless to say, he has the money to employ professionals to take care of his problems."

"And I'm a problem." Again, no emotion. She merely stated a fact. Joseph approved of the strong woman she had grown into. Em cleared her throat. Joseph grabbed a bottle of water from the cup holder and handed it to her. "Was the guy in the bar part of this?" That wanna-be Dom? Too fucking stupid. "No, I don't think so. The man at the bar seemed to think you were a submissive without a Dom. Stupid ass-wipe. If you're wearing a collar, you're already owned."

"What? A collar? You mean my choker? That's what caused him to be such an ass?"

"Yeah."

"How do you know that, the collar thing?"

"Been around that block more than once."

"Are you into that? Are you one of those Doms? Like those books that all the nurses were talking about? What was the name? Shades of something?"

"I have no idea what you're talking about." Not going there with you—ever. "We need to focus on critical issues." His clipped reply was probably harsher than it should have been. Damn. He wasn't good at this conversation thing. But he had to admit the majority of the people he had one-on-one contact with were dead within minutes of meeting him. His knife skillfully silenced any opportunities for casual chit-chat. Yeah, not much chance of conversation with a corpse.

She took a deep breath and blew it out. "Okay. Isn't the Morales Cartel the one responsible for the mass murders along the Mexican border and the hit squads killing border patrol agents?"

He nodded, his eyes scanning the rear view mirror. "Yeah, that's the one."

"So it wasn't law enforcement who called the hotel was it?" He looked down. Her hand lay in his comfortably. His thumb stroked circles over the back of her hand. Damn, how long had he been doing that?

Her question… "Ahh… no, as far as I know, all law enforcement agencies have been given a cease and desist order in connection to you." He looked over and shrugged. "Looks like you're stuck with me for a while, Em."

She closed her eyes and sighed, and Joseph watched her battle fatigue. She was crashing, no doubt the adrenaline pushes of the day waning now that she was safe. He had experienced the same exhaustion too many times to count. She wouldn't last long. She couldn't quite keep her eyes open.

"I think it is the other way around Joey, I'm not going to let you go. You couldn't get rid of me now if you tried."

Joseph chuckled. He lifted the center arm rest and patted his thigh. "Lay down. You're exhausted."

"Hmmm… I would love to, but before I do, is there a woman that's going to kick my ass for using you like a pillow?"

He smirked when he looked over at her. "No. Half of the world is terrified of me. The other half is blissfully ignorant."

Ember took off her boots and curled up on the seat putting her head on his thigh. She snuggled closer to him resting her hand on his leg near his knee.

"I've never been afraid of you, Joey."

He reached down and ran his fingers gently through her silky black curls. "I know, Em. I know."

The powerful car effortlessly put distance between them and the last place she'd been seen. Her silky smooth curls molded around his fingers. Mindlessly he ran his fingers through her hair while she slept. The dashboard lights illuminated her face. Her thick and extraordinarily long lashes rested on her high cheekbones. Darkness hid the freckles that dusted over her nose. She hated them. He didn't. Her full luscious lips parted as she slept. Angelina Jolie, you've got nothing on these lips. He ran his thumb over the pulse steadily throbbing in her neck. It had been almost sixteen years since he'd held her. It had been a simpler time, when he'd had dreams and a shot at a future. It seemed like forever.

Few cars shared the road and the lack of an adversary allowed his mind to wander. His finger traced the collar on her throat. He knew exactly what the leather signified. That she didn't spoke volumes about her. Hell, her body may have matured, but Em still reminded him of the sweet girl he knew so many years ago.

The miles and hours slipped away. During the night, she'd tossed and turned during the drive. Now she lay on her back with her head on his leg. He knew the second she woke. Her breathing changed. Her body tensed slightly. She relaxed then smiled without opening her eyes. Lifting her hand, she stroked his arm. "God, you feel so good, Joey."

He chuckled and squeezed her shoulder. "We're approaching a rest stop. Need to freshen up?" She nodded and sat up, stretching her arms and rolling her neck.

"Sorry the accommodations weren't better."

She laughed and slid towards him kissing his cheek. "My compliments to the management. That was the best rest I've had in years."

She wormed her way next to him, scooting against his wounds. He lifted his arm and she snuggled into the crook before she put her head on his shoulder.

Okay, this closeness? This needed to stop, this snuggling thing she had going on. The sudden lovey-dovey shit could be damn easy to get used to. Ignore the warmth. Ignore the perfect way she fits next to you. This can never happen. Ember deserved better than he could give her. He cleared his throat. Time to get back on course. "We'll get some breakfast in Sioux Falls before we turn onto I-90 heading west. The safe-house is another twelve to fourteen hours away."

"Don't you need to get some sleep?"

"The work I do has provided me with vast experience in dealing with very little sleep. When we get to the cabin, I'll let you stand guard while I hibernate for a day or two."

Joseph exited the highway into a rest stop and parked. Ember pulled her satchel into the front seat and opened the zipped pouch inside. Pulling out a small silver capsule, she pushed it at him. "Here, you take that, I don't want it. I don't want to know what's on it, and I don't want to be associated with it."

He nodded and got out of the car putting the flash drive in his front pocket of his slacks. He stretched, careful not to wince. "Too late, you're already associated with it, but I'll take care of it until we can upload it to a secure server."

Ember cocked her head looking out the open door as she pulled on her boots. "Okay, you've got all day to explain that secure server comment, but right now I'm heading to the ladies' room."

Joseph walked with her into the building. He used the facilities and splashed his face with cold water hoping to reduce his growing temperature. Sitting outside in the early morning sunshine, he waited for her. The muscle spasms, shaking and even the fever he was nursing remained manageable. He suspected by tomorrow he would be in a world of hurt, but by then they would be at his cabin. She exited wearing faded jeans and knee high boots instead of the mini skirt. Her curves were sensational and he wanted nothing more than to peel the skin-tight denim off her body. Ahh… just fuck me now. I'm so screwed. A groan rumbled in his chest. At her questioning look he admitted, "You've grown into a beautiful woman."

She leaned up and kissed his cheek. "I was just thinking the same thing about you, Joey."

Moving away from her before his body could betray where his mind had taken him, he responded, "I'd never live it down if my brothers heard you say I'm a beautiful woman."

"What? No, ugh, you know what I meant. You're a total stud muffin. You always have been. Please don't tell me the King brothers are still maneuvering for the most macho award?"

He shook his head as he got in the car. "No, not really, but there's a definite pecking order. Justin is a businessman. He owns six very successful restaurants. He's the only one of us who's never been associated with Guardian Security. We no longer fight over who is most macho because we all agree. Justin lost hands down."

She laughed as he programmed the GPS for the nearest restaurant and pulled onto the interstate. "So you work for Guardian too?" He threw a glance her way before he nodded.

Ember slid closer to him once again forcing his arm up so she could snuggle next to him. Her body, her scent, her sexy voice—God, what a fucking distraction. She placed her hand on his thigh and squeezed slightly. "What do you do for Guardian? Your mom said you worked overseas."

He didn't respond. What the hell was he supposed to say? Instead, he pulled off the interstate and motioned towards a small restaurant. "Breakfast."

She crinkled her nose and erupted in a throaty chuckle. "Stop ignoring the question. What do you do?"

Oh, nothing much, I kill evil mother fuckers who deserve to die. "I have assignments abroad." Congratulations, it wasn't a lie.

"So you work for Guardian overseas doing what?"

He stopped the car, put it in park and turned his head towards her. He didn't move his body more than necessary. "I eliminate security concerns. Stop bad situations from getting worse." Yep, with practice he could actually hold a conversation.

She smiled at him, "Is this what you pictured when you joined the Marine Corps?"

He leaned back gingerly on the door and leveled a very pointed stare at her. "We had a very naive view of the world back then, Em. Nothing about what I do is that innocent. I perform a necessary function, without which hundreds if not thousands of innocent people would perish."

He watched for her reaction. Her brow furrowed as her head cocked. "What could you possibly do that would stop that much suffering?"

"My job."

CHAPTER SIX

JOSEPH DISSECTED THE DINING ROOM, A HABIT HE couldn't stop after years of living on the edge of society. The waitress served them coffee, took their order and left while he determined the possible threats.

Ember leaned across the table and placed a hand on his. She lowered her voice to a whisper, "Is there anyone here we need to worry about?"

He nodded and drew his eyes to hers. "Two men, seated separately—one at the entrance, the other near the bathrooms. Based on the number of cars parked outside, and accounting for the staff and patrons grouped into clusters, they could be together. They seem to want to give the appearance they aren't."

She never looked away from him and calmly asked, "What are we going to do?"

Brave girl. He shook his head and leaned forward towards her. "We are going to eat breakfast and push on. If they're looking for you, they won't know you're with me. Hopefully, they're not aware you've changed your looks."

Time to change the subject. No need someone hearing something they shouldn't. "So tell me how your Aunt Caroline is doing." His field of vision held both of the suspicious men.

"Ahhh well…she died four years ago. It was a sudden, massive, myocardial infarction that irreparably devastated the heart muscle. There was no chance of survival."

"God, I'm sorry. I don't remember anyone telling me that." Damn it King, you really do suck at small talk.

She shrugged. "Death is part of life. Nobody has tomorrow guaranteed."

"I take it by the terminology you used that you did go to medical school?" He covered her hand with his and once again stroked the top of it with his thumb. And, no, thank you, he didn't want to know why he felt the need to do that.

"Went to, graduated from and currently practice emergency medicine. Or at least I did until yesterday."

Reality. He could deal with reality. "I can get someone at Guardian to make a call and get you a leave of absence if needed."

She shook her head. "Nah, that won't be necessary. I just resigned my position. I'd reached a point where I wanted a change. I planned to take the next year off. I had the foolish notion I wanted to travel the country and see all the sites. While I was soaking in the Americana experience, I was going to look for a smaller hospital, one where I could actually have a life, you know? Outside of work, I mean. I was supposed to drive away today on my long anticipated hiatus."

Joseph kept silent until the approaching waitress deposited their breakfast plates, refilled their coffee and left. "Do you still enjoy medicine?"

Ember cut the blueberry pancakes and swirled them in the maple syrup she had pooled on the plate. With the fork halfway to her mouth, she paused before she smiled radiantly.

God, she was amazing.

"Absolutely. I love what I do, but the way I was doing it was draining my energy, my essence. I felt almost… I don't know how to explain it, but I felt dead inside. It's hard to put out there because I don't want to be a complainer. But when you're good at something, sometimes, you allow people to put you in a position that keeps taking that skill from you until you burn out. Believe it or not, it's human nature. Well, if not human nature, it's at least my nature. I was asked to accept more responsibility, work longer hours and take on additional shifts." She stuffed the pancakes in her mouth and chewed for a while before she continued. "All of which I did without complaint. That left me with almost no time to figure out who I was or what I wanted. I floated, doing exactly what people expected of me. I was content or at least ignored my dissatisfaction until I saw a way out. The friends I made in college are all married. They have families and their lives are filled with children and love. All I have is a storage unit full of taped up boxes. I want more."

And didn't that sum up the way he had allowed his profession with Guardian to suck him into nonexistence? The parallel was uncanny on so many levels–too many to be comfortable with.

Putting another bite of the blueberry studded pancake in her mouth she closed her eyes and hummed, "Delicious!"

Hell yes, she was delicious and, damn, he may just have to sample a bite. "I agree."

She opened her eyes and cast a glance at his stack of pancakes. "Joey, you haven't even taken a bite."

"I'm not hungry for food. I'm talking about you. I bet you're absolutely… delicious." See? Ember was a distraction. Trouble with a capital E.

Just like in high school, her blush built up from her chest and swept over her cheeks. She peeked through her long lashes at him.

He chuckled and pushed his food around his plate. Well, you started it King. Don't stop now. "I'm betting the recipe may have gotten better with time. With age and maturity the flavor has had time to develop additional spice."

Ember winked at him. Between bites, she teased, "Nice. Call a woman old and then complement her on her spices!" Her laughter peeled around him. He had to shake his head in disbelief. She hadn't changed at all.

"So, mister-open-mouth-insert-foot, just how do you propose to savor said spices?"

He frowned at the food on his plate and put down his fork. "That depends. Is there a man who is going to try to kick my ass when I make love to you?"

Ember cocked her head and looked at him narrowing her eyes. He recognized that look. He'd seen it many times when they were younger. She pointed her fork at him.

"When you make love to me? Don't you mean if you make love to me?"

He shook his head. His eyes devoured her luscious body. "If I'm completely honest? I'm not entirely sure. Still contemplating whether or not that would be a good move for either of us. Answer my question."

She blushed vividly and suddenly found her pancakes very interesting. He struggled to hear her soft reply.

"There's nobody and hasn't been for a long time. Remember the work rant I just bored you with?" She threw a radiant smile his way. "Half the world doesn't know I exist and the other half only values me for my medical skills."

His foot knocked hers under the table like he used to do in high school when he wanted her full attention. "I happen to know you exist and at this second I don't need a doctor."

"Really? Have you had a routine need for a doctor in the past?" She ate another forkful of pancakes as he watched.

He shrugged and regretted it immediately when pain skipped across his shoulder and back. "More than I care to admit."

Ember kicked his foot under the table. He glanced at her while taking a drink of coffee. Her eyes were bright with laughter.

She purred, "Hey, Joey, want to play doctor with me?" Coffee spray showered the table as he choked on the hot beverage. Her squeal of laughter ripped across the restaurant. Picking up her napkin, she wiped her arm and tossed it at him. "Damn, Joey, you lost all cool points on that one!"

He couldn't help it. He laughed. It had been forever since anything had struck him as funny. Dropping cash on the table, he stood up offering her his hand. "Maybe, but that was one hell of a loaded question."

She giggled, stood up and walked out the door with him, "That would be true. It was. So? Are you going to accept?"

He got in the car and waited until she had fastened her seatbelt before he put it into gear. As he pulled out, he answered. "Do I want to? Hell, yes. Am I going to? Look, I'm not politically correct and I don't play games. I'm putting my cards on the table. I'm not the kid you used to know. I'm not what you need. I would end up hurting you, Em. I don't do normal."

"Normal what?" Her eyes were wide as she stared at him.

"Normal relationships. I guess you could say I have unique desires." Damn, could she blink maybe or look away? How in the hell did I get into this conversation?

"Oh. Ohhhh! Like the Dom thing you wouldn't talk about last night?"

He shook his head. "No, not like that and I'm not getting into this with you. You probably couldn't handle what I need."

"Are you gay?"

He couldn't stop the laugh. Damn, she tickled him. "Far from it. Not that I give a shit who a person is attracted to, but guys don't do it for me."

"Then what is it you need I couldn't give you?" The innocence of the question defined everything she couldn't give him.

"I'm not into regular sex, babe. You couldn't cope with what I want from a sexual partner."

He purposefully didn't look at her. He couldn't bear to see the expression on her face.

Her voice was calm, almost clinical. "You do the thinking for everyone, or am I just particularly lucky?"

He shot a quick look her direction. "Babe, what would you say if I shoved my cock down your throat and held you so tight against me you couldn't breathe? Or fucked you up the ass or pounded into you so hard you screamed? I like it when it hurts, when it frightens and when it's rough. No, I won't play doctor with you. I don't play." He risked a look at her and did a double take. He hadn't expected to see desire. He'd expected disgust.

"Oh, really? What makes you think I wouldn't get off on that?" She threw the challenge his way and damned if he wasn't going to accept it. Deadpanning, he responded. "One, your ignorance about the significance of that collar you wore says you are pure vanilla. Two, I dated you for over a year. I know what got you hot and it wasn't me hurting you. And three, there is no way this, what's happening here, has a snowball's chance of becoming anything other than a one-and-done. I'm never in one place. My job is dangerous. A relationship is a weakness I can't afford."

Quite proud of himself for remaining in control of the situation, he gave himself a mental pat on the back. He did well. He defused the situation and let her down easy. Her foot started tapping the floorboard. Oh, God... not the foot tap. He risked a glance at her. Her eyes blazed. Her jaw was set, and her face had turned the color of cooked lobster. Oh, fuck me. Here it comes.

"You self-righteous, smug son-of-a-bitch! Let's examine your bullshit-filled list why don't we? One—just because I don't know about the Dom thingy lifestyle doesn't mean I'm stupid, frigid or sexually stunted. I learn damn fast. Two—for your information, my fucked-up Romeo, you may have dated me for a year, but you never fucked me. I can tell you this, Joseph Theodore King, while what we did was sweet, it did absolutely nothing towards getting me off! And three—you arrogant asshole, did I ask you to marry me? No, I don't think I did. Your one-and-done? Okay by me, Mr. God's-gift-to-women! I merely offered to fuck you into next week. For that, I get a lecture on my lack of sexual knowledge. Gee, thank you so much for your self-denial at my expense, you self-centered, conceited prick! Do me a favor? Stop doing me favors, you… you chauvinistic asswipe!"

Well shit, when she puts it that way. "Ember…"

"No. This conversation is over. When we get to where ever it is you're taking me, I'll call one of your brothers to come get me. Calling you was a mistake. Huge! Massive! The biggest fucking mistake I've made in sixteen years. I had to have been fucking nuts… conceited son of a… "

He reached over and grabbed her chin in his hand pulling her face toward him. The pressure hurt, he knew it did, yet she did nothing to make him stop. "You do not get to call me that twice in one day!" She glared at him but remained silent. "There is no way one of my brothers is coming to get you. If anyone is going to protect you, it's me."

He cast a look at the road before he pulled her towards him and kissed her. He kept an eye on the road as his lips punished hers until she mewled under him. That whimper was what he lusted after. It could get him off quicker than just about anything. He lived for those cries of surrender, and from Ember, the small whimper lit him up like a fucking roman candle on the Fourth of July. He released her chin and seat belt before he pulled her across the seat firmly tucking her next to him. When she started to pull away, he growled, "Sit there and be absolutely silent until I tell you to speak or I'll whip your sassy ass. And believe me, I'll enjoy every second of that!"

Uncharacteristically, Ember complied. She sat quietly beside him with her eyes downcast. The only movement he saw was her bottom lip being repeatedly pulled into her mouth. God, not like that was distracting after the kiss they just shared. Casting his eyes to the rear view mirror, he watched the truck with Texas plates. It still held its distance. Great. All this fun and a couple of douchebag wannabe druggies.

Joseph drove for miles waiting until the area surrounding the interstate became remote. A plan coalesced before he spoke, startling the pouting woman next to him. Making his move away from potential witnesses was going to require some ingenuity on his part.

"Ember, we have a tail. I'm going to stop to get gas. When I ask you to freshen up go into the station and lock yourself in the women's restroom. Do not open the door until you hear my voice. You got that?"

She looked up at him before she nodded and rubbed her arms as if to ward off a chill. Those beautiful green eyes showed her lust and more than a little confusion. Joseph hated that he didn't have time to finish her little lesson right now, but other things, aka douchebag wannabe druggies took priority.

"Reach behind me and take the phone out of the front pocket of my pack. Take it with you. If I don't come get you in twenty minutes, power it up, push the redial button and tell whomever answers the phone your name and that I need assistance. Whatever you do, don't leave that bathroom."

"Are they going to try to kill us?" Those big green eyes were now wide with fear.

"Those two? I doubt it. They're probably hoping for a snatch and grab opportunity. The unknown is how they knew we were heading this way and if they have reported us as a suspected contact. I'm going to have a conversation with the gentlemen while you powder your nose."

JOSEPH VEERED INTO AN ANCIENT GAS STATION AND pulled up to the pump. His pale face was drawn tight, and he was sweating. "Go. Don't come out for any reason."

Em nodded her head simply because she couldn't speak. Terrified of the men who followed them, she walked into the station going straight to the back of the building and locked herself in the lady's restroom. Leaning against the wall, she waited. Her nerves jumped at every sound she heard in the adjacent store as the minutes stretched on. Ember tried to breathe deeply to counteract the anxiety, but the exercise just made her nauseous. Pacing in the tiny room, she lurched and cupped her hand over her mouth to stifle a scream when a knock sounded on the door. She held her breath and waited. A woman's voice asked, "Excuse me miss, is everything all right?"

Ember's voice shook as she responded. "Yes, thank you. I have an upset stomach. Could you give me a couple minutes, please?"

"You betcha, hun. Just checking on you. You've been in there for a while and you haven't paid for the gas that was pumped.

"Yes, ma'am. I'll come out and pay. Just not right now." Ember flushed the toilet to punctuate her comment. It must have worked. The woman didn't say anything else.

Time seemed to stop. Ember checked the minute hand on her watch more than once to ensure it hadn't started to run backwards. The noises from the shop attached to the gas station muted as the minute hand struck the time Joey had instructed her to make the call. She cradled the cell phone and turned it on. Her finger trembled as it hovered over the redial button.

"Em, open the door, babe."

She leapt at the accompanying sharp wrap on the door. The phone flew out of her shaking hands. Plastic and metal became a skittering bullet on the painted cement floor. She chased after and picked up the escaped phone. Em threw back the bolt and launched into Joseph's arms. Burying her face in his neck, she finally exhaled. "Joey, I was so scared. Are you alright? Did they hurt you?"

He tensed immediately and loosened her arms from around his neck. "Come on. We have to go." He threw several bills on the counter for the clerk as he grabbed her arm and pulled her out of the gas station.

He got in and pulled out onto the interstate. Once again, his training superseded his desire to stomp on the gas and get the fuck out of Dodge. Drawing attention to the car now wouldn't help their situation. "Joey what happened? What took so long? I was just about to hit the redial." She held up the phone providing evidence of her intent.

HE LOOKED AT THE PHONE AND SIGHED. THE woman beside him vibrated with anxiety. A bundle of nerves. Taking the phone from her, he put it up to his ear. "Jacob, it was a false alarm. Em got a case of the jitters. You can stand down."

He glanced towards Em. Her eyes were huge as she realized she had somehow placed a call. He pointed to the seat next to him. She moved over immediately. "No, we're fine. When Ember dropped or picked up the phone, it must have redialed the last number used. I'll authenticate if you need me to."

Jacob shouted on the other end of the line, "Yes, damn it. I need you to authenticate. I pass you—Gulf." There was no doubt Ember heard his little brother's pissed off response.

Joseph replied calmly, "And I respond—stream. Now, would you please stand down?"

"Alright, but damn it man, put a strap on that phone. I had half the world heading toward… Sioux Falls, South Dakota?"

Joseph cast a glance at the woman next to him. "No problem. It won't happen again. I had to make an adjustment and Em got spooked."

Jacob cleared his throat. "How much of an adjustment?"

Joseph scanned the rearview mirror as he replied, "Adjustment is perhaps the wrong word."

"Did you remove the threat or delay it?"

Joseph's laugh was evil, caustic. "Oh, I removed it. Permanently."

"Joseph can the removal be traced to you?"

"As if." He snorted his brother's insinuation. Damn the little man was starting to piss him off.

"Is there something you're not able to tell me, Joseph?"

"Able to? No. Going to? Yes."

Jacob glanced at Ember as she bit her bottom lip and watched him intently. He nodded towards the water bottle. She opened it and took a drink waiting to pass it to him. "We are good to go for now. I need a truck, four-wheel drive, not this sedan I was forced to rent in Kansas. Park it at the Rushmore Mall in Rapid. South side parking lot. This car won't make it up the trails to the cabin."

"Alright, done. I'll have a truck positioned for you. I'll text you the plate number and a description. The keys will be in the usual place."

"Thanks. Later." Joseph powered the phone down and gave Ember a withering look. "Just what I needed to do…soothe the little man's frayed nerves." He gave her a lust filled glare. "Do you still want to fuck me into next week? Because, if you do? I'll play doctor with you."

CHAPTER SEVEN

EMBER GULPED DOWN ANOTHER SWALLOW OF WATER AND handed the bottle to him. The idea of sex with Joey, any kind of sex, had her wet. She only hoped it wouldn't show through her skin-tight jeans. Panic assailed her. Instead of answering him, she asked, "What happened to those men?"

He looked over at her and shook his head. "Evasion? Alright, I get the hint. Nothing happened that you need to worry about. I replaced our Missouri plate. That may give us some more time."

She put her hand on his and lightly touched his knuckles that were swollen and red. "You said removed them permanently. Did that mean you killed them?"

Joseph shrugged and Em noticed a wince. "I did my job. Let it go."

Ember put her head on his shoulder needing his warmth, but he didn't put his arm around her or allow her to get any closer. "I'm sorry, Joey."

"Sorry you offered to play doctor with me?" His hand rested on her thigh and squeezed.

The man had a one track mind, zero to sex in a second flat… or he was trying to change the subject on purpose?

She shook her head. "No, I'm not sorry about getting you to look at me as a woman and not the girl from your past. What I am sorry for is getting you mixed up in my drama. For making you drive half way across the country and for having to protect me from people who want to kill me."

He squeezed her thigh again and leaned over to kiss her temple. "Kinda glad you called."

She put her hand on his and patted it. "So, for my sanity's sake… when will you realize that I'm, in fact, an intelligent person?"

He chuckled. "Really? What have I done to indicate I think you're not an intelligent person?"

Ember turned in her seat so she could see his expression. Okay, put on your big girl panties and throw it out there. "You kill people for a living."

Nothing. Not a tick of movement from him. He blinked once and then turned his head toward her. "And?"

Wow. Just wow. Oh, my God. Oh, my God. Oh, my God! Breathe. In and out. Think! The boy she grew up with, the person she measured everyone else against, and the man who she wanted so bad her insides hurt, had just admitted to being an assassin. How? When? Why was he doing that? Was he a criminal? "Uhhh, Joey… I really need you to explain why you killed them. Couldn't you have just knocked them out and tied them up, or something?" Crap. She could hear the tremor in her voice.

His eyes never left the road unless he was checking the review mirror. He didn't respond and she didn't push the question. He drew a breath and cast a look at her.

"Alright, the truth is those two men would've been paid a lot of money had they killed you. They had the intent and capability but not the opportunity because I stopped them. That's what I do, Ember. I eliminate threats. Due to the injuries they sustained, neither were conscious or able to exit the crashed vehicle. Investigators will find a ruptured fuel line, nothing more. Our vehicle description and plate number were compromised. Your appearance modification threw the idiots. However, you looked similar enough to the photograph dispersed to all of the cartel's minions that they called in the suspicion. They didn't get a good enough photo of you in the restaurant for a definite confirmation. You weren't supposed to be traveling with a man, so their leadership isn't convinced it's you. They were told to take you out if the opportunity arose or follow and to call back tonight. When they don't call, it will cause an all-out search for this car. By that time, we will be in a truck somewhere in Wyoming." He delivered the information in a plain brown wrapper. No fuss, no muss—no emotion.

"How do you know all this, Joey?"

"We had a conversation. They told me."

"A conversation? You did something to them to make them tell you, didn't you."

"Well, they didn't volunteer the information, Ember."

She should shut up. She didn't want to know. Did she?

"But how did they find us?" Her voice cracked. Ember quickly looked out the side window hoping the flat prairie would help her process everything or anything.

"Pure unadulterated luck. The cartel moves drugs via the interstate system. They have personnel, semi-routes, smaller cargo shipments and safe houses set up to move the drugs. The DEA or state and local drug interdiction officers can't stop them. The infrastructure and communication are intricate. I'm speculating here, but I assume when Morales figured out you had the information, he put a picture of you out to every one of his familial contacts. They in turn sent it out to the network. Anyone eliminating a problem for Morales would become a very important person."

Em's rational and not-so-rational sides collided. A waterfall of emotions cascaded through her mind. The man next to her had just admitted he killed two men—to protect her. Minutes ticked by. Mile after mile of interstate passed. Her mind worried the information the way her teeth chewed at her fingernails. She took a shuddering breath and looked back at him trying to conceptualize the type of man that would or could kill another.

His black hair seemed darker. No. He had a pallor to his skin tone that wasn't there earlier. His facial expression showed nothing, but perspiration saturated his shirt collar and beaded his forehead. Red flushed his high cheekbones. A response to physical exertion? True, but it had been at least a half hour since they'd pulled out of the gas station. Joey was a fit male. His heart rate should have stabilized and lowered within minutes of getting into the car. An uneasy concern prompted her forward to get a better look at his pupils. She never made it that far. "Joey?"

"Yeah?"

"You're bleeding."

He pulled his coat over his side and nodded. "It is just a scratch, nothing to worry about. We need to put some distance between us and them before we stop again."

She reached over and peeled the jacket back. She stuck her forefinger through a hole in the luxurious material above the hip pocket on the right side of his coat. "This looks like a bullet-hole. Joey?"

"Yeah, for wannabe's the fuckers were well armed. The silencer was probably Russian."

She grabbed his arm and ordered, "Drive with your left hand." Pulling the jacket off, she unbuttoned the cuff of his designer shirt. Moving closer, she undid the front buttons and peeled the material away from his ribs. An angry red gash furrowed along his rib and bled freely. Ember lurched over the front seat and grabbed his pack from the back. She pulled a t-shirt out and ripped it in half. Pouring some water from what remained in the bottle, she quickly wiped the area. Rolling the other half of the t-shirt she put it against his wound and placed his hand over the makeshift bandage. "Hold this."

Launching over the back seat to her satchel, she pulled out her mini skirt. Ripping it from the zipper to the hem, she turned it and laid it over the bandage. "Sit away from the back of the seat." Joseph complied as she fed the rolled material around his ribs moving his shirt out of the way as she pulled the roll around. Taking both ends, she tied the cloth tightly over his wound.

"Damn woman, how am I supposed to breathe?" He adjusted his position and grimaced. She looked at the knotted shirt again to see if she had tightened it too severely. It took a couple of seconds before she realized what she had missed when she had only focused on the grazing wound from the bullet. When reality hit, she gasped.

He jerked and looked at her at the same time that he pulled the side of his shirt back to cover his body again. "Ember… it isn't as bad as it looks."

Holy heavenly father, she had never seen such massive dermis disruption. Pushing the shirt back again, she held it away from his body. How could he function? The excruciating pain those types of injuries produced were normally treated with massive doses of narcotics. Yet, she'd seen him take nothing. She pushed the shirt off his shoulder and down his arm. The atrocity of his wounds lay bare to her eyes. She reached out a hand almost touching the multitude of injuries, scabs and remodeling tissue that covered his chest, shoulder, and ribs. "Oh, God, Joey. Who did this to you? These wounds?"

He grabbed her hand and lifted it to his lips. "Shhh. We can talk about that later. Will you get me a t-shirt out of my pack? I'll pull over and put it on and we'll ditch these clothes."

"Who did this? They tortured you. Didn't they?"

He slowed down and pulled to the side of the road. Putting the car in park, he cupped her face in his large hands. "Ember, I exist in a dangerous world. The important thing is I'm here with you now and you're safe."

He lowered his lips to hers and kissed her softly, almost reverently.

His forehead rested on hers. Short panting breaths brought her eyes back to his face. His color was almost ghostly white as he whispered, "Em, baby, please get me a shirt out of my pack, moving right now is not enjoyable."

She nodded and leaned over the seat getting a black t-shirt. He unbuttoned the other sleeve and pulled the jacket off. His shoulder holster came off next followed by the white dress shirt. Em helped him take off the shirt and saw the devastating injuries that marred his back. The damage to his flesh had barely healed in some places. In others, infection and untreated wounds wept. She helped him pull on a t-shirt and his shoulder holster.

Joseph nodded to the back. "There are some jeans, hiking boots, and a black button down. Pull them out for me will you?"

She retrieved the clothes, helped him take off his shoes and pull down his slacks.

"Damn it, can you loosen the bandage? I can't breathe." His small huffs for air paid stark testimony to his complaint.

Em assessed him and reacted immediately. She lifted his eyelids. The extreme dilation of his pupils told her he needed help and stat. He closed his eyes and dropped his head back on the headrest. She took his pulse and mentally logged the other symptoms he presented. "Joey, what are you taking for the pain?"

He shook his head keeping his eyes closed. "Nothing now. At first, I was given some locally milled heroine. That kept the pain from driving me crazy until I got to civilization. I've been eating oxycodone since then. But, I quit taking them."

He struggled with his jeans and she semi-straddled him helping him snap and zip the Levis. "Cold turkey, Joey? When did you stop?"

"Yesterday, when I got back to the States. I was going to detox in the hotel room. I didn't have time to get anymore after you called."

"Joey, move over into the passenger seat. I'm driving, you need to rest."

He shook his head, "No."

"Damn it to hell, Joey. You've been shot. You're going through withdrawal and if we get pulled over we have stolen plates. Let's not forget to mention you have a concealed weapon… or should I say cannon? What the hell is that thing?" Ember's eyes flashed as she moved him towards the passenger seat.

As he started to answer, she threw up her hand to silence him. "No! Never mind, I don't want to know. Just slide over and let me drive."

He lurched for the passenger door throwing it open just in time to vomit on the side of the highway. Ember let him void his stomach as she rolled up his bloody shirt, jacket and slacks and put them back in his pack. She picked up the black button down shirt and waited for him to sit up. She handed him the water bottle, "Rinse your mouth out." When he returned the bottle, she helped him put on the shirt, covering the shoulder holster.

After adjusting the seat and mirrors, she pulled out onto the interstate. With a flick of her finger, she put the car on cruise control at the posted speed. She grabbed his hand. A firm pull tugged his head to her thigh.

Stroking his sweat-dampened hair from his face, she automatically detected the fever that consumed him. "Shit, Joey, the adrenaline from this morning's activities acted like a catalyst to accelerate the purge of opioids from your system. There is no controlled burn with this detoxification. Your system is on automatic. You're crashing hard and you're not going to have a soft landing, honey."

He grimaced. "There's no such thing as a soft landing in life. And why the hell do you need to sound like a medical encyclopedia?"

"I'm sorry. I do that when I'm nervous. A former colleague pointed out it's my comfort zone. I retreat there when I'm scared… and damn it, Joey, I'm scared now!"

He writhed in pain. Taking shallow panting breaths, he spoke slowly, "I know. Listen Em, just keep an eye on the rearview mirror. If someone is always staying the same distance from us, that's a problem. Even cruise control varies the speed. If they're not losing or gaining on you, they're stalking you. We'll be okay."

"Alright, Joey. I'm going to have to trust you on that. I'll wake you up if there is a problem or we get to Rapid City." She looked down to see if he had heard her and shook her head. He labored to breathe. He was either unconscious or asleep. He groaned and shifted. She sighed. God, please help me. I'm so scared for him and for me.

Ember knew the physiology of the physical pain he was going through. Her mind whirled with the clinical terminology and her brain automatically began alphabetizing the terms. A defense mechanism. Dr. Sebastian was right. It allowed her to distance herself from the emotional pain of her patients. Only it wasn't working this time. She glanced down at Joey. At this point in withdrawal, his body would be aching. Within twenty-four hours, his joints would feel as if the muscle was being pulled from the bone. Because of his fever, violent shivers would rack his body, creating more muscle distress.

When the gas gauge registered half a tank, Ember pulled into a truck stop and fueled the car. She paid cash. She used the bathroom and bought more bottled water, a couple of protein bars, and four packets of Tylenol. Going back to the car, she unlocked it and slid onto the seat, putting his head back on her thigh. He was still out of it when she forced him to take the analgesic tablets and sip some water. The effect of acetaminophen on his injuries was like slapping a Band-Aid on an arterial hemorrhage, but it was all she could do. Praying his body would hold down the medicine, she pulled back out onto the interstate.

Ember gripped his shoulder lightly as she entered Rapid City. "Joey, I need you to wake up."

His eyes opened and he bolted upright. He tried to stifle the exclamation of pain. Slamming his fist viciously and repeatedly against the dash, he ground out another moan. "Fuuuuck!" he hissed. "Remind me not to do that again." Clenching his eyes closed, he fought the effects of the pain. Joseph opened his eyes again as he lay back against the headrest. "Em, take the second turn to the off ramp. The mall is down about a mile on the right. Pull over and park in the south lot near a lot of cars."

She nodded and followed his instructions.

"You stopped for gas?"

She nodded again concentrating on driving the unfamiliar streets.

"Did you see anyone trailing us?"

"No, there was a car back there for a while, but they pulled off at a tourist stop. Wall Drug? I haven't seen them since." She pulled into a parking spot and turned the car off.

"Joey, how are we going to find the truck?"

"Turn on the satphone. Jacob was going to send a description and plate number."

Ember reached back, pulled the phone out and hit the power button. The text came through and she memorized the information. "Alright I got it. Let's find the truck and go."

He chuckled humorlessly, "No. You need clothes. We have to go shopping."

"You are insane. I don't think so, my friend. You can barely sit up, how in the world are you going last while I go shopping?"

He turned his head towards her. "Em, I'm asking you to make quick selections and only get the basics, but you do need to have some clothes. We don't know how long we'll be at the cabin."

She nodded at the store they were parked in front of. "I can get the basics here." She reached over to the floorboard and pulled his hiking boots towards her. "You stay here. I'll be right back."

"Not happening. I'm going with you. I can't risk leaving you alone." He lowered slowly toward the floor board, reaching for his hiking boots.

"Fine. Let's get you dressed and go shopping."

Ember found a bench for him and stood unmoving in front of him until he agreed to sit down. "I promise to keep within your line of site. The store is closing in ten minutes and there is nobody here but the cashier. She's at least sixty-five. I'm not in any danger."

She quickly selected clothes and walked to the register. Paying for the items, she put the bags next to him and smiled. "I have to buy some shoes, Joey. As much as I love them, these heels probably won't work where we are going. The shoe department is around that corner. Give me five minutes and if I'm not back, you can send in the cavalry."

He stood and physically paled before he bent over and grabbed the shopping bags. "Like hell I will. I feel like I've been hit by a car, but I've lived through worse." He nodded in the direction of the shoe department.

"Men. I swear, a feather would knock you down right now and you think you are going to protect me?"

"No, Em, my forty-five is going to protect you. I may be under the weather, but I'm still better than ninety-five percent of the people they would send after you."

"Yeah? And what about the other five percent?"

"Unless Morales pays over two million, they wouldn't bother."

Em looked up at him. He was dead serious. Dead being the operative word.

"Glad I'm not worth the effort then."

"Oh, I have the distinct feeling you will be worth the effort." His small evil laugh left no doubt of his meaning. Even beaten to hell his mind went from zero to sex in a second flat. Ember visibly shuddered, earning another roll of the wicked laughter.

CHAPTER EIGHT

EM WATCHED HIM HUNCH OVER THE STEERING WHEEL of the truck in obvious distress. He tried to play off the pain, but she knew. She knew only too well.

"Joey, do you want to get a room here and get some sleep? Or maybe I could drive?" He shook his head and started the truck.

"No. I'm taking back roads. We need to make it to the cabin tonight under the cover of darkness. The area we are going to is desolate and I need to know for sure we're not being followed. If someone is tailing us, we'll see them. Once we get there, we're uploading the data to the server in Virginia and then we're going to lock the doors and go to bed for a couple days."

She laughed gently. "I'm game, tiger, but I think you may need a few days of sleep first."

The perspiration soaked edges of his hair clung to his face making the pallor of his skin almost ghostly in the fading evening light. "Actually, I was talking about sleeping, Em. I think I'm pushing my limits right now."

She put her hand on his forehead. Heat radiated from him. Infection or withdrawal, either way, the source needed to be addressed. "Can we stop at a drug store on the way out of town? I want to get some over the counter medication, decent bandages and antiseptic for your wounds and a temporal thermometer. You're burning up. I have to know how high that fever is. I'll make it quick." If I were licensed in this state, I could write a script for antibiotics and painkillers. But that process took forever, which wouldn't do them a damn bit of good tonight and would leave a trail to her. Right now, she agreed with Joey. It seemed nothing in life was easy.

They left the city behind after a stop at an all-night drug store. The drive through the Black Hills, in the dark, seemed eerie yet beautiful at the same time. The moon illuminated the white granite peaks contrasting with the looming black of the huge pine trees that towered over the roads.

They passed Mount Rushmore and Ember caught a glimpse of the grandeur of the massive monument. The pictures she'd seen failed epically to portray the majesty of the stone carvings. Yet despite the beauty and awe-inspiring sights, she couldn't relax or let down her guard. Joseph was in pain. His breathing labored in harsh contrast to the silence in the cab of the truck. He groaned involuntarily when he was forced to engage his large muscle groups.

They hit the Wyoming state line and continued west until just before Sundance. Turning north on a dirt road, he drove into a Wyoming spur of the Black Hills. Joseph turned off the headlights and traveled slowly using only the moonlight to keep them on the gravel track. Ember feared for him.

"Your temperature is too damn high." Ember cleared the digital readout. One hundred and three. If it gets higher your bodily functions are going to fail. You need help, Joseph.

His glassy stare remained on the road. "I'm not stopping."

Fear and concern churned deep inside her. "If you won't stop, at least let me drive."

"No."

"Joseph—"

"No." She settled into her seat and crossed her arms. "You are an idiot… a single-minded, determined idiot. I can't remember when I've seen someone so hell bent on killing themselves."

"Welcome to my life." Joseph muttered and then lapsed into silence.

The road behind them remained dark. No headlights trailed them. After about forty minutes, Joseph slowed even further and turned down a trail that was marked by a dime-sized red reflector on the side of a massive pine tree. He followed what Ember assumed passed as a road, although as vague as it appeared, she couldn't be sure. It appeared he followed a faint set of tire tracks barely discernible by the overgrowth of vegetation. After fifteen minutes, the truck bounced around a curve and he stopped in front of a fence and gate. The grey metal tubing formed a huge rectangle barrier blocking the dirt road. A chain and padlock wrapped around the metal blocking any further travel.

He put the truck in park and collapsed on the steering wheel. "Em, I'm going to go open the gate. Drive through so I can shut it after us alright?" She nodded and watched as he slowly exited the vehicle. She could not imagine how he functioned through the physiological rigors. Driving through the gate, she put the truck in park and waited. The darkness obscured her vision but the muted sounds of metal against metal hinted at his location. She listened intently for his approach, but as the seconds dragged and the noise at the gate ceased, panic flashed through her. Em pushed the door of the truck open and practically fell to the ground in her scramble to get out. As she stood, she saw him, silhouetted in the faint light of the moon. He'd crumpled to his hands and knees and swayed. His head hung limply from his neck. She ran to him and dropped beside him. His eyes were closed and his breathing came in shallow pants. Even in the pale light she could see the perspiration dripping from his nose and chin.

She put his arm over her shoulder. "Joey, you have to help me. You have to stand up." He nodded and struggled to stand as she lifted him. She walked him to the passenger side door and helped push him up into the cab. Getting into the driver's seat, she turned the high beams on. To hell with being stealthy. She wanted them alive when they got to the cabin. She crept the truck through impenetrable black, her eyes riveted on the two ghostly white ribbons that passed as the road. Fifteen minutes later, she pulled up in front of a log cabin. It took her several moments to unwrap her hands from the steering wheel and relax enough to move.

Ember managed to get the barely coherent man out of the truck and into the cabin. They struggled up the split log steps onto a massive porch that wrapped around the entire dwelling. The moon shone through the windows and provided the only light as she struggled to hold up his ever-growing weight. Joseph disabled a security system with the press of several keys before he pointed toward the right where she found a bedroom. She tried to lower him slowly to the bed, but his weight was far too much to handle. The best she could do was control his fall. He grimaced and groaned in pain but grabbed her wrist before she moved away. "Em, get Jacob the information."

"I don't care about that damned information right now, Joey. You push yourself any further and you may not make it. You need medicine and rest. Jacob will just have to wait until morning. You're too sick to be worried about that right now." She pulled the comforter off the footboard and covered him with it. "You're home, Joey. I'll take care of you. Now go to sleep. We're safe."

He grabbed her hand again and held her tightly, almost painfully. "Em, call Jacob."

"Alright, Joey. I promise I'll call him. Now, please rest."

He laid his head back and in the next instant, he was out.

After ensuring his respiration and heart rate was stable, she wet a cloth, stripped him down to his boxers and set about cooling his overheated torso. She performed basic first aid measures and prayed his body was strong enough to beat both the infection and the detox that ravaged him. Satisfied when his temperature finally lowered, Ember took a few minutes to empty the truck. She threw the bolt on the front door and found the kitchen. Had she been less stressed, she probably would have marveled at the modern stainless steel appliances and granite counter tops. Instead, Ember pulled the phone from his pack and turned it on. Angry and frustrated at her inability to help Joey, she jabbed the redial button and waited.

"Alpha." The deep voice at the other end answered. From the gravel sound of his voice, the man had been sleeping. Well, good for him.

Ember puffed her cheeks in exasperation and said, "May I please speak to Jacob King."

"Ember? This is Jacob. Where are you?"

Bitterness swelled, contaminating her voice. She needed to blame someone for what was happening to Joey and Jacob became the available target. "We're at the Wyoming cabin." The silence at the other end of the line was frustrating, but two could play at that game so she remained silent.

"Why isn't Joseph making this call?"

"There are actually several reasons, speaking from a strictly medical perspective. First, he was shot this morning. Although it is just a flesh wound, the path it traversed aggravated the damage that was done by the recent torture."

"Excuse me? What the fuck did you just say?" Jacob's voice boomed across the connection.

"Tortured. In my estimation due to the repair, remodeling and infection that has occurred, the trauma was inflicted within the last ten to fifteen days. And let's add a cherry to the top of the unfathomable suffering he has endured, shall we? He stopped taking his pain meds cold turkey. So he is going through clinical opioid withdrawal without the aid of any mitigating medications to lessen the crash. At the moment, he is unconscious with a fever of 101." Her throat closed up and she struggled to keep her tears at bay. "So I guess that's why your brother is not making this call."

"Tortured? My God, Ember, are you sure?"

"Oh, I'm sure. I'm an emergency medicine physician. I see trauma daily. I deal with car accidents, bullet wounds, knife wounds, burns, severe beatings, and abuse. But in all my years in the ER, I have never, repeat never, seen the extent of trauma your brother has endured. From the evidence on his torso, it appears as if someone succeeded in flaying the skin off ninety-percent of his back."

The silence at the other end of the line was unbearable. "Did you hear me? Did you hear what I said?"

"I heard you. Is there anything I can do?" His voice broke as he asked the last question.

"Yeah, Jacob, you can keep him safe. No work until he's healed. The world will just have to spin on its own. I'll take care of him. We'll send the information when he wakes up. But his body is going through a massive shock. He needs antibiotics, pain killers, and a solid week of rest. He needs time to recover."

"Em, I didn't know. He didn't say anything. It wasn't in his reports."

She sighed. It would be like Joey not to let anyone know. Regretting her tantrum, she swallowed her pride. "Okay Jacob.

Hey, look… I'm sorry for assuming you knew. I've unloaded the truck and locked up the cabin. I'm going to take care of his wounds, get him to hydrate some more and then go to sleep. I'll have him call when he wakes up. We can upload the information then. If the cartel finds us tonight, they can have us." How can I be so tired?

"Em, you're safe for now. Joseph's home is off the grid. Nobody will know you're there. Hell, until last night I didn't know where it was. I'll get you help ASAP. Get some sleep and call when you can."

"Goodnight, Jacob."

She turned off the power to the phone and retrieved the bag from the drug store. With an effort, she roused Joey enough to take more Tylenol and forced him to drink most of the bottle of water. I wish I had something better to help you, Joey.

Em covered him with the comforter and turned off the light. Undressing quietly, she slid into bed next to him. Turning towards him, she snuggled close, giving him the warmth his body needed. Ember put her hand on his chest. His heartbeat felt strong and regular. Reassured, she fell asleep almost immediately.

THE SUN SPILLED INTO THE CABIN THROUGH THE skylight in the bedroom too soon. Ember woke slowly and squinted, her eyes trying to focus. With a sudden realization of her surroundings, she looked to her left and smiled softly at the man sleeping beside her. Some of his color had returned. His breathing was even, deep and steady and his face was relaxed. She marveled at how the boy she knew had become such a magnificent man. His hair hung over his brow making him look seventeen again. The multitude of lesions on his shoulders and chest were livid, red and puckered. She could not imagine the pain he must have endured. Em fought the tears that threatened to spill. The injuries were so severe and yet, he came for her. He'd put aside the anguish, the pain, flown halfway across the country and then had driven all night just to make sure she was safe. No matter what he said or how he said it, he cared for her. That thought bolstered her spirits and allowed a small upward tug of her lips as she brushed the hair from his forehead.

She slipped out of bed and went into the bathroom to shower. Shampooing removed most of the black rinse out of her auburn hair. Wrapped only in a towel she tiptoed across the floor and out into the kitchen where her new clothes sat in shopping bags. She dressed quickly. Rifling through the cabinets, she found an unopened can of coffee and coffee maker. After a fifteen-minute search for a can opener, she found it mounted under the cabinet. Laughing at herself for missing the obvious, she started a full pot.

A picture window framed a meadow that spread out behind the cabin. The view of the Black Hills and the yellow and purple wild flowers scattered throughout the field was breathtaking. A gentle breeze blew the flowers and tall grasses. They swayed in time to nature's own dance. She rinsed out a cup and filled it with coffee.

Now armed with the caffeine her body desperately needed, she peeked into the bedroom. Joseph's steady breathing reassured her he was still asleep. Ember walked to the back door and left it open as she sat down on the edge of the porch and dangled her legs in the morning sun like a little girl.

Ember leaned against the pole and breathed in the warm air. Pine, sunshine, and freshness invaded to a cellular level. Finally, she relaxed from the drama of the last two days. Her only plans for the day were drinking at least one more pot of coffee and exploring the house.

She walked softly not wanting to make any noise to wake Joseph. A quick observation showed the "cabin" was a two-bedroom, three-bathroom home built with care and craftsmanship. Every room boasted a beautiful view of the hills and was furnished with sturdy furniture that fit the rustic feel of the house.

Making another carafe of coffee for herself, she walked back to the bedroom and peeked in the door. Joseph lay awake and stared at the ceiling. Ember walked in and sat down beside him. She gently pushed the hair off his forehead and smiled. "Hey, how are you feeling?"

He closed his eyes and swallowed. "Like I've been run over by a semi-truck… a couple of times." He put his hand on her waist and opened his eyes again. His voice was soft, "Your hair is red again. God, how long have I been out?"

"It's okay, you haven't been out long." Ember whispered as she lay down beside him and caressed his cheek. "The color was a temporary rinse. I shampooed most of it out this morning. You faded out on me last night at the gate. We managed to make it to the bed and then you were gone. It's just as well. I am glad you weren't conscious when I cleaned and redressed your wounds. It's late afternoon now. You need to drink some water."

He shook his head and reached over pulling her closer. "No. I couldn't hold it down. I need to call Jacob and let him know we are safe."

She chuckled. "You told me to do that last night. I called him. I think he wants you to call when you're feeling better."

Joseph closed his eyes and nodded. "Alright, but not right now."

She lay still as his body relaxed again and he drifted back to sleep. Exhaustion was a symptom of opioid withdrawal and the sleep was good for his mending body. She waited until he was in deep REM sleep before she slid out of his grasp.

Her mind ticked off his physical progress. No fever, better color, no respiratory distress—all good signs that his stamina and conditioning were fighting to pull his body through.

She turned the corner into the kitchen and froze. A large man leaned against the counter in the kitchen drinking a cup of her coffee. Of American Indian descent, she thought. He looked menacing, but passive. Something in his casual repose fueled her courage. Ember picked up her coffee cup and walked to the pot. Pouring a cup, she turned. "Are you here to kill us or help us?"

"If I wanted to kill you, you'd both be dead now. Jacob sent me."

She took a drink of her coffee. "My name is Ember."

The man nodded. "Yeah, I know. I'm Mike, but everyone calls me Chief. I have a cooler of food and some other groceries in the truck. Doc sent some medical supplies. He nodded toward the small package on the counter. Said you'd needed that."

She opened the packet examined the sealed vials of medication. "Joey needs these antibiotics."

Chief nodded and put the cup down. "You make good strong coffee."

She smiled as she opened a syringe from the sealed pack. "No sense in drinking it if it tastes like tea."

"You got that drive? I'll send in the documents."

Ember stared at him and shook her head. "Sorry ace, nice that you know names and appear to be a good guy, but until I get permission you don't get squat."

He looked at her and laughed. His entire personality transformed. "Okay, call Jacob and ask or go back into the bedroom and wake up Joseph. He can vouch for me."

Ember looked at him and growled protectively. "There is no way in hell I'm going to wake him up." She walked to the satellite phone and powered it up. Looking up at the huge man, she pushed the redial button. It rang twice before Jacob answered.

"Joseph?"

Ember responded, "No this is Ember. There's a huge man standing in my kitchen drinking coffee and he said you sent him."

"Yeah, I did Em, his name is Chief and he's my friend. I trust him with my life. He'll stay with you until Joseph is better."

"A little heads-up would have been nice."

"The satphone was off. Besides, after you told me about his injuries, I knew Joseph needed help. Chief can upload the documentation, and we can start to get some resolution to your situation. By the way, did you say your kitchen?"

Ember glanced at the big guy as he poured another cup of coffee. "I believe I did. Thank you for sending us help. I'll have Joey call you when he wakes up."

A low rumble resembling a laugh came through the phone. "Joey? Jesus, I haven't heard that in a while. Thank you for taking care of him. If he had his way, he would have healed up and left the country without anyone knowing he was here. He's…well, he's protecting us by not bringing his world into ours. We know it, and what sucks is that you've spent more time with him in the last two days than I've had with him in the last ten years."

Ember blinked back the tears that filled her eyes at the thought of the loneliness Joey must live with. "Yeah, he's alluded to the fact he doesn't do relationships—even with his family." She cleared her throat and bounced back to her comfort zone again. "Look, I get that you didn't know about the abuse. There is no way I can verbalize the extent of the trauma he has endured. Honestly? I'm surprised he wasn't mainlining morphine."

"Okay, please ask him to call me when he can. Chief will take care of your security until Joseph kicks him to the curb.

Once we get the documents, we will start defusing the time bomb that Dale primed."

Ember disconnected the phone and got the drive for Mike. She watched as he set up the computer and placed inline encryption devices on the system that would secure the data transfer. As the documents uploaded, they unpacked his truck and Ember gave Joey a dose of antibiotics before putting the groceries away.

She finished preparing dinner for herself and Mike and checked on Joseph throughout the evening. Over his protests, she force-fed him a few spoonfuls of broth and a bottle of water. When Mike headed out to check the access road for any activity, she went to bed. She slipped in between the sheets and moved next to him. Joseph reached out and pulled her closer. "God, you feel so good."

She chuckled and snuggled closer to him. "Go back to sleep, Joey. You're not strong enough to do anything your mind might be imagining."

"Mmm… don't go anywhere. When I wake up in the morning, you're going to see just how strong I am."

"Hate to tell you this champ, but your body is going to be really sore for the next couple of days." She traced his lips with her fingers.

His voice was soft and she could tell he was falling back to sleep. "Yeah? Been there done that… got the scars to prove it."

She put a hand on his chest and kissed his lips softly. "I know, Joey. I know."

His breathing had evened out before she pulled her lips from his. She lifted her hand and brushed his hair from his forehead. She still loved him. Oh, not in the sweet innocent way she had when she was eighteen. No, he was the epitome of everything she wanted desperately to avoid. Drama, stress, anxiety, and fear. Yet, he was everything she needed. Strength, loyalty, kindness, and compassion.

Joseph King was a dichotomy rolled in danger and served with a huge side of sexual tension.

"I'm so screwed. How can you still mean so much to me?"

CHAPTER NINE

EMBER SMELLED THE AMAZING AROMA OF STRONG COFFEE long before she walked into the kitchen. God bless Mike for making coffee the right way and for getting up earlier than her to do it. She walked out onto the back porch with a steaming mug in hand. She stilled immediately when a doe and two fawns raised their heads from grazing in the meadow. Sitting down with a slow and quiet intent, she watched the gentle creatures dip their heads to eat, oblivious to her intrusion.

Mike's voice from the kitchen carried in a low whisper, "They're upwind. If they could smell us, they wouldn't be anywhere near here."

Ember glanced over her shoulder and smiled. "They're bigger than any deer I've ever seen. So beautiful."

"They're mule deer. See how large the ears are? They resemble the length of a mule's ear, hence the name. They're the largest breed in the States."

He walked out slowly and leaned against a post as they watched the animals feed on the tall grass. Ember sighed and looked up at him. "I'm sorry to pull you out here, Mike. I am assuming you had other reasons for being way out here in no man's land?"

He shrugged his shoulder. "I was in the area. Joseph and Jacob have pulled my butt out of the fire many times. It was the least I could do. The Kings are my family. I'd do anything for them."

Wait. Hold on a minute. "I thought Joey worked alone."

"He does. Normally." The man drank his coffee obviously not going to expound on his answer.

"Would you care to elaborate? I don't have a nifty security clearance, but I've figured out what he does."

Chief took a draw of his coffee examining the bottom of the cup as if searching for the words to use. His shoulder lifted in another shrug. "About a year ago, a rescue mission we were on tanked. It was bad. Two of us were taken by hostiles. Jacob, Joseph and another brother stayed in country to mitigate the damage and recoup the losses. Losses…hell I was the loss. Me and a teammate, Doc. Jacob and Joseph were able to track the ones who took us. The bastards didn't stand a chance once those two showed up."

"He's really good at what he does, isn't he?" She didn't try to hide the admiration in her voice.

"No ma'am, that'd be an obscene understatement. He's the best there is. Period."

"Are you married, Mike?"

He shook his head and laughed. "Whoa, whiplash on the conversation vector there. No, ma'am, I'm not. I don't think it's fair to ask a woman to take on my lifestyle unless she's part of it, like Jacob's wife."

A small smile tugged at her cheek. "Really? Don't you think that should be left up to the woman?"

"No, ma'am. I don't. It would be incredibly selfish of me to ask any woman to put up with my life. Hell, physical training and involvement with the teams I train impact any down time

I have. Plus I'm subject to immediate recall if the situation warrants. What would give me the right to ask someone I care about to put up with the loneliness and the danger? What kind of woman would say yes?"

Ember stood and looked down at her empty coffee cup. "One like me would say yes in a heartbeat. One that understands there are no guarantees but is willing to take a risk on having a happiness that others desperately seek and rarely find. Yeah, I guess a woman like me." She leaned against the railing and looked towards the meadow. "Women are so much stronger than you testosterone-filled alpha males give us credit for."

She slid a glance his way and winked. "Take some unsolicited advice from a woman who knows just a tiny bit about your life. If you have someone, stop wasting what precious time you have on this earth by protecting her from your lifestyle. Tomorrow isn't going to come for everyone. What happens if she walks out the door one day and never comes home because an accident takes her away from you? Would she know how you felt about her before she died? Trust me, Mike. You need to let her have the opportunity to enjoy you. And you? You better love her while you can. My mom once told me life isn't about the millions of breaths you take. It's about the individual moments that take your breath away."

Ember turned to walk into the house but froze at the site of the gorgeous man standing in the doorway wearing nothing but low-slung jeans. Joseph. Evidently, yesterday's re-bandaged wound dressings didn't make it through the shower. His hair freshly combed and still wet shone jet black in the morning sun. He lifted his coffee cup in a mock salute. A slow smile spread over his face. Mike turned to follow Ember inside but when he saw Joseph, he too, stopped. Chief nodded acknowledging his friend and immediately turned, dropped off the porch and headed toward the front of the house.

Ember felt her face flame red as Joseph sauntered towards her. The mesh of livid wounds across his shoulders, chest and ribs couldn't detract from the sexual magnetism he exuded.

He pulled her toward him gently and lowered his lips to her neck. "Having a good conversation with Chief?" he whispered.

He trailed light kisses along her neck sending rivulets of pleasure throughout her body. She melted into his arms, moving her head to the side giving him access to her neck and sighed. "Yes, he's nice."

"Nice? Huh. Not a word I've heard to describe Chief before." His quiet whispers were interspersed between delicious feathery kisses. His hands traveled down and cupped her ass pulling her closer to his apparent desire. He nibbled on her ear. "What were you talking about?"

The feel of his body against hers and the heat from his hands and lips enveloped her. Damn, did he ask a question? "Hmmm? Oh…God, you feel good. Ahh, we were talking about you…I mean… oh… your work."

He chuckled as he moved to nip and kiss her jaw, slowly making his way to her lips. "Oh? That's not what I heard."

He lifted his lips over hers hovering above them as he whispered, "Is it true? All I have to do is ask a woman like you?"

Her eyes opened and stared into his. Yes. "Maybe."

He smiled and lowered his lips slowly towards hers. He swept over her lips softly exhaling as he teased her, pulling away before he kissed her. His arms tightened around her almost crushing her to him. "I won't ask. I can't. You know I can't give you forever. This is for now, this moment in time only. But I find at this moment I want to take your breath away."

He finally lowered his lips and captured hers with a warm press of lips. He tasted of morning coffee and an indefinable flavor only Joseph possessed. Memories of long summer nights spent testing and teasing each other flooded her senses as it had happened only yesterday. Ember lifted to her toes, pressing her body close in an answer to his demanding call. Immediate need flared inside her just as it had when she was in high school. The knowledge that today her need would be filled roused the ache no other man had ever fueled.

He smiled and lifted his hand to her face, stroking her bottom lip with his thumb. "Let's go into the bedroom. I don't think we need Chief to walk in on us."

"Joey, you shouldn't. You need to rest and let those wounds heal." God, it cost her to say that. She wanted him, but the physician in her raised its hackles and screamed in disbelief at what the wanton woman in her was considering.

Taking her hand, he led her into the bedroom and shut the door. Crossing to the bed, he pulled her closer. He slowly unbuttoned her shirt as he kissed her neck, his voice low and thick, "I've slept for over twenty-four hours. My wounds are better and I'll be damned if they're going to stop me from making love to you. Tell me you want this. You want this moment in time."

Her hands traveled over his shoulders and chest feeling his muscles ripple under her touch. "I want you, I need… But…"

"No buts. No future. Just us. Now." He covered her mouth with his as he dropped her shirt from her shoulders. His kiss pulled her dizzyingly higher as he unhooked and pulled off her bra. She clung to his arms as he unbuttoned her jeans and pushed them over her hips dropping the material to the floor. Holding her tightly, he continued to kiss her as he laid her under him on the bed.

Her eyes traveled his body and his obvious arousal. As a doctor, she'd seen hundreds of naked men. But damn this man's sexual equipment was the finest she'd ever seen. "Mr. King as a health care professional I would be remiss if I did not remark on the distinct attributes of your spectacularly endowed physique. You've grown into a fine specimen of a man."

He chuckled and lowered over her. "Dr. Harris as a man who appreciates true beauty, I would be remiss if I did not tell you I have never seen… touched… or kissed… a more beautiful woman." He punctuated each word with a kiss as his lips slid from hers, to her neck, to the top of her breasts. His thumb rubbed the top of one nipple as his lips covered the other. His teeth nipped and tugged her tender flesh. She gasped and arched her back toward him to encourage the exploration of his mouth. He transferred his attentions to her other breast and lowered his hand seeking her center.

Ember stilled as he touched her. This wasn't what he had described wanting, but God it was so good. Joseph lifted his head and kissed her neck softly. "You're so beautiful. I've wanted you for so damn long. Just us, baby. You and me. Right now. So good."

His hand continued to explore, opening her. He covered her lips with his and immediately deepened the kiss matching his hard finger strokes with the invasion of his tongue. Her body tensed, arched to his touch as she moaned under him. His mouth on hers consumed her sounds of need and desire.

The degree of the growing tightness in her catapulted from intense to inescapable. His fingers speared her as his thumb continued to stroke her clit, driving her towards orgasm. Never before had anyone set off the unmatched heat raging in her body—not like this. Where his hands and body touched her skin, intense feelings ignited. Her body tightened and convulsed under his hand as waves of deep pulling sensations drove through her core and exploded within her. Her cries consumed by his lips rent the quiet of the room. He pushed into her relentlessly with his fingers and rode out her orgasm never leaving their kiss. Joseph slowed his hand and the fervor of their kiss as her body calmed. Tremors shook her. Apparently, lingering aftershocks were a byproduct of phenomenal sex. God, who knew? A deeply sated grin covered her face when he finally pulled from the kiss. She watched him as her expression registered. He lifted himself over her and moved his knee between her legs.

"You look so damn sexy."

Sweet Jesus, his deep baritone whisper set off another aftershock. "Mmmm… Feeling so good right now, Joey."

"Woman, I'm about to rock your world."

"Promises, promises." She ran her hands through his hair and pulled him back down to kiss him. She loved the way he tasted—the dark, bitter flavor of coffee accented the wonderful essence of the man he had become. His hips settled between her legs and he nudged the head of his thick cock against her.

"For the love of God, tell me you're on the pill." He groaned his words against her lips.

"We're protected, and if you tell me you're clean, I'll trust you."

He nodded against her neck. "I'm clean."

Her body arched towards him, encouraging, begging him to continue. He slowly pushed forward, just barely entering. He lifted his chest away from her but took the bud of her nipple into his mouth. Slowly he increased the pressure of his bite on her breast until her body pulled away. The pain radiated from where his teeth clenched and yet he didn't stop.

With his teeth still around her nipple, he growled, "Brace, yourself." His cock split her in one monumental thrust, wrenching a gasping cry from her. Her body lunged trying to escape his penetrating thickness. His fingers bit into her shoulders and held her onto his cock. "Stop, baby girl. You're going to take me now. Good girl, now look at me." His words bit into her over-stimulated brain. She pulled another ragged breath and tried to move away again. His size was too much. The discomfort was almost unbearable.

"Ember, stop pulling away." He pinned her mouth with his and punished her with the press of his lips against hers. She could feel the tears welling in her eyes. And then he moved. Oh God, a moan ripped from the fabric of her soul as he slid out of her only to slam back into her recesses. She couldn't explain the sensations. The pain was intense and yet... she wanted... no... needed more? Over and over, his cock impaled her as his mouth held her, silencing her cries. His arms pulled her to him as his shaft drilled into her. His kiss refused her the oxygen she needed and she desperately pulled air through her nose.

Finally, he lifted his head. Instinctively she drew large gulps of air into her lungs.

"That's right. Breathe, baby girl. You feel so good, so fucking tight."

He lifted onto his knees and pulled her legs over his thighs. Joseph grasped her hips, curling his fingers into her flesh and moved, driving in and out of her at various angles but always with a mind-numbing force. He drove his shaft into her impaling her with an assault like none she had known before. Ember couldn't stop the cries his forceful mating drew from her. She tried, God knew she tried, but the sensations were too much.

"Fuck yes, let me hear it. I love the way you sound when I'm taking you."

Ember saw the excitement in his eyes. The same passion she loved and wanted but he'd refused to give when they were younger. Yes, she wanted this. She wanted him to take her just like this. Why? Her body once again tightened as the deep pulling of her core clenched around his cock. Each slam drove her closer to release. She bucked against him before she screamed, claiming her own ecstasy.

He buried himself painfully deep. "Oh fuck! Jesus, Ember!"

She barely registered his cry joining hers, shattering the silence of the house.

Joseph lowered his spent body on top of her. Shared perspiration formed a slick layer between them. Panting in an effort to catch her breath, she stroked his shoulder, careful to avoid his tender wounds.

He rolled onto his uninjured side pulling her with him, still buried deep within her.

His hand grasped her by the nape and his thumb stroked the pounding pulse point at the base of her neck. The tender touch struck her as the complete antithesis to his treatment a few moments ago.

"Holy hell, Ember, I think I've died and gone to heaven."

Her answering chuckle muffled in his chest. "Yeah, that was phenomenal sex."

"Not bad for a kink novice. You have exceeded my expectations. I'll have to push the envelope next time." He grunted and slapped her ass, gripping it tightly, pulling her closer.

"Next time? So you're keeping me around?"

"Oh, hell yeah, I'm not letting you go."

She purred and moved closer to him, relaxing. "Hmm… you better be careful, Mr. King. I may mistake that comment for an offer of a relationship."

He leaned over and kissed her, running his fingers through her curls. His grip tightened holding her immobile. "If things weren't as they are now, I would be more than alright with that, Dr. Harris. But this is for now. I don't have a future to give you."

"I know, Joey. I accept your stipulation that this won't last." She lowered her eyes as her hand traveled down his bulging muscled arm. "Do you realize it took us almost sixteen years to make love to each other?"

He leaned forward and traced her jaw with his tongue before he whispered against her lips, "You were worth the wait." Pushing her onto her back, he pinned both of her arms over her head with one arm. "But I'm done waiting."

Joseph walked out of the bedroom hours later. Starving, thirsty, and for the moment, sexually sated, he wandered into the kitchen. Those feelings were a hell of a combination and one he could do over and over again. *Yeah and you did do her over and over again, didn't you, King?* Shaking off the lingering thoughts of sex, he turned to the mission at hand. Food and drink first, then he needed to call Jacob.

Yeah, right. His mind wandered back to the woman lying in his bed. He left Ember asleep in the bed after a marathon session of the best sex he'd ever had. Damned if that woman wasn't everything a man needed. Soft, giving, caring, smart, sexy and if today was any indication—insatiable. Even with the fatigue, stiffness and the nagging pain of the injuries, he felt better than he had in months. He took several cookies from an open pack on the counter and picked up the satellite phone hitting redial. Jacob answered immediately.

"Alpha."

His mouth full of cookies, Joseph asked, "Were the documents what you anticipated?"

"Joseph?"

"Yeah. Well, were they?" He shoved another cookie in his mouth, walked to the refrigerator and pulled out a half-gallon jug of milk.

"The documents are exactly what were indicated. The Morales Cartel has some extremely influential people on their payroll. The FBI has launched a joint task force with Homeland Security. They anticipate several of the higher ranking people will talk if they're promised immunity and protection."

Joseph drank a quarter of the milk straight from the container as he listened. "What is the word on the hit?" He stuffed two more cookies in his mouth.

Jacob paused. "Jared is working it, but it seems the order came from Morales himself. Even though we have the documents, Morales wants the woman who was able to escape his reach. According to intelligence, one has taken the assignment. All others have pulled off."

Joseph put the cookie he was about to eat down and tensed. "Who?"

"The identity has not been confirmed by secondary sources."

Joseph paced around the kitchen's granite topped island and growled, "Damn it, Jacob, who?"

"Indications are the Scorpion has taken the contract."

His gut clenched at the revelation. The Scorpion was a ruthless assassin who skillfully used various methods to complete his missions. Meaning he couldn't anticipate how the killer would do the job. Joseph's voice became ice cold as he quietly responded, "That Spaniard doesn't work in the States."

"True, and as I said, it hasn't been confirmed, but then again you don't work in the States either."

Joseph pulled his hand through his hair and sighed. "He's an international level professional."

"Yeah, he's good, but we both know you're better. I've talked with Gabriel. From what he can find, there may be a family connection between the assassin and Morales. The Scorpion and the leadership of the Morales Cartel have been coded for assassination and targeted through the appropriate channels. We have a green light to take them out. When we get proper intelligence, I'll send a team in."

Joseph glanced behind him to make sure Ember wasn't listening. "Like hell you will. If they're coded, that makes them mine. Don't you dare send in a team. They'll be slaughtered."

Jacob paused. "Then I'll send in another shadow operative. I'm not allowing you to go, Joseph. Ember told me about your injuries. You're on medical hold until I get you cleared. You don't have permission to work this case."

"Damn it to fucking hell and back! See, this is why I didn't write it up. I knew you would pull me out. I'm only going to say this once little brother so get it through your head, now. I. Was. Not. Compromised. I didn't break and the fucker that messed me up is dead. I'm fine now so what's your fucking beef?"

Joseph swiped his hand through his hair again in frustration. "This conversation is why I didn't think it was necessary to report in. Quite frankly, I don't give a flying fuck if you give me permission to work this or not. Morales and his hit man are threats to Ember and neither she nor I will be free until said threat is eliminated. You and I both know I'm the only one capable of doing this without additional loss of life on our side."

"Ember said you were going through opioid withdrawal."

"The operative terminology there is 'was.' Yeah, I took pain killers. I ate them like fire consumes gasoline. I stopped the day I landed back in the States. I don't know if I was addicted, but I'd built up one hell of a tolerance. Believe me, it was not fun getting off them. But I'm drug-free now and I don't feel any dependency."

"Yeah? Are you still in pain?"

"No more than usual, little man."

"If you're allowed to take this case, and that is one hell of a big if, it could take months to conclude. How can you protect Ember from the Scorpion if you're tracking Morales?"

Joseph's mind had already calculated the first moves of a chess game he knew only too well. He spoke slowly and clearly as his eyes scanned the hills behind his house. "The Scorpion will make his move on her here. It's what I'd do."

"How can he find you? You're off the grid."

Joseph sighed. "The two I took out called in a possible sighting. When that duo of dipshit didn't report in last night or… the night before… anyway, when they didn't report in, we gave away the general location. Would you like to guess how many satellite telephones there are in the Tri-state area?"

Jacob sighed heavily into the phone. Joseph didn't have to tell his brother they'd handed their position over on a silver platter every time they powered on the damn satphone. The Scorpion would pinpoint the location of the calls, eliminate the locally-issued numbers and be on his way. The assassin was one of the elite—not one of the minor league operatives who wouldn't know how to track a satphone. He'd use the signal like a GPS.

"Two days?" Jacob's question pulled Joseph back to the conversation.

"Maybe, but I doubt we have any longer."

"For fuck's sake old man, take Ember and get out, head to the airport at Rapid City. We will move you out to a secure location."

A dry, resigned chuckle floated across the room. "Jacob, if I don't take him out now, he'll track us. He'll be relentless. I know because that's what I'd do. He wants her. It's a vendetta now. She's his focus. The silver lining? He doesn't know who I am. That is our only advantage. Once I take out the Scorpion, Guardian can protect Ember and I'll go after Morales."

His voice lowered as he closed his eyes. "I'm going to need Chief for a couple days. The two buttheads who reported me passed on a general description. Chief's build is similar—a big guy with black hair. I need Chief here, close to Em, to protect her while I do what I need to do. When I go after that son of a bitch Morales, Guardian needs to get her to another location."

There was silence at the other end of the line. Finally, Jacob spoke, "We can take her to…"

"I don't want to know where you take her. I won't be coming back for her. After I finish this, I'm walking away. No more shadows. No more missions. I'm out of it. All of it."

Severed throats, sleeping in the filth and cold or enduring days of scorching heat and thirst, living on pain pills only to detox yet again—this had become his world. He couldn't believe it, but he'd reached the end. Fuck. Two days with Ember and he'd crash landed. Nothing felt good. Nothing felt right. He wanted out. He wanted to be out and be safe. With Ember. Fuck.

"Alright. I understand. But before I release you on Morales, Doc is going to give you a physical. I'm not sending my brother into an assassin's way without knowing his exact condition."

"I don't need—"

"No. I'm your supervisor and your brother, damn it. You can have Morales, but you'll go through a complete physical, a go/no go evaluation and you will follow reporting protocols. Period. Is that understood?"

"When I have eliminated the Spaniard get Doc out here. I'm not sitting on my ass while you get people in position."

"He's close by. Keep yourself alive, old man."

Joseph hung up the phone and took a long drink from the milk container finishing it. Old man? When did that happen? Joseph knew Chief had heard most of the conversation. Without turning he spoke, "I'm using you and Em as bait. I'll leave tomorrow morning and ghost into the hills. If he was overseas when he got the assignment, I should have at least another full day before he's in the area. I'll try to stop him before he reaches either of you. Don't leave her alone."

Chief walked to the coffee pot and poured a cup. "Got it. Are you going to be able to hang? I mean physically?" The Cherokee nodded towards the remodeling flesh on his ribs and shoulder. "You need to heal."

"Fuck, man—I got no choice."

Chief grunted in acknowledgement. "I'll take care of your woman when you go after the Cartel. I figure you'll have to trail them and learn the organization before you can infiltrate and neutralize him. Use that time to regain your strength. Call me when you're ready to go in the morning. I'll be camping out on the perimeter. You need some time with your woman." He turned to the back door and looked out at the meadow. "Fury, I got your back, man. I promise I'll keep her safe until you take out Morales.

Joseph nodded, not giving Chief's use of his code name a second thought. "I can't risk waiting. Once the hired gun on her is neutralized, we have to move. It won't be easy to get into the Cartel and it could take several months or longer to work my way to Morales."

Chief drank the steaming hot coffee like ice water, finishing the cup before he spoke. "I owe you my life. On that debt of honor, know I'll keep her safe."

Joseph turned, put a hand on the Cherokee's shoulder, and squeezed. Words couldn't express what he was feeling. Dropping his hand, he walked back to the bedroom.

He'd tell Ember, but not now. Now he needed her. They were going to have a few good memories of their time together. He'd make sure of it. Hell, they both deserved at least that much.

Joseph opened the door and smiled when he heard the shower running. He dropped his jeans near the bed and took off his t-shirt throwing it on the chair as he passed into the bathroom. She was standing under the water with her eyes closed but smiled sensing he was there. "I'm so glad you're here. I need someone to wash my back for me."

He walked up to her and pulled her front into him holding her as she bent backwards rinsing her hair. God he could lose himself in her soft warm body. Years of loneliness pulled at him. The emptiness he existed in ceased when he took her in his arms. He lowered his head to her throat and alternated between kissing and nipping the steady pulse of her neck. Her heartbeat filled his senses and for once he allowed himself to pretend he could have something this good. She pulled forward out of the water leaning into him giving him the opportunity he wanted. He'd pay for the emotional attachment he allowed himself, but right now he didn't fucking care. He lifted from her neck and captured her mouth. Her softness molded against him as he took her mouth forcefully.

The knowledge he'd be leaving her soon amped up his desire and perhaps motivated his aggressiveness now. Yeah, not really. He wanted her. Period. If he had the next fifty years to discover her secrets, it wouldn't matter. His hands traveled her body, caressing, holding and pressing her against him. This woman symbolized everything good and whole in his life. She represented a time before all he knew was death. He would never be able to get enough of her.

Bending down, he lifted her and walked her to the shower wall. He leaned her back against it as he continued to use his hand to discover her body.

"Wrap your legs around me, babe."

"No, your wounds will open up again. Put me down, Joey, I have an idea."

He lifted away from her and slowly smiled. Interesting. By all means—tell me how you want it. "Okay, baby girl, what's your idea?"

She lifted her eyebrows and smiled. Turning around, she put her back against him and leaned back. "Hold on to me."

He grabbed her waist with one arm and cupped her breasts with the other. She spread her legs and pushed her ass back against his raging cock. They aligned perfectly and his cock took immediate notice. "Jesus, woman, don't destroy me before we get a chance to try your new position."

She laughed as he grabbed her ass with both hands. "Come on, old man. I want you to take us to the moon. Think you can handle that?"

"You wicked, demanding wench, who are you calling old?" Her sultry laugh barely registered as his attention was one hundred percent riveted on that perfect ass pressed against his painfully erect cock.

She leaned forward against the shower bench. Reverently he smoothed his hands over her soft cheeks before he buried his fingers in her flesh. "Oh God, I have always fucking loved this beautiful ass." He lifted her away slightly. Bending, he pushed his rock hard cock into her hot, wet core and damn near came right then from the tight heat of her body. Ember's head fell forward as he pulled back slowly only to thrust deep inside her again.

"Harder, Joey. I want you deeper and faster!"

Oh God, what this woman did to him. His control snapped with her words and he pummeled into her, pulling her back to meet his cock as he buried deep inside of her. Her tight body opened to take his entire length, and he pounded her softness.

"God, don't stop!" Her panted plea turned into shattered cries as he felt her body clenching around his cock. He slipped a hand around her and fingered her clit. She came screaming his name. His control broke and he crashed into her, grinding through her orgasm. He pulled out of her, still rock hard. He wanted, no needed something more. His dark desires ran deep.

He reached behind her and turned off the water. Reaching out the door for a towel, he slowly dried her, stopping to kiss every area he rubbed dry. She shook from head to toe by the time he moved slowly back up and dried her hair. He dropped his lips to hers. "So responsive to my touch. So beautiful. Such a good girl for me."

He straightened and pulled away. He wrapped a towel around her and reached for another to dry himself. "Dry me off." He held the towel out to her waiting for her response.

EMBER TOOK THE TOWEL SLOWLY. 'GOOD GIRL' ECHOED in her mind. Unfathomably the thought of being called his good girl made her happy. She felt her skin heat at the implications of being possessed by this man. His to care for, his to use, his to take. His approval and praise struck a chord deep inside her. At that moment, she would have done or given anything to earn his approval, to be called his good girl again. God, what did that say about her?

While her mind dissected and examined his words and her feelings, she used the same method to dry him that he'd used on her. Kissing his shoulders, biceps, pecs and abs after the towel, pink from the wounds that still hadn't fully closed, she dried his skin. The injuries that marred his body were invisible to her. She kissed the man, not his past.

Em dried his erection, her smile faltering as she lowered herself to her knees.

"Why didn't you finish? Wasn't I enough?"

"I'm not done with you yet, little one. I want something— more," His desire for pain. His unspoken desire sent a chill down her spine.

She slid her fingertips down his chest and abs. His muscles contracted and shuddered under her feather light touches. Ember smiled to herself. She had discovered in college that she had little to no gag reflex and the few boyfriends she did have raved about her ability to take them deep down her throat. Comparatively speaking, they were boys. This was a man, but she wanted to try. Taking hold of him, she kissed the dark pink head of his hard cock. She moved her attention to the sensitive underside, licking and kissing all the way down to his tight balls. The feel of the soft, wrinkled, skin covering the heavy weights and the quiver of his legs when she sucked one into her mouth flipped a switch in her body sending a cascade of her own juices down her leg. Her desire combined with lust filling her with a base, raw hunger to gratify the man before her.

Em looked up at him and smiled when his intense blue-green eyes met hers. He watched as her tongue laved its way back up his shaft. Taking the head of his cock, she sucked it into her mouth and caressed the bottom with her tongue. His body thrust forward and a growl sounded deep in his chest. Her tongue and hands worked together as she opened her throat and took him as deeply as she could. His hand dropped to her wet hair and entwined in the riot of curls. Her mouth and hands worked in unison, coaxing and caressing his sensitive skin, taking her time to stoke his desire and work her way down his shaft. When her throat relaxed enough, she braced her hands on his thighs and pulled forward taking him to the root. She wanted to smile as a low guttural moan echoed in the bathroom. His arms tensed and he momentarily held her head against him and shuddered around her. Joseph pulled completely out of her mouth surprising her. She gazed up at him, silently asking for the reason he stopped. The emotion in his eyes blazed back at her.

"Baby girl, if I take your mouth again I'm not going to stop. I want to fuck your lovely lips hard. Have you ever had anyone fuck your face? Anyone force you onto them and shoot down your throat? I'm giving you one chance to get off your knees."

Em saw his muscles shaking as he stood over her. Oh, yeah. She wanted this. She wanted to be his good girl. Em lowered her eyes to hide the embarrassment that flooded through every fiber of her body with that realization. "I want you to take my mouth. I want to taste you. I want you to…" To be proud of me? To call me your good girl again? How could she say those things?

Instead of saying anything, she leaned forward and licked the head of his blood engorged shaft and swallowed him until his cockhead hit the back of her throat. That's all it took. Immediate forceful stabs of his massive shaft ripped past her lips stopping only when he could go no further. She struggled before she could relax her throat enough to take him. It didn't matter. He used her hard, chasing his release. His hands gripped her hair tightly. The pain excited her more. His hips surged forward relentless and demanding. When she could take no more, he held her at the root of his shaft. She started to panic when he didn't release her. Long seconds passed before he withdrew. She drew great gulps of air into her burning lungs.

"Good, so damn good." Over and over he rammed his cock deep and held her tight against his body, using her throat for his pleasure. She fought for air when he pulled away, desperate for oxygen. Her eyes watered and saliva ran from her mouth as he took her throat. Depraved? Demeaning? God, she had no idea, but she was pleasing him. Right now, that was all that mattered. As if hearing her thoughts his words fell on her calming her, rewarding her. "So good, baby girl. Yeah, just like that. That perfect mouth. Ahh… take me. That's so fucking good. So hot."

His words of encouragement wrapped around her spurring on her efforts to surrender everything to him. Time stopped. Thoughts stopped. One goal consumed her mind and body. His pleasure.

"Oh, such a good girl. I feel you, so hot and wet. That's right, let me have your body. Let me take it. Let me in."

He pulled out enough for her to breathe. "Open your eyes Em. Take a deep breath. Another. Good. No, look at me don't close your eyes."

His fingers stroked her cheek, cool trails on her overheated, tear-soaked skin. "So beautiful with my cock in your mouth."

His hand threaded through her hair again and he smiled that wicked, sinister grin. Fingers grasped her hair tightly and his grip pressed her forward as he thrust into her throat holding her against him. She couldn't breathe and yet her heart flew when he praised her, desperate to please him. "God, yes! Look at you wrapped around my cock. Now take me deeper. No, all the way in. More. Stay there, don't move." His fingers pulled her hair holding her head still. "Yeah, that's it. No, you can't breathe yet." He held her tightly. The lack of oxygen tinged her world with black spots. She began to push on his legs desperate for a breath of air.

Hot jets of cum burst into her throat. Lips sealed against his cock she tried to swallow his musky seed but choked sending a white trail seeping down her chin. His hands pushed her back allowing her to breathe. Her rational, medically trained mind knew he'd edged her close to unconsciousness—but he hadn't crossed the line. He was an assassin. He knew the fine line intimately, and he hadn't crossed it. He knew exactly how to balance her on the edge of danger. Refusing to pull away from his shaft, she coughed and licked him worshipfully while sucking air into her lungs. Lost to anything but him, she continued until he cupped his hand around her neck and moved her away from him.

Joseph dropped to his knees in front of her and lifted his hand to her face wiping his cum off with his thumb. Em turned her cheek into his hand and licked his thumb clean.

"Amazing. Just amazing, baby girl. Thank you for trusting me. Are you alright?"

"I'm fine. Did I… I mean… was I?" Damn it, she hated when her voice trembled.

"Perfect, baby girl. You're absolutely perfect. Come on, let's go lie down."

His body shuddered, a last tremor of passion and then he stood, strong, alpha, and vastly more coordinated than she felt. His hand stroked her hair. "Are you okay?"

"Hmmm… better than okay." Her body lacked any skeletal structure and the blissful aura that settled around her made his movements seem all the more abrupt. "Whoa, I hope you don't think I'm moving that fast anytime soon. Did you go drink an energy drink or something? Not that I'm complaining mind you."

"Energy drink? Hell no. Years of physical training, the promise of mind-blowing sex and a couple days sleep did the trick. I did drink half a gallon of milk and ate a couple dozen cookies. Maybe it's the sugar." He offered her a hand up. "Now I believe we were headed to bed."

Her laughter pealed across the room and became contagious as her legs almost gave out. "Well, if I could stand without help that would be an excellent idea. That is, of course, unless you need more sustenance. Once I get feeling back in my legs, if I still have legs, I can make us some lunch or dinner. I honestly have no idea what time it is."

"It is too early for dinner and too late for lunch. I vote bed for at least another hour or so, and then we can worry about food." His lips found hers in a soft, warm, coaxing kiss.

"Hmmm…it is unanimous. Bed, now, Mr. King."

She watched as his features hardened and changed. He stood and offered her a hand, "Yeah, come on. We need to talk."

Ember lifted her eyes to him. A frigid shaft of fear pierced through her contented cloud of post-orgasmic bliss. "Talk? Why? What's wrong?"

He wrapped his arms around her loosely. "We have new intel. Let's go into the bedroom."

She let him lead her out and slid into bed next to him. He covered them with a quilt and positioned her next to him. She memorized the feel of his body warm and hard against her.

"Please tell me what's going on." Her hand drew small circles on his stomach almost hoping he wouldn't answer.

"There's been a contract placed on you and it was accepted by a professional. The good news is I know the man and he has no idea that I'm protecting you. I am better than he is but in order to keep you safe, I'll need to leave. I'm taking the hunt to him out there in the hills where I have the advantage. Chief will stay here with you. After I take care of the contractor, I'll come back, gather what I need, and then go after Morales. Chief will take you away from here and watch over you until its safe."

"A contract on me?"

"Yes."

"Why? I'm nobody. I don't have any idea what was on the drive."

"No, but you did manage to allude Morales. You're everything he can't allow. You're an embarrassment to him. You're a woman. A woman who is smart and strong. A woman who escaped his grasp. He can't allow you to live simply because you've damaged his reputation."

"You said you know him? I mean the guy they hired to kill me. You know him?"

"I know of him. People in our profession don't get friendly. Life expectancy plummets when introductions are made."

"But he's here? He's in the Black Hills? How did he find us?"

His fingers pushed back a boßunce of red curls so he could see her eyes. "There are ways to track anomalies. The use of our satphone is an anomaly. He's very good. I have no doubt he's aware of our location."

"Can't we just run? Hide somewhere until they forget about me?"

"No, baby girl. This man will find you, and he'll kill you unless I stop him. Your only hope for a normal life right now is me—doing my job."

"I'm not going to lie, Joey. I'm really scared right now."

"Do you trust me?"

"With everything I am."

He pulled her to him and wiggled his eyebrows suggestively before he said, "Maybe I should've had that energy drink."

CHAPTER TEN

EMBER WALKED THROUGH THE THICK WAVES OF THIGH-HIGH prairie grass and plucked another dainty violet flower adding it to her bouquet. She knew Joey was somewhere in the hills surrounding the cabin. He had left early before the morning sun could shine over the peaks of the beautiful mountains. She walked further and gathered more of the blossoms.

"Ember, please don't go out any farther. Joseph isn't expecting our guest for a day or so, but he would kick my ass if I let a bear get you." Chief's warning caused her to pause and look back at the house. She had, in fact, walked longer than she intended. She smiled and waved to him turning back towards the cabin. Spying a lovely cluster of the beautiful purple flowers she walked over. The profusion of violet waved happily in the light breeze of the late spring afternoon.

Chief dropped off the porch and headed towards her. She smiled up at him. "Mike, I'm sure you'll protect me from any wildlife that may venture out of the hills. Look at the flowers. They're so beautiful!"

He smiled and shook his head. "Women! How can weeds be beautiful?"

Ember laughed. "Beauty is in the eye of the beholder. Haven't you ever heard that? It's the middle of June and the flowers are still blooming!"

She dropped to her knees to pick some more of the blossoms. Ember heard a buzzing whizzing noise and looked up in time to see Mike's body jerk and fall before she heard the report of a gun. If she'd still been standing, she'd have taken a shot to the chest. She saw the bullet explode through Mike's jeans. She heard him roll from where he'd fallen as she dove into the grass after him. Taking his cue, she tumbled to the left violently and froze when she heard the slap of another bullet hit to her right.

She whispered, "Oh God! Mike? Mike? Can you hear me?"

"Yeah. It's going to be okay. Stay where you are Ember. Don't move. The grass is thick and high enough to camouflage our position. Don't move. He has the upper ground and will see if you move an inch."

"You're hurt. I need to take a look at that wound."

"If you move, you're dead. You being dead wouldn't help either of us, now would it?"

Her heart pounded loud in her ears. Okay, that's true. "What do we do? I need to assess your wound!"

Chief's chuckle was dry and reassuring. "Well, now all things considered, I think our best course of action is to wait. I don't believe the bullet hit an artery. The bleed isn't that fast. Don't worry. Joseph heard that report. The guy up there has no idea he is being hunted. When it gets dark, we'll move, but for now, we stay absolutely still. Do you understand?"

"I'm not moving. How bad is your leg?" Her mind replayed what she had seen, a thigh wound, outside. It might not be life threatening, but it would be excruciatingly painful.

"The bullet hole doesn't seem to have a problem. I, on the other hand, would like a very stiff drink."

Ember laughed despite their situation. Silence extended for what seemed like hours. Chief was close. She could hear his rhythmic breathing. "Tell me about your woman, Mike. What is she like?"

There was a long pause before he responded. "Desiree. Her name is Desiree. She's a good woman with a very kind heart. She's never been more than a hundred miles from home. Innocent and beautiful inside, you know what I mean?"

"Yeah, I do. That's important, being a good person. How long have you two been together?" Ember fought the urge to wipe the ants off her hand and instead blew them off.

"Together? We aren't. But I've known her for almost two years now. I met her when Jacob's wife brought him out here to heal. She is young. Younger than I should be hanging around. She just turned twenty-four, twelve years younger than me. I told her there was no future for us, that she needed to find someone better for her."

Their conversation lulled, both lost in their own thoughts. A strong hiss from his position brought him back into focus. "Mike, what's wrong?"

He groaned and answered through what sounded like clenched teeth. "Muscles are cramping in both my legs. Not. Pleasant."

Ember closed her eyes. The physiology of the wound and the cramping indicated bleeding in excess of what he was letting on.

"How much blood are you losing?" Ember inched forward towards him.

"Couldn't tell you, Ember, I can't see and I'm not moving to find out. Don't you even think about moving!" His words were clipped in warning as he spoke to her.

Ember dug her toe in and pushed herself another six inches in his direction. "Wouldn't dream of it. God knows I always do what I'm told."

A bullet slapped the ground to her left, slamming down in front of her, kicking dirt up in her face. The report of the shot followed seconds later.

Mike's frantic whisper was immediate. "Ember? Are you alright?"

"Yeah, not moving another centimeter. I promise!"

"Damn it, Ember if you move again, he will kill you! I'm okay. I've been hit worse." His voice rasped to her through the thick grass.

"Mike? Is Joey better than this guy?" She struggled to hold her fear at bay and to keep him talking to her.

Chief's voice was perfectly calm as he replied with a breathlessness that had her worried. "Ember, Joseph is the most skilled assassin in the world. He… he is death. The man in those hills has no idea how close to his maker he is at this moment."

THE FIRST OF TWO MUZZLE FLASHES FLAMED TO his left and up about two hundred feet. The first bullet must not have found its mark. Joseph's eyes searched the area near the house. He couldn't see Ember or Chief. They were either in the cabin or concealed in the tall grass. If he couldn't see them, the assassin above him couldn't see them either. The most direct path to the assassin's position would place him in the hit man's peripheral vision, the most sensitive of all vision fields for an assassin. Moving away would cost him time, and he wasn't sure how much time Ember and Chief had. He looked again at the field. If the killer thought he'd scored a hit, he would be on the move towards the meadow. There was no movement. Thank God.

Joseph slowly worked another hundred feet to his left and then started a very methodical and controlled climb up the mountain before he veered right again. A shift in the lower area around a pine tree caught his attention. Freezing automatically, Joseph's eyes moved in a strip and grid search of the terrain. The bush beside the tree moved slightly and Joseph discerned the shape of the sniper's rifle supported by a rock at the base of the tree. The gun jumped in the killer's hand. The sharp report echoed down the valley. He closed his eyes, momentarily listening for the telltale soft thud of a bullet going through flesh and bone. All assassins knew the tone. He counted the seconds it would take to reach the valley floor but heard nothing. His focus once again landed on the man at the base of the snarled pine tree.

Joseph thumbed the safety loop off his favored kill weapon. His blade. The balanced hilt sat in his hand perfectly. A steady inhaled breath aligned his target and his attention. Joseph could feel the beat of his heart. He ruthlessly pushed the flittering of birds from limb to limb into the background of his mind's eye. The assassin became his only focus. Forward. Each foot placement became the difference between life and death. Forward towards the man who wanted to take Em from him. Adrenaline jacked his system. His training and experience had turned him into a lethal weapon. He became hyper-aware of every detail surrounding him, his target and the area they both occupied. His target's attention focused on the field just as his centered on the assassin. The man moved slowly, carefully adjusting his scope. Joseph could tell he had located either Ember or Chief. The hit man inhaled a steadying breath. Joseph's silent approach went undetected. He'd plotted a collision course to eliminate the man trying to kill the woman he loved.

Discipline forced emotion from his mind. Joseph's knife slipped around the neck of the man who knelt at the base of the tree. He pulled it tight against the Spaniard's throat. "I hope you have made peace with your God, Scorpion. You went after my woman and for that I'll kill you."

The man's muscles tensed against the razor sharp edge of Joseph's blade. A trickle of blood dribbled down his neck. The assassin's quiet hiss carried far enough for Joseph to hear him. "Who are you? How do you know of me?" The certainty of the assassin's death was the only reason Joseph answered.

He pushed his knife deeper against the Spaniard's neck sending a thicker stream of blood over the blade. "I have many names. I'm the Guardian."

Realization widened the man's eyes as he sneered before he spat, "You're Fury. Had I known she was yours, I would not have taken payment for the job. I would have raped and tortured her just to draw you out. Your death would be worth so much more than the killing of this whore."

Joseph's sharp pull across the jugular ended the conversation. He held the man's head up as his body slumped down. He watched with an unemotional detachment as life literally drained out of the assassin. No, there was no emotion, no regret. In order to survive, others died. Others died. Not him. Not Ember. Not Chief. Not today.

The dying declaration of the assassin provided proof positive that Joseph could not involve Ember in his world. The life he led would follow him until the day he died. The idiocy of thinking about an ordinary life with Ember mocked him as he did what he was trained to do. He scanned the area methodically and waited to ensure he was alone on the mountain. Segmenting the terrain, he visually cleared it, ensuring there was no further threat before he stood.

Looking down at the dead man he called out, "Ember?"

There was silence and then Ember answered, "Joey? Chief's been hit. He's unconscious. Blood loss I think. I can't see him."

"It's safe to move. Help him."

He watched as she lunged forward and dropped into the

deep grass again. "Ember can you handle the situation?"

He waited for an agonizingly long period of time before she yelled back. "Yes. He's alive, but he's lost a lot of blood! I'm going to need help getting him into the cabin."

"Take care of him. I'll be there soon." Joseph picked up the dead man's bag and started rifling through the assorted weaponry. He glanced up when he saw her run towards the cabin. His eyes followed her and waited until she emerged again with a pack and raced back toward the meadow.

Going through the man's equipment, he found a rugged laptop and a black ledger. He paged through the ledger and scanned the information. Joseph drew a deep breath and replaced the computer and book. Taking the assassin's backpack, he strapped it on before he bent, lifting the man onto his shoulders.

Pain ripped through his body. The sensation of ten thousand knives piercing his back and shoulder forced him to his knees. He dumped the body to the forest floor and gasped for air. The warmth of blood flowing over his wounds confirmed the damage the dead man's weight had wrought. Fighting the black spots that invaded the edges of his vision, he pulled another rasping breath. Rage filled him. Anger at his weakness and physical limitations seethed deep and powerfully. Resentment of his body's deficiency fueled his weak-assed attempt to move the man's body. Grabbing the man's collar, he pulled the man towards a rocky canyon. Joseph unceremoniously shoved the corpse over a ledge and watched as the body plummeted to the rocks below.

There was no way down into the crevasse. He swept the ground where he had pulled the dead man's carcass with pine tree boughs and erased all evidence of his movement. With a methodical dedication, he worked the trail back to the tree where the assassin had hunkered down. Joseph policed the brass from the assassin's rifle and pocketed it. He scattered dirt and pine needles over the blood soaked ground. Finally, he worked a strip and grid pattern search to ensure nothing could indicate his or the assassin's presence on the mountain. Even if the man was found, there could be absolutely no connections made. The sun had sunk behind the granite topped mountain before he walked out into the meadow.

His approach behind her was silent. She didn't see or hear him come to her side. She had fashioned an IV holder out of a stick and had it hanging above Chief's head. Ember had cleaned and bandaged the wound and was taking his pulse when she looked up. Jumping to her feet, she grabbed him. His wounds screamed at the touch. His body seized. He pulled away barely stifling a groan.

Joseph dropped his hands to his knees and braced himself in an attempt to remain standing. Nodding towards Chief he asked, "How bad is it?"

Ember shrugged pulling her hands through her mass of curls. "Sit down before you fall down."

Only because he was going to fall down anyway, he sat down hard on the earth next to Chief.

His girl knelt on the ground again. "Have your wounds reopened?"

He nodded and drew a shaky breath. "Yeah. Bad this time. How is he?" Ember's manner automatically transitioned. Her briefing was professional and to the point. "It was a through and through. The high caliber bullet from the rifle made one hell of a mess. The saving grace—it didn't hit the bone. I stitched it up while he was out. He came to and was determined to move once I told him you said it was safe. So to prevent his macho ass from ripping out the stitches I just finished, I pushed some morphine in the IV. He is out for at least the next two to three hours. I've given him plasma, ringers and antibiotics for the infection."

Joseph looked at the medical bag beside her. "Where did you find that?"

"Mike brought it. Said someone named Doc heard you were in poor shape and thought I might need it. It's the best-stocked medical kit I have ever seen outside a hospital environment."

Her hand reached over the sleeping man. "Joey, is he gone? The guy with the gun?"

He nodded and looked her in the eyes. "He's gone. We need to get Chief in the cabin and call Jacob. This lug is going to be out of action for a while and I have to make a report."

Joseph was exhausted beyond any comparison he could recall. Getting Chief into the cabin proved to be misery rolled into anguish and tied up with suffering, but he managed without passing out. Barely.

Once Chief was stabilized, Ember forced him face down on the bed and for the next two hours stitched Joseph's lacerations closed. He refused anything other than a topical cream to lessen the pain. He had to stay alert until reinforcements arrived.

She made no attempt to hide her emotions. She caressed his cheek with her fingers. "You should be on IV antibiotics Joey. Your wounds are infected. If you don't let me treat you soon, you will have wound sepsis and possible blood poisoning."

He grabbed her hand and kissed her palm. "I'll submit to whatever treatment you need me to as soon as someone arrives." Drained of all energy, he sat emotionless as he watched Ember move from the living room into the second bedroom where he could hear Chief mumbling in his morphine-induced slumber.

Joseph concentrated on the task at hand. He hit redial and waited.

"Alpha."

His response flat and to the point. "The contractor has been eliminated."

"Area, connections, and visibility?" Jacob's mind was obviously ticking off the boxes Joseph's actions this afternoon had already covered.

"Area is clear, no connections and visibility is outward not inward. One non-lethal casualty, guarded condition with a seven point seven six millimeter round through and through to the left thigh, member sustained traumatic blood loss. Medical on scene apprises the member is down for at least a month."

Joseph's concise report provided a shockwave of information yet Jacob's professionalism never slipped nor did Joseph's. "Define outward visibility."

"A paperback ledger showing payments and apparent routing or bank account numbers associated with the payments. Additionally, a computer was found. As the com specialist is down no access to the hardware has been attempted."

"I'm sending a courier to secure the outward visibility, team members and primary." Jacob's voice changed as he asked, "When are you considering engaging the target?"

Joseph closed his eyes and drew a deep breath. "I need help, little man. I'm tore up, I need rest and antibiotics. I have nothing left to give. I'll hold out until you can get someone from the Annex out here. Once I'm patched up, I'll work the target."

Jacob's pause lengthened. "Is there helicopter access?"

Joseph looked out to the field. "Yeah, meadow behind the house."

"Help is on the way. Hold on, bubba. I got your back."

"Jacob?"

"Yeah?"

"I love you."

Joseph cut the call before his brother could respond and looked at the email he had composed to his brother Jason, indicating a change to his last will and testament. Ember was to be his sole beneficiary for all his property and possessions. She would never have to worry about money as long as she lived. He watched her walk out of the kitchen as he hit the send button.

She came over to him and placed a warm hand on his cheek. "How long?" He pulled her towards him and rested his head against her midriff. "They're dispatching a helicopter from the Annex. Maybe an hour or less depending on who is flying and what type of bird it is."

CHAPTER ELEVEN

EMBER HEARD THE HELICOPTER BEFORE SHE SAW THE shadow of the massive machine drift over the cabin. The noise from the blades pulsed with a whopping thrum, shaking everything in the house. Loose grasses and leaves from the meadow launched in a frenzy of botanic debris as the massive dual rotor aircraft sank onto the field. Before the helicopter settled, two men jumped from the open side door. A hand held stretcher slapped the legs of the faster man as the two men raced towards the back porch.

Ember watched them both vault the three steps to the landing. A tall blond wearing an eye patch saw her first and headed directly to her.

"Dr. Adam Cassidy."

"Dr. Ember Harris. Chief is stable but critical. Extensive blood loss. No broken bones that I could determine. Massive tissue damage. I performed primary field triage and sewed him up the best I could. He will need surgery to clean him out and assess the actual damage. I have him on a morphine drip, plasma, and lactated ringers. The idiot tried to macho up and move, so I put him out."

Both men followed her into the second bedroom where Chief lay unconscious.

"Roger that. Dixon and I'll get him ready for transport. Where's Fury?"

Ember's mind went blank. Huh? "What the hell is Fury?"

Both men stopped and looked at her as if she had three heads.

The doctor seemed to search for his words before he replied, "Umm… Joseph?"

"Joey? He finally agreed to take something for pain. He may have thought it was Tylenol. He is in the other bedroom."

Doc chuckled and shook his head as he and the tall, sandy haired man easily moved Chief onto the stretcher. His words came slow and measured… almost hesitant. "Let me guess. It wasn't."

She suspected the doctor might have a slight speech impairment. His mind was sharp though.

Ember eyed the doctor and shook her head now leery that the man might report her deceit in dealing with her patient. "Drugging a patient without informed consent would be considered unethical. Anyway, you'll need to run some labs but the wounds are definitely infected. His strength had returned and his injuries were repairing nicely until he went out into the hills. Whatever he had to do up there, it ruptured every laceration that had been remodeling. I believe he may be in the early stages of septicemia. Now that he is out I have him on IV antibiotics."

The doctor flew into a flurry of sign language and the younger man nodded and bent to lift the stretcher. As the men carried Mike out of the room, the younger one spoke. "Alright we'll get Chief to the chopper and come back for Joseph. Pack everything you need. You won't be coming back here. The location has been compromised." Doc nodded in agreement.

"Ma'am, Fury… I mean Joseph… he recovered a backpack with a computer and a notebook this morning. We'll need that too."

"It's all by the back door. Joey made me pack everything before he would take anything for his injuries."

She watched the men make quick work of the transport and return quickly. They transferred and loaded Joseph and the bags before bundling her into the aircraft. Doc secured the side door and helped Ember strap in after he assisted her with her helmet.

"We're heading to Guardian's new training facility in South Dakota." He looked out the window as if attempting to recall something. Just before they lifted off the ground he yelled, "A ranch in the middle of nowhere."

"A ranch? Really?" Ember shouted back.

"Yeah. Good people."

A disembodied voice came over the speaker in her helmet. "That's affirmative, ma'am. The Marshall ranch is our new training and recovery site. Chief runs it that's why he was able to come out here to assist you."

Ember had no idea which one of the two pilots spoke. She watched as the two men's hands flew over switches, buttons, and LED displays. Doctor Cassidy sat between his two patients and performed all the tests she would have performed.

Left to her own thoughts, Em moved her foot to touch Joey's as he lay face down on a stretcher. The mere contact grounded her. His wounds wept through the dressings. Looking out over the mountainous terrain, she fought back the tears that suddenly threatened. Seventy-two hours ago life had been so easy. Three days later the tally stood at four men dead, one man critically injured and Joey fighting off toxic infections sustained at the hands of God knows who. Joey. Fury. Assassin. Protector and lover. A deluge of realization hit her jolting her mind with the cold hard facts of exactly who Joseph King was. Oh God! No, no matter what he was, what he had done—she loved him. A single tear rolled down her cheek unchecked. So many lives wasted. So much pain and suffering endured.

∽

EMBER SAT IN THE SAME PLACE SHE'D BEEN for the last seventy-two hours, Joey's bedside. The plastic chair left a lot to be desired in the way of comfort. She needed sleep. Her judgment on any level was compromised. That's why she pretended not to hear the exchange between Doctor Cassidy and the man who entered the facility. Frank Marshall had checked on the men several times in the past three days.

"Frank, do me a large and get these women out of here. Dr. Harris hasn't slept more than a couple hours in days and Desiree is a wreck."

Frank gave Doc a once over. "I can do that. What about you? You look like shit."

Doc gave a humorless chuckle. "Sorry I don't meet the Miss South Dakota beauty pageant standard." The doctor nodded towards Ember. Frank waited as the doctor searched for the words his mind knew but couldn't get his mouth to say. Ember had done the same since he told her about his brain injury and the lingering effects. Finally, he spoke. "Get them to stand down. I'll stay until Dr. Harris comes back and then I'll catch some sleep."

"Ahh, huh… sure you will. I'll send over some food. You need to eat."

"I don't need food."

"Yeah? Well, I say you do. You'll eat it too or I'll come back and feed it to you."

Ember closed her eyes and tried not to smile. The older man looked like he could follow up on his threat. When she opened her eyes, the gruff man's demeanor had changed radically. His expression softened before he put a work-worn hand on Desiree's shoulder and shook her gently. "Dee, honey, come on. Mike is sleeping comfortably. You won't do him any good if you're so tired you can't be here when he needs you." He looked at Ember. "Ain't that right, doc?"

Ember nodded wearily. "He's right, Desiree. Mike's resting comfortably. He isn't having any issues. You should get a shower, some sleep, and food. When he wakes up and gets ornery, you'll thank us for making you take a break."

The man smiled. "Same goes for you, Doctor Harris. Joseph is resting… now. The restraints will keep him from fighting anyone or hurting himself. You need to crash so you can come back and relieve my boy Adam over there."

Ember's sly glance his way ended with a raised eyebrow. "Mr. Marshall, I applaud you. That was very well played. I didn't see that one coming at all." Her sarcasm held humor and the man's expression told her he got it. Ember lifted off the chair, bent down and brushed a kiss on Joseph's temple and stretched. She yawned as she said, "Alright, come on Desiree, food, shower and sleep."

Desiree lifted from the chair. She bent over and carefully placed a kiss on Mike's cheek before she took a long deep breath and turned her chocolate brown eyes towards Frank.

"I know Mike doesn't want me here. He told me last week he didn't think we should see each other anymore. Felt he couldn't give me what he thought I deserved. When they flew him in, I was here to tell mom I took a job working at the Hollister Ranch. I thought maybe…."

She pulled her hand through her long brown hair apparently gathering her thoughts. Desiree cleared her throat and finished her thought. "I thought I would stay until he woke. But in all honesty, I don't want to hurt like this anymore. I can't." She looked over at Ember and gave a tenuous smile. "Thank you for taking care of him. He is a good man, even though he'll never believe that about himself." Desiree swiped a finger under her eyes as tears brimmed over and fell down her suntanned cheeks. Yet, she straightened her back and nodded as if confirming her own internal convictions. "Bye, Uncle Frank." She stood on her tiptoes and kissed him before she walked out the door.

"It probably isn't my place to say anything, but I think he does love her. He talked about her after he was shot."

"Hell, Doc, everyone at the ranch knows Chief loves that soft-spoken little sprite. The big man is going to have to scramble to get her back. Once a Marshall woman has made up her mind and set sail, God and all the forces of creation would have a fit trying to alter their course. Almost serves the idiot right for pushing her away. Almost." He put his hand on the small of Ember's back and gently urged her out the door. "One thing you will learn about the men from Guardian…they will fight Satan's demons through the burning mazes of hell simply because it's the right thing to do. But place them in the vicinity of a good woman? Four out of five times they'll screw it up."

"Four out of five times?" Her low chuckle and inquiry got a sly smile in return as they exited the little hospital.

"Yes, Ma'am. Jacob got it right straight out of the chute. Figured out what he wanted and didn't stop until he got her. Swept my daughter Victoria off her feet and never looked back. Doc, Chief, your man, and the rest? Far as I can tell, all those boys are in serious need of a kick in the ass."

Ember stopped and looked at him. She gave him a tired wink and a smile. "Mr. Marshall, I believe you may just be the man to do it, too." Ember saw a flush rise to his cheeks.

"We all have our crosses to bear ma'am, taking care of these boys is mine. And the name is Frank. We don't stand on ceremony around here."

THE HAZE THAT PULLED AT HIM LESSENED. HE needed to get up. Get out. His mind demanded his body move and yet it wouldn't. The uncertainty and confusion multiplied when he felt his muscles flex. He was tied, flat on his stomach. Fuck.

Where am I? What op were you on? Think, damn it, King! What is the last thing you remember? Holy Fuck! Ember! Where the hell was she? Joseph forced his eyes open and pulled against whatever was keeping him down. The florescent lighting jarred his eyes. He blinked rapidly to focus. Tile floor, white walls, stainless steel tray. A sweating plastic cup with a straw sticking out the top. No instruments of torture, no hypodermic needles. Fresh cold water. He was safe. Probably in South Dakota. But why the fuck couldn't he move? He tensed again and pulled with all his strength. The bed groaned. Restrained. Joseph pulled against the restraints again in a quick sharp snap of movement.

"I'll take them off when you tell me who you are and where you are." Doc's voice was low and soft, but Joseph recognized it immediately.

Joseph slowly turned his head towards Doc. "I'm the man who is going to kick your fucking ass if you don't come release me from these restraints."

"Yeah, threats of aggression aside, tell me who you are and where you are." Doc gave him a seriously jacked up sneer.

"Joseph King. I was in Wyoming, but I'm assuming I'm now at the Annex on Frank Marshall's ranch in South Dakota." He face-planted into the soft pillow. "Where is Ember? Why was I restrained? I have a bitch of a headache." The pillow rendered his questions in to a muffled, rumbling and snarfing noise.

Doc chuckled and Joseph felt him release the restraints. "Don't roll over. It will screw up all our work on your back. And I don't speak pillow. Repeat that?"

Joseph turned his head just far enough to be understood. "For the second time, where is Ember? Why was I restrained? I have a bitch of a headache."

"Yeah, okay. Joseph, look at me."

Joseph turned his eyes towards him. Doc used American Sign Language.

I have lingering issues with my speech. This is an easier way for me to communicate.

When Joseph nodded his understanding, Doc continued.

The headache is probably because of the fever that caused your delirium. The delirium is the reason you are in restraints. Your woman knocked your ass out until we could pump enough meds into you to lower your temperature. Frank convinced Dr. Harris to stand down. She hasn't slept much in the seventy-two hours we've been back.

"Longer than that. She needs to sleep." Joseph pulled his arms under his body when Doc released him. "How's Chief?"

Doc sat back down and shrugged. "SNAFU."

"Situation-normal-all-fucked-up. Ain't that the perfect metaphor for our lives?"

"That or FUBAR."

"Fucked-up-beyond-all-repair? Yeah, that one would work too." Joseph adjusted his position on the pillow cradling his head with his arms. God that felt so much better than the strapped down position he'd been in.

Doc grinned and nodded. "He'll be okay. Your lady's a… good doctor."

Joseph closed his eyes. The pain Doc's statement caused was immediate. "She's not mine. Used to be a long time ago. Now I can't risk contaminating her life with the death and destruction that surrounds me."

Doc gave a short whistle. Joseph opened his eyes. Doc

signed, I've read the reports. About what happened over there? I don't remember. Tell me what you saw.

Joseph cleared his throat and thought back to the weeks they had spent in country waiting for Doc to get better. "You had a massive head trauma when we pulled you out of the Afghani camp. The first couple of days, you responded well to rest and what little medication I had squirreled away in that God-forsaken wasteland. The enemy forces had us holed up. We couldn't leave, not just because of you, but because of Jared. He screwed up his ankle. Bad. We all lived on rations meant for one and it weakened all of us. You started to get worse. Your eye? Well, I honestly don't know if we could have saved it even if we got out the first night."

Joseph watched Doc focus on one of the granite tiles between his feet. Waves of exhaustion poured over him. He could barely keep his eyes open. "Did you ever tell her?" Joseph felt his eyes close and damned if he could do anything to keep them open.

"Who? Did I tell who what?" Doc's voice brought him back to the edge of consciousness.

"Huh? Oh yeah, Keelee. You couldn't talk so you signed when you were in the cave. The night I watched you towards the end? You kept signing you needed to tell her you loved her." Joseph heard some sort of mumbled reply, but he couldn't focus anymore. His body felt like it was floating. The waves pulled him over the edge and oblivion took over.

CHAPTER TWELVE

EMBER SNUGGLED FURTHER INTO HER BED. SOFT. So soft, warm and comfortable. Oh, the bliss of waking up in one of those perfect positions that you never want to move from because your body hovers in complete relaxation. No stress, no aches, no reason to get up. Hmmm… why is the light so bright?

Ember bolted to a sitting position, blinking rapidly, pushing her hair out of her eyes. The unfamiliar room confused her. Memories of the previous week shoved themselves into her mind. The ranch. She was at Frank Marshall's ranch in South Dakota. Guardian's training and recovery facility. Joey and Chief! No… no it's alright. They're okay. The clock on the bedside table explained the sunshine. Noon. Flopping back on the pillows, she rubbed her face.

Double bags of dog crap! She was supposed to have relieved Doctor Cassidy after a nap. Ember flew into the bathroom barely cognizant of the fact she should be exhausted. She beat her patented five-minute shower time by at least a minute. Clothes on, hair and teeth brushed in less than three.

Ember ripped open the door, launched out of the room, and slammed face first into a hard, immovable object. The force of the collision landed her directly on her ass. Not a dainty sit-down. Oh no, this was a boink-rebound-smack-splat that ended in a full double-ass cheek plant of Olympic proportions. Man, hardwood floors hurt like crazy.

A man's hand presented itself in front of her face. "Dr. Harris, I presume?"

Ember pushed her curls out of her face and looked from the hand, up the well-muscled arm, past to the massive chest on to the dark hair and laughing brown eyes of a rather mature looking man. She wouldn't call him old, but the grey at his temples and the lines around his eyes indicated he was older than his well-conditioned body let on.

Ember accepted the hand up. Without any dignity, she reached back and massaged her sore posterior. "Ahhh… yeah, that would be me. I'm all about making great first impressions. I didn't dent you or anything did I?"

A warm rumble of laughter filled the hall. "No, I think you received all the damage during that collision."

Ember felt the blush rolling up to her cheeks. "Yeah, I think you're right. Good thing I have ample padding. You Guardian guys are like freaking brick walls."

Again warm laughter rolled from the man. "Well, I'm not quite sure how to take that. Are we built like brick walls or mentally as thick as them?"

Ember did a double take at the man. "Honestly, from the guys I've met so far, I'd have to say a lot of the built and a little of the other. Do you work or train here?"

The man shook his head and motioned towards the grand stairway. "Neither, my name is Gabriel. I run Guardian."

Ember stopped at the top of the stairs. Ahh… the boss. "In charge of everything? Everybody? That means you could tell Joey not to go after the cartel."

Gabriel put his hands on his hips and gave Ember an assessing look. "Yes I could, but I won't."

What? Why not? "But he's exhausted. He's been injured and is recovering from a massive infection! Can't someone else go?"

Gabriel motioned down the stairs and Ember fell in beside him. "I'll ensure he's recovered and medically cleared before he's released to finish this assignment. There isn't anything in this world that could stop him from taking out the man who put a contract out to kill you. I'd rather he have the support in the field that we, at Guardian, can provide."

Ember shook her head as he held open the screen door and accompanied her down the porch steps. She started towards the clinic. He kept her leisurely pace not seeming to be in any hurry. The silence wasn't uncomfortable, but in addition to the dialog stuck on repeat in her head the lack of conversation teetered on awkward.

Finally, she blurted out what she had been thinking. "I wish I'd never called him. If I had just gone to the police or turned the thumb drive over to Dale's employers, none of this would've happened. Four men are dead because of that damn drive. Dale, the two men on the way to Joey's and the man they sent to kill me. Chief was shot and Joey was pushed to the limits of his physical endurance." She stopped on the crushed rock path before they reached the hospital.

"Look, I know I don't have the right to ask you not to allow him to go. He would be pissed if he knew I had. But I've come to the hard cold realization I love that man. What he has done? I mean the work he's done for you? Is it… I mean he's still a good guy, right? He hasn't killed anyone that didn't… I guess what I'm trying to ask is…"

"Let me help you out here. Joseph is a scalpel. My organization uses him to surgically remove cancerous lesions that if left in place, would allow abominations of humanity, beyond our civilized world's limited comprehension, to flourish.

He is the best in the world. Period. And as to your point about none of this happening had you not contacted him? Yeah, you're right. It probably wouldn't have. But Dale would still be dead. You'd be dead. That, my dear, is a certainty. Also, an absolute fact—the corrupt politicians, judges, law enforcement officials and businessmen who channel those drugs into our nation would still be making money hand over fist. And every man, woman and child who are addicted to the cocaine, 'H' and weed would still have easy access to the drugs that will eventually destroy their lives or kill them. But because you called, that network is now in ruin, those filthy participants are either on the run or in jail. And as an added bonus two confirmed murderers and one ruthless assassin are no longer part of my world."

He turned towards the clinic and started walking towards the front door. "Yep, you sure screwed up when you called Joseph."

Ember blinked rapidly at the older man's unconcealed sarcasm. Gabriel's words ripped out guilt she tried desperately not to show. She felt responsible for three deaths. Yet had she not called Joey she would have been dead herself. Was it better that others died so she could live?

As a doctor, she'd been trained to do everything humanly possible to save lives. The man that she loved beyond all measure had been trained to take lives. Ember's analytical mind tried to process what Gabriel's comments implied. Stripped raw and in the stark light of day the facts were irrefutable. Her Joey was a good man doing a horrible job. If she hadn't called, she'd be dead and the drug network would still be fueling the nation's addiction. Easy to repeat. Difficult to internalize.

Gabriel stood patiently holding the door until she looked up at him. "It doesn't make any difference in how I feel, but thank you for the facts."

"If one does not use fact and reality to navigate through life the consequences can be intolerable. When decisions are influenced by emotions, the results are at best skewed and in the worst case scenarios the results are devastating." His eyes hardened and his voice carried an edge of sharpness that hadn't been there before.

"Are you speaking from experience?" Ember mentally slapped both hands over her mouth. Stupid, stupid, stupid. Why did she even open her mouth? God, sometimes she was her own worst enemy.

"Indeed. An emotional decision made by a person who was trying to protect me nearly cost me my family. But that is a story for another time and place. I need to speak with Joseph and you—together. The course forward has been charted and I need both of you to be aware how things are going to play out." The warm demeanor he displayed in the house vanished.

Ember shuddered at the menace of his words. His attitude left no doubt this man was the driving force behind Guardian.

He motioned towards the door for her and waited for her to enter. If the course he had charted involved Joseph and the Cartel, she knew the way forward was riddled with heartache and complications.

JOSEPH WATCHED EMBER AND GABRIEL CROSS THE DISTANCE from the main ranch house. They had stopped before they entered. The conversation seemed intense. He watched Ember carefully. She was completely out of her element, yet the woman still amazed him. Smart, adaptable, sexy, and his. At least for the time being. He harbored no illusions. Once he left the ranch, he would never be able to see her again. Any number of nations or criminal organizations would pay to have the distinction of erasing anything the assassin Fury cared about. Even the remotest possibility of someone making the connection between his alias and his real name was too much of a risk to take. He rarely saw or contacted his family for that reason. Weeks of precautions, misdirection, doubling back, covering his route and watching for shadows preceded any physical contact. Electronic communication was easier, but it, too, had risk.

He was lost in thought, staring sightlessly out the window, when he heard them come into the small ward.

"You're supposed to be in bed resting." Ember's reprimand didn't hold any bite. He looked over his shoulder and raised an eyebrow.

Adam walked into the room pushing Chief in a wheelchair. "Couldn't keep him in the bed any longer. In fact, I'm surprised he's still in the building."

Joseph turned and placed his hands on his jean-clad hips looking down at his bare chest and feet. "I wouldn't be here but somebody decided to leave my boots and shirt at my cabin in Wyoming."

Gabriel laughed. "I'll have to remember that trick." He walked over and extended a hand. Joseph gripped his boss's hand shaking it firmly. "I need a sit rep, gentlemen."

Joseph nodded toward Doc, who immediately began the briefing. "Chief is on limited duty for the next four to six weeks." The doctor's effort to speak without a stutter or pause forced his speech to slow. "I'll monitor the bullet wound, but it will take at least that long before he is deployable. Joseph needs to remain here for the next seven days so I… can… ensure he finishes his course of antibiotics. He needs a 'go/no go' done and then I'll release him for duty."

Ember cleared her throat and all four men looked her way. "Ahh…excuse me but 'go/no go'? I've been a trauma doc for a while now and I've never heard that term."

Joseph noticed the men all shifted their gaze to him, deferring the response. "After every mission people in my career field are required to pass a psychiatric evaluation to ensure we haven't lost our link to humanity. Most people doing what I do have borderline psychological tendencies. The 'go/no go' evaluations help Guardian determine if we are a 'go' or a 'no go' for the next mission."

"Oh. Will the psychiatrist come here or do we go to him?"

The corner of Joseph's mouth raised slightly at the implication she would be following him. He could get used to this woman being with him wherever he went. Gabriel sat down on Joseph's bed before he answered. "Dr. Wheeler is located in Hollister. He is on staff and will come to talk with all of you." Gabriel held up a hand to stop the comments. "Doc, you haven't kept an appointment since you came here. I will no longer tolerate that avoidance tactic. You will attend each meeting or answer to me." Gabriel's dark eyes bored into the tall blond before he received a barely perceivable nod. Turning his attention to Chief he continued, "You've got a facility to run, I want to make sure there are no issues. No arguments."

Chief shrugged and winced as he lifted his leg, resting it on the bed across from his boss. "Roger that, sir."

Joseph watched with interest as his boss turned to Ember. "You, young lady, have been close to four deaths, two injuries and countless stress-filled hours. You will talk to my doctor and you will follow his directions or I'll keep you on this ranch until you do. You're under Guardian's protective custody."

Joey watched it happen. Ember's eyes narrowed and her face flushed a torrid shade of red. Her arms crossed. He couldn't help the smile that spread across his face. Better you than me, Gabriel. He leaned against the window frame careful to keep his back away from the sharp edge of the molding.

"Oh, really? I need a psych eval? Me? Because I've been associated with four deaths and had several stress-filled days? Is that right?"

Gabriel tensed before he nodded. Joseph knew his mentor had just figured out the little minx had bared her claws.

"Well, let me educate you, Mister Gabriel. I'm a board certified Emergency Medicine Doctor. I routinely work fifty-six hours straight. I've been buried elbows deep in a patient's open chest massaging their heart while my other hand plugs hemorrhages waiting for another doc to sew them up. I have watched people die from a tooth infection and I watched them die after being blown to hell in a chemical plant explosion. Don't even talk to me about stress, Mister Gabriel. I may be under your protective custody, but I'll be damned if you will direct any medical procedure for me. So thank you very much, but, no thanks."

Joseph dislodged himself from the window sill and walked over to stand directly in front of her. The fury in her eyes lit him up. The fire inside him continually burned high for her, but damn the thought of mad sex with her put gas on that fire. He loved the feisty little spitfire. Shit. Admitting it made it real. He did love her. Probably always had.

He put both hands on her shoulders and kept his voice low between the two of them. "Nobody doubts your abilities, little girl. In the trauma center, you don't know the people you treat, right? You knew Dale. You saw the two men who were going to kill you. You saw what the assassin did to Chief. You helped me go through some pretty serious shit. Whether you want to admit it or not, it's different this time. If you won't see a shrink because it's the right thing to do, see him because it would make me feel better. Help me focus on what I need to focus on rather than worry about you."

Ember's eyes searched his face. Her features started to relax and he felt the anger begin to melt from her tense frame. She nodded.

He reached up and cupped her neck in his hand running his thumb over her cheekbone.

She closed her eyes and pushed into his hand. He lowered his lips to hers and brushed a soft kiss along her lips. "Thank you. Now, would you do me a favor while I talk with Gabriel?"

"I'd do anything for you, Joey." Ember's whispered reply hit him in the gut slugging the air out of him.

He smiled softly. "That's my good girl. Go back to the ranch house and get me a shirt and a pair of boots. Dixon and Drake should have something I can wear."

He kissed her one more time before he spun her around and pushed her towards the door. He watched her leave before he turned around.

The amused looks from the three men in the room immediately pissed him off. "What?"

Gabriel's smile taunted him. "Wow, when a King falls, he falls hard."

"I have no idea what you're talking about. There can never be anything between us. An assassin can't afford to have a life. You know that as well as I do."

Gabriel nodded. "True. Which is why we need to focus on the mission at hand and your exit strategy."

Joseph's eyes darted toward his boss. The man was up to something. He had never given any input to Joseph's operations. Joseph was a loner. He planned his own insertions and exit strategies. Gabriel's comment lingered ominously. The man outlined his vision for the op and Joseph accepted most of the ideas, modifying the timelines, working the logistics and rearranging the events to work within his skill set and capitalizing on his talents. As the plan unfolded, Joseph smiled. Gabriel was a certified genius. The plan was set and the countdown started. Joseph's biggest obstacle? Not getting killed.

CHAPTER THIRTEEN

EMBER SAT IN THE PORCH SWING, HER MIND lost in thought. After she had taken Joey clothes and a pair of boots, she'd had absolutely nothing to do. It was a foreign feeling. Nobody to watch over, no patients to see, no laundry list of things that needed to be accomplished. After walking around the training facility and as much of the ranch as she felt comfortable traversing, she sat down on the huge porch swing at the main house. She gazed out at the pasture filled with brown and white cows. Horses stomped their massive feet in the corral by the barn. Ember shivered. Those huge animals scared her, but the sweet old collie that sat next to her seemed to know she needed comfort. Ember was lost in thought and didn't notice the woman until she spoke.

"Hi. I'm Keelee Marshall. My dad owns this ranch. I run it. Are you with Guardian? One of the Security Officers or a team member?"

Ember jumped in surprise sending the porch swing in motion and the dog trotting to the woman who spoke. She blinked and gawked at the Amazon standing before her. Long blond hair pulled back in a ponytail framed beautiful blue eyes. The woman possessed a body Ember would kill for. Ember had always wanted to be a thin, athletic type, but God 'blessed' her with an abundance of curves. She watched the gorgeous woman scratch the dog behind the ears.

"Ummm… no, I'm Ember Harris. I'm a doctor." Ember scooted over so the woman could sit down with her.

The woman looked up and gave the dog a final pat. "You're a doctor, too? Yeah, well, that just about figures doesn't it." Ember detected an immediate chill in the woman's attitude.

"Okay, look I'm not sure why that would make a difference. I'll be here for a while and I don't want any uncomfortable situations. Did I do something wrong?"

Keelee cut her eyes towards Ember and Ember felt the aggression as if she'd been slapped. Finally, the woman shook her head and gave a sigh. "No. I don't have any right to be jealous, but just to be fair you should know. I used to love him."

Ember paled and felt sick but forced herself to ask, "Did Joey love you, too?"

Keelee jerked her head back and raised both eyebrows. "Joey? Who's Joey? No I'm talking about Adam."

"Adam? You mean Dr. Cassidy? Why would I need to know you love him? I'm here with Joey."

Keelee looked at Ember blankly before she broke into a relieved laugh. "You mean I've been worried sick for the last three days about you and Adam, and there is nothing between you?"

"Obviously. Who told you there was?"

Keelee dropped her head into her hands and rubbed her face. "I saw him almost carry you off the helicopter when it landed. He kept his arm around you even after the patients were unloaded. I guess I misread the whole thing."

"I was exhausted. I was airsick and terrified of the blades on that helicopter. Dr. Cassidy was nice. He was a complete gentleman." Ember bumped Keelee's shoulder with her own. "Why didn't you ask him?"

Keelee dropped back onto the cushion of the seat and stared at Ember. "That story would take a bottle or two of wine. Got any plans?"

"God, no! Go get the wine. Believe me, I could use a drink about now." Ember waved towards the door.

Keelee lifted gracefully to her feet and Ember once again marveled at the beauty of the woman. "Be right back. Red or white?"

Ember chuckled, "As long as it will get me drunk it could be green and I wouldn't care."

"Got it. Whiskey it is."

Ember pushed off, setting the swing into motion again. Looking towards the little hospital, she chided herself. She loved him and had no idea what to do with it. Should she tell him? What if he went after the cartel and died without knowing? If she told him, would he reject her? Lord he already had, hadn't he? There is no way this, what's happening here, has a snowball's chance of becoming anything other than a one and done. She finally understood the meaning behind his warning. God what a mess. What was she going to do?

Keelee came back out to the porch and handed a glass to Ember then poured a dark liquor into her tumbler. She poured a generous portion for herself and settled back into the swing cushion.

"First let me apologize again for the jealous scene earlier. It's hard. Harder than I could imagine trying to pretend I don't know him."

Ember was taking a sip of her drink when Keelee's last comment registered. She swallowed quickly and coughed at the deep burn from the whiskey going down wrong. Keelee laughed and patted her on the back waiting for Ember to breathe.

"Why would you pretend not to know him? You said you loved him. I'm sorry, but I don't understand."

Keelee sighed and took a healthy sip before she rolled her eyes towards Ember. "About two years ago my sister, Tori, brought Jacob, her now-husband, and his team to the ranch. Jacob had been injured and he came out here to heal. Adam was a part of that team, and he and I had an immediate attraction. We were moving cattle from the upper pastures, the weather was nasty and my bad chest cold became pneumonia. The four of us, Jacob, Tori, Adam and I, were up at a line shack a day's ride from here. There was some bad weather coming in, but I was laid out and needed rest. So, Adam stayed at the line shack to take care of me while the others finished the cattle drive."

Keelee swirled the liquid and took another drink. "I guess the best way to explain it is I had more of an attraction than he did. He turned me down in no uncertain terms. Some things were said that couldn't be unsaid." Keelee sighed and looked out towards the Black Hills. "He tried a couple times to talk to me about it afterwards, but God, I was so humiliated. I built a wall so tall and broad nobody could get around it. He left with his team and then was injured." Her eyes misted up and she waved towards her own face indicating her eye. "He lost his eye and according to scuttlebutt around here he lost a portion of his memory. He doesn't remember me, and I can't forget the rejection or the humiliation. I've avoided him. It hasn't been hard. He has shown absolutely no interest in getting involved with either the training Guardian does here or the ranch itself. So, I just go about my day-to-day life and pretend he isn't here. I pretend I don't know him. The guys tell me he's changed. He used to be such a happy person. He never smiles anymore. Did you know he has dimples so deep they look like slashes? I don't know if he has smiled since he's been back."

Keelee finished her whiskey and refilled both glasses. "So that's why I need a drink. Why do you?" She sat the bottle back on the rail of the porch.

Ember pointed toward the training complex. "Joseph is over there doing something with his boss, Gabriel. My problem is that I love him and I know he doesn't love me. He has spent an inordinate amount of time telling me whatever is between us ends when he leaves. I don't know whether or not I should tell him how I feel." Ember took another drink of her whiskey. The burn no longer registered. Damn smooth stuff.

"You want my advice? Not that I'm in any position to give it." Keelee pushed the swing, setting it swaying again.

"I'll take any advice I can get." Ember's eyes never left Gabriel and Joey's progress across the clearing to another building beyond the clinic.

"Don't put up walls. I'll never know what Adam wanted to say to me. It haunts me."

Ember sighed when Gabriel and Joseph entered the building. Holding her glass out to Keelee she nodded and clicked the other woman's glass. "No walls. Good advice."

Joseph left Gabriel in the communications office after he had gotten the information he needed from Jared. The plan had a chance of succeeding. The earth, moon, and all the planets had to align correctly, but it was the best chance at ending Morales' reign and keeping Ember safe. He had seven days of meds and a psych eval before he would force himself to leave her.

Joseph had stopped by the small pharmacy before he headed back to the house. He had plans for his woman tonight. He heard them before he saw them. Ember and Keelee sat on the porch swing and laughed riotously. He paused and chuckled at the overt mannerisms of the two women in front of him. They both had evidently been drinking. Joseph looked at the setting sun. Drunk at six thirty? How the hell did that happen? Better question—why were they drunk? Her beautiful auburn curls bounced around her face. The woman's body should have been illegal. Her curves killed him. And that ass? God, he'd crawl on his knees for ten miles behind her just to enjoy the view.

He sauntered forward until Ember saw him. Her face lit up. "Joey! Hi! Do you know Keelee? Keelee, this is Joey."

Keelee broke into giggles and pushed Ember, nearly upending her from the swing. "Yeah, I know him. He's a King! That makes him my sister's brother-in-law." She stopped and looked over at him with an entirely befuddled look on her face. "Right?"

Joseph couldn't help the smile that pulled on his lips. "Surprisingly, yes. How about I help you ladies into the house?"

Ember scoffed at him. "No, you're the injured one. We should be helping you into the house." Joseph stretched forward and steadied Ember as she stood.

Keelee sniggered. "Nah, I'll sit right here. Besides, Clint is supposed to come by tonight." She scrunched her nose in distaste. "He jus' wants to date me 'cause he's after my daddy's ranch. Not happening no matter how lonely I get."

Ember pulled her arm from Joseph's hand and teetered over to Keelee. She dropped to her knees in front of the other woman and gently patted her knee. "You gotta knock down the walls, Keelee. No more walls. We clear?"

Keelee smiled sadly and nodded. "No more walls. Gotcha."

Joseph tried valiantly not to laugh at the women. He helped steady Ember when she stood up. She spun and leaned into him grabbing his belt loops and plastering her soft voluptuous body to his. "No walls, Joey. Can't have any walls or it jus' won't work."

She ground her hips into his hardening cock and purred. "You don't want any walls between us do you, Joey?"

Sweet Jesus, how could this woman want him? And why in the hell was he looking a gift horse in the mouth? He reached behind her and cupped her ass pulling her tighter against him. "Walls are the last thing I want between us. How about we go upstairs and make sure those walls stay away?"

The short trip from the porch up the stairs took far longer than Joseph wanted. A drunk Ember proved to be very talkative and seemed to have grown four or five extra sets of hands. Not that he minded that little addition. By the time he finally wrangled the woman into her bedroom any curiosity about the wall comment was a thing of the past. Her naked with his cock buried in her was the only thing that mattered. He was able to rid her of her jeans and panties before she started to giggle almost uncontrollably.

"Baby girl, we need to talk about your drinking problem."

Ember's eyes grew large before she burst out in a laughing fit. "I don't have a problem drinking. I managed just fine. I drank. I got drunk and now I'm really horny. Is it okay for me to want you, Joey?"

Was it okay? Hell, yeah. The things he wanted to do to her? Damn, it was a good thing she wanted him. Otherwise things could get awkward. He removed her shirt as he nipped her neck and kissed her on that sensitive spot just under her ear. With a shiver, her body molded into his. Her little moan when he got rid of her bra, ramped his need up ten or twenty notches.

"Wanting me is perfectly okay." He pulled away and lifted her chin up looking at her intently before he spoke. "I don't wish to take advantage of you. Make no mistake, I want you, but you've been drinking. I need you to look at me and tell me this is what you want. That you want me to take you."

Ember's green eyes opened and searched his face. "I'm feeling real good Joey, but I'm not so drunk I don't know what is going on. I want you. I want you the way you like to take me. I like it when…"

Her face turned a deep red with the heat of embarrassment. Ember pulled her chin away in an apparent attempt to try to escape his gaze.

He grasped her chin and pulled it back to him. He wouldn't let her hide. "No looking away from me, little one. What do you like, Em? Tell me everything you like."

He held her gaze and waited, wondering if she would tell him. Finally, she whispered, "I like you doing those things to me. I like it that you're strong and that you take me—that you don't give me a choice. You make me feel so good when I give you what you ask for. I like the harsh way we make love. I like it when you tell me you're proud of me. I love you, Joey, and I don't want anyone else to be your baby girl."

Well, shit. You asked, King. Time to man up and tell her the truth. "You make me very proud Ember. I have never called anyone else baby girl and I never will. Only you."

He lowered his mouth and took hers. No gentleness. He didn't want gentle. His demand was nothing but raw possession. She opened to him allowing him to take what he needed. And God did he need. "Turn around and bend over. Grasp the edge of the bed." He waited until her gorgeous body was bent in front of him. "Spread your legs. More. Good. Stay there. Don't move."

He ran his hand down the hot skin of her back. Her muscles shivered at his touch. Joseph retrieved a small tube he'd acquired at the pharmacy from his clothes before he knelt behind her. His hands ran up the back of her thighs before his mouth followed his hand's track. She jumped and moved her legs. Joseph slapped the inside of her thigh. "Do not move again, little one."

His hand separated the folds around her labia. He blew over her hot glistening sex. Her hips squirmed slightly against the sensation. Slowly he started his trail of small kisses interspersed with sharp bites along the inside of her thigh. Her body trembled by the time he reached the apex of her leg. With both hands, he spread her sex open wide to him. Unable to hold himself back any longer he stroked one side of her with his tongue. Her clean, sweet taste was an unbelievable aphrodisiac.

He began to torture her with long, languid strokes of his tongue that never quite reached her clitoris. Her body wept with need and he gladly lapped up every bit of her essence. Ember's low throaty moan and the nearly constant shivering of her muscles urged him on. He lifted on his knees and moved away from her heated center to circle her small tight opening with his tongue. Her body tensed abruptly and her head jerked up. Kissing the soft skin of her ass, he whispered his words against her. "This body is mine to do with as I wish, Ember. Be a good girl and make me proud and I'll take you to heaven."

Her head dropped back down between her arms. "Perfect, baby. So good." He lowered his head and circled her pucker with his tongue pushing in slightly, nipping around the edges of the sensitive nerve endings. One hand found her vaginal opening. He entered her with his fingers at the same time as he circled pressure on her clit. She bucked back against him, her actions begging him for release.

Joseph speared her puckered circle repeatedly with his tongue and loosened the tightness slowly. Her body clenched and her breath caught. She teetered precariously on the edge of orgasm. Joseph stood, centered himself and thrust deep into her. The head of his cock hit her cervix. Ember choked off a cry and whimpered as he bent her further changing his angle so as not to injure her. He liked inflicting pain, but he would never seriously hurt her. He set a sharp, rapid pace, pumping her with fierce intent. Her channel clenched tightly around him as her hips moved in an orgasm-driven reaction. He felt the tight squeeze of her walls, but he refused to be pulled over the edge. No, he wanted more.

He stilled and unscrewed the cap of the lube spreading a thick line along his fingers. He used his slicked fingers to open her virgin ass while his cock remained buried in her. He thrust two fingers into her. She didn't even try to muffle her cry. He slapped her round butt cheek with his free hand leaving a bright red handprint. "I love the sounds you make. I want to hear them." His fingers scissored, working and stretching the straining ring of muscles opening her further. The insertion of a third finger and more lube forced a deep groan from her.

"That's my baby girl. Let me take what I want." He lifted his hand further, placing two fingers in her mouth. "Suck them." Her hot wet tongue swirled the cream covered fingers and her suction pulled her taste from his skin. "Can you taste how good your cream is?"

Her moan reverberated around his fingers. "That's right. Don't stop." He released his fingers from her hot back channel and pulled her against him. He withdrew his cock from her cream soaked pussy and immediately moved up pushing through the painfully tight ring of muscles guarding her entrance. He held his hand over her mouth, quieting the cry his entrance forced from her. Her ass was so damn tight he knew she was reeling from the burn of his cock impaling her. The intense pleasure of her constricting hot ass almost forced a climax before he seated himself completely. Joseph thrust up burying himself in her and stilled until her body loosened. He could feel her shudder as she struggled to adjust to the fullness of his girth. She whimpered and tried to pull away from him. Her movement echoed deep in his balls. God, the ache to come nearly overtook him. When he regained control, he slid out a scant inch only to press deeper inside her. His hand muffled her gasping cry, keeping the delicious sound for himself. God, the grip of her tight body and those sexy as hell little cries. So damn good.

"That's right. This luscious body is mine. I've wanted this ass for over sixteen years. You're so damn tight. God you feel better than I ever thought you could."

He moved in and out of her vise-like confines and groaned against her neck. "So fucking good, baby girl."

His hand lowered from her mouth to her mound where he worked his fingers through her folds finding her weeping hot sex. "Oh hell, yeah, you like it too, don't you?" Her 'yes' fell in a guttural sob. He concentrated on bringing her to another orgasm while trying to hold off the molten lava of his own. Her body spasmed. Her muscles clenched with a gripping intensity around his cock and when it did, he erupted inside her again.

Joseph held her tight against his chest while they both pulled ragged lungfuls of air. When his cock softened and slipped from her body, he gently maneuvered her forward toward the bed. Once he got her situated in the middle, he went into the bathroom and cleaned up, bringing a damp cloth back to care for her. Joseph threw the towel toward the bathroom before he lay beside her, careful not to pull any of his repairing wounds. He ran his fingers through her silky red curls.

"You're a gift."

Ember turned towards him and snuggled close to his chest. Her muffled voice responded, "I'm not sorry I told you I loved you, Joey. I do." She lifted up on her elbow and looked down at him. "I used to think love came with a white picket fence. Now I know it comes with an expiration date. It hurts, Joey, not being able to have a normal relationship."

He could see her internal battle and the hurt that drifted across her expression. He lifted a hand to her cheek and moved her curls from her face. "Who gets to say what normal is, little one? Who gets to decide what love is or how long it lasts? Who can say with absolute certainty that love is only traditional sex between traditional couples? I believe God made each person unique. Who's to say each person's reality of love can't be unique too? Does what we do and what we have right now, at this moment in time, make you feel good?"

He watched as she searched his face before she lowered her eyes and nodded. "I've never done the things I've done with you. I love the way you make me feel. I love it when you use my body to make us both feel good. But, I'm not going to lie. I want forever."

He pushed a random curl away from her face and pulled her closer. "Forever is the one thing I can't give."

CHAPTER FOURTEEN

EMBER SAT QUIETLY ON A BENCH OUTSIDE DR. Cassidy's office at the clinic. In her opinion, Guardian's mental health expert had come way too early to conduct his sessions. Ember's head ached miserably. When she woke this morning, a bottle of water and two aspirin were on the bedside table. Joseph taking care of her, no doubt.

Her head did ache, but worse, she couldn't find a comfortable position to sit. Every time her body moved, her aching muscles reminded her of last night, of Joey. A smile lingered on her face as the warm feeling once again flushed through her body. She had told him she loved him. The freeing sensation that hit her last night still lifted her like a kite on a strong wind. Her heart soared with buoyancy until reality crashed around her. He would be gone soon. Gone from her life—forever. How could she possibly deal with that?

Keelee's advice landed right on target. She would never regret letting him know her feelings, no matter the personal cost. She sincerely hoped that somehow her new friend would be able to tear down the walls in her own world. Ember slowly leaned back against the back of the couch and closed her eyes.

With an effort, she diverted her mind's wandering from her personal issues to the door across the hall. Doc had been in with the clinical psychologist for a long time. Chief had already had his session and had called her when he was finished, almost an hour ago. Joseph was scheduled to go in after her. Ember jumped when the cushion suddenly sank next to her. She gasped and hit Joey in the arm. "Don't sneak up on me!"

His laughter carried through the small sitting area. "Feisty this morning aren't you, little girl?"

Ember immediately blushed as he pulled her onto his lap. She positioned herself to sit on her hip rather than her bottom. He nuzzled her neck and whispered, "Are you sore?" Joseph's hand moved down to her backside where he held her softly, undeniably claiming what he knew was his.

Ember melted inside. This massive man, an assassin, who had endured more pain in his life than she could ever imagine, held her like she was a priceless object. The way they made love might be rougher than what she'd once considered proper, but she wouldn't have it any other way. She snuggled against his chest and rested her head on his shoulder. "I'm a little sore. But I like being reminded of what we did."

The door to Doc's office opened. Ember tried to move off Joey's lap, but he held her securely. Adam walked out giving both of them a distracted nod before he headed down the hallway and out the door.

"Good morning, sunshine! How the hell are you?" Ember jumped when she saw the doctor who followed Adam out the door. His greeting was the same one he used every morning for a year during their rotations together.

"Oh my God! Remi Wheeler! What are you doing here?" Ember launched from Joseph's lap and jumped into the arms of the massive tattooed doctor who loomed in the doorway.

"I could ask you the exact same question, Red." He pulled her tight and twirled her around before setting her down and planting a kiss on her upturned lips.

Ember laughed and turned to Joseph still hugging the newcomer. "Joey, this is Remi Wheeler. He and I were on the same rotations during medical school. We put up with the same doddering old doctors and dealt with the same hospital politics and med school bureaucracy before we went our different ways."

The doctor released Ember and held out his hand. "Dr. Jeremiah Wheeler. I take it you two are friends."

Joseph extended a hand and grasped the doctor's. "No, she is more than a friend. In the interest of full disclosure, if you kiss her like that again, I'll kill you."

Holy shit! Ember's head whipped around at the comment. No laugh followed Joey's statement. Aggression rolled off him in waves. She had to give Remi credit. He didn't flinch.

"Yeah? Well, if you kill me it won't be sanctioned."

Ember watched the two men square off. She moved over and stood beside Joseph. He wrapped his arm around her shoulders and tucked her close to his side.

"True, but the idea of an off-the-books hit doesn't bother me right now. Make an informed decision, Doc. It may be your last." Ember trembled at the threat, but Remi threw back his head and laughed.

"Fair enough. You have no worries. I have a woman in Hollister that would string me up by the balls if I stray off the reservation. Now, since I sense absolute zero trust from you big guy, why don't we do our session first and if Ember agrees you can sit in when I talk to her about last week?"

Ember rushed to agree. "That's fine. I think I'd actually prefer Joey to be with me." She felt his muscles relax at her response and said a silent prayer of thanks. Remi always could read people.

❦

Joseph sat in the chair across from the shrink. The dude looked more like a biker. Tall guy, six three, athletic—favoring his left leg—he wore his black hair long and loose almost hiding a snake tattoo slithering up the right side of his neck. Two forearms of very impressive ink were revealed when the doctor pushed his long sleeve t-shirt up toward his elbows.

"Done measuring me?"

"Yes." Joseph had learned early the only way to get a "go" on any evaluation was to be brutally honest.

"Tell me. What do you see?"

"Clarify the question."

"You sized me up. What do you see?" The man leaned back in his chair.

"You appear relaxed. You're not. You limp slightly on your left leg. I would exploit that weakness should I decide to kill you. Your heart rate is elevated. Your repetitious clicking of that pen indicates you're nervous. Smart man. You've read my file, and my relationship with an old friend of yours has upset you. Most likely because of what you've learned from that data. You've been around hard people. You're comfortable in that environment. You're not comfortable around me. Probably because what I do upsets your morals."

Joseph watched the effect of his words. The doctor stopped clicking the pen and put it down gently on the notebook on his lap.

"You're very astute, Joey."

Fuck you, asshole. You don't get to call me that. "If I weren't, I wouldn't be alive. Knowing my environment and my enemy is essential. My name is Joseph."

"I'm not your enemy and Ember called you Joey."

"You're not my friend. Therefore you're a potential enemy.

She is the only one who calls me Joey."

"The fact you limit your friends isn't surprising. Why is Red the only one who calls you Joey?"

Because I love her, fuckwad. "I allow her to do so."

"Do you have to control everything? Even what people call you?"

Well, no shit, stupid. "Yes."

"Why?"

"I want to live."

Joseph waited for several minutes. He knew this game too. The doctor was waiting for him to add more to the conversation. Keep waiting, doc. Hell will freeze over first.

Finally, the man spoke. "You almost didn't live. Your last assignment almost killed you."

"Yes."

"Tell me about it."

"Clarify the question."

"Tell me what happened after your cover was blown." The shrink crossed his leg at the ankle and leaned back into the chair willing to wait for an answer.

"I was taken."

"And then?"

"I woke in a dungeon with my hands tied to a wooden pole. They didn't secure my legs." Joseph stopped and focused his vision just left of the man's ear as the doctor wrote a note on his pad. "That was their second mistake."

"Go on."

"Things got uncomfortable. You read my file. You know very well what happened."

"How did you endure the pain?"

Joseph blinked and looked back at the man. "Clarify the question."

"According to the medical records your skin was peeled off your back. The pain must have been excruciating. How did you deal with the pain?"

"I focused."

"On what?"

"Killing the mother fucker."

"And did you?"

"Yes."

"How?"

"I freed my left hand and severed his carotid artery with a scalpel."

"How did you escape?"

"I ran."

"Just ran? Nobody said anything to you about the strips of skin hanging off you? The blood? That must have been obvious."

"An old woman saved my life. She hid me underneath the floor in the kitchen of the compound where I was held. Two days after she moved me out of the crawl space, they found it. She refused to tell them where the women of the village had hidden me. They pulled her into the town square and raped her–broke every bone in her body and then eviscerated her alive as a warning to others never to help the enemy again."

"Intelligence reports indicate all the men in that compound were mutilated and dismembered."

"Do they?"

"Yes. Did you do that, Joseph?"

"No."

"Then who did?"

"I don't speculate."

"Ah heck, just this once, give it a try. It'll stay between us."

Joseph stopped looking past him and focused on the man. He noted the way the doctor shifted uncomfortably under his stare. No different than any other man.

"I killed them, doc. Clean, quiet. When I finished, I opened the compound gates and drove one of the guard's trucks away. The women must have done what is indicated in the reports."

"Women? You believe old women committed this…this atrocity?" Rampant disbelief dripped from the man's inquiry. Inquiry… hell it was an accusation.

"Aside from the fact that it takes a fair degree of strength to dismember a body and I was not at my best, those men took everything from that village. They murdered husbands and sons. Daughters as young as eight vanished into the compound never to return. The women spoke of the screams they heard at night, the helplessness and guilt they lived with. Those bastards kept them alive to be servants and the dogs were treated better than they were. I'm an assassin, Doctor. They were victims. I made it safe for them. What they or anyone else did after I left isn't my concern."

"You're very matter of fact about this abomination."

Joseph laughed. He watched the doctor flinch. Yeah, the man may be tough, but he didn't do evil well.

"I don't fabricate drama or surround myself in fantasies, doctor. You asked for the facts then you asked me to speculate. I provided you both. How you process the information isn't my concern. Your outrage is your baggage. You deal with it."

The doctor paused and glanced at his notes before he underlined a word and cleared his throat. Twice. "Okay, let's backtrack for just a second. You said leaving your legs untied was the enemy's second mistake. What was the first?"

"They didn't kill me immediately. Rank amateurs."

"Tell me, do you care about the lives you took?"

"Bingo. The money question sprung after a distraction. Do they teach that in Shrink 101? Every fucking one of you have the technique down. I don't have sociopathic tendencies, doctor.

Why don't I save us both some time and effort? Do I value human life? Yes, I do. Would I have taken those lives if it were not for the requirements of my job, for my safety, or to protect those women? No. Did I have average family attachments growing up? Yes, I love my family. They're big, noisy, and messed up, but they are mine. Do I have healthy relationships with women? If you asked me before Ember came back into my life, I would say no. I used women for sex. Do I have problems dealing with what I do for a living? Absolutely not. I have never had a sleepless night. I trust my handlers at Guardian implicitly."

"Since Ember came back into your life? You knew her before?"

"Yes."

"Would you care to elaborate?"

"No."

"You threatened to kill me if I kissed Ember again. That is territorial and in direct conflict to your stated reasons for killing—your job and safety."

"Yes."

"Please explain."

"Ember is a part of me and you threatened that part."

"With a simple kiss?"

"Yes."

"Don't you trust her?"

"Of course I do, but I don't trust you."

"Why not? Guardian does. Gabriel does. He directed you to talk to me."

"If a complete stranger did the same to your woman in Hollister would you trust him?"

Doctor Wheeler shook his head as a smile parted his lips. "No. Can't say that I would. But I don't think I would threaten to kill him."

"No, you'd just think it. The difference between me and your polite society? I act."

"And still you maintain you have no sociopathic tendencies?"

Joseph chuckled and shrugged. "I've been tested. The results are in the records you hold. Now can we cut the hypothetical bullshit about what I would or wouldn't do?"

"Alright, let's talk about this past week. How many people have you killed in the last seven days?"

"Three."

"How many were sanctioned kills?"

"One."

"The other two?"

"Had the intent, opportunity and capability of killing Ember. I prevented that."

"And why would they want to kill Ember?"

"If you needed that information it would have been provided to you. Not my place to fill you in on the specifics, doc."

"You act as if this is a game, Joseph. How many of these evaluations have you gone through?"

"Is that a roundabout way of asking how many people I've killed?"

"Yes."

"If you needed to know, it would have been provided to you."

The shrink blinked repeatedly. "Pat answer and a complete cop out. How many lives have you taken Joseph?"

"It doesn't really matter. What matters is that I need to be cleared to take at least one more."

"Why? What is so relevant about your next kill?" The doc leaned forward intently.

"It'll be my last mission." Joseph leaned back in the chair. He had the doctor exactly where he needed him.

"Clear me for this last mission, doc. After it's over, I'll never have to be cleared again."

"That's not how this works."

"Sure it is. You and I both know I passed every objective of this interview. Do your job and let me do mine."

Joseph watched the doctor push his fingertips together apparently thinking before he spoke. "Tell me how many people you have murdered or assassinated, Joseph."

"Two different topics. Murdered? One. Assassinated at my country's request? Fifty-three."

"Fifty-three assassinations. How many more were collateral damage?"

Joseph shrugged. "None that were innocent civilians."

"Alright. Who did you murder?" The doctor's question lingered for several minutes.

"The piece of shit that killed my father. I was sixteen. And yes, if I had to do it again, I would."

"Have you asked yourself if you can walk away from this? Turn your back on the massive adrenaline spike? Will you be able to leave this life and death power behind?"

"Leaving it behind won't be an issue. There's little likelihood I'll return from this mission. Next to zero. This is the end of the road for me."

"Then why are you going?" A puzzled expression masked the doctor's professional demeanor.

"If I don't, they'll find Ember and they'll kill her. If the choice is her or me? The answer will always be her. I'm willing to die so she can live."

"Does she know?"

"That I'm leaving? Yeah. She knows I won't contact her again. I've told her from the start our relationship ends when I leave. She doesn't know this is my last mission. She doesn't know

I don't expect to come back alive. She doesn't need to know the choices I made to keep her safe and give her a future. If you know her, then you know such knowledge would eat her alive. So, those sociopathic tendencies you think I have? They aren't too much of a concern any longer, are they?"

"No. Loving someone so deeply would eliminate that concern."

"Huh. You don't say."

Joseph lifted from the chair and walked to the door. The fact the doctor didn't stop him gave him the information he needed. He'd get a 'go' for the mission. Ember gazed up at him when he opened the door. She looked like a scared kitten. He offered a hand to her. Her smile removed any lingering aggression he felt from his little talk with her friend. He pulled her into his chest and lowered his face into her curls.

"You didn't hurt him did you?" She barely concealed the concern in her voice.

"No, little girl, your friend is alive and well. Let's go in and talk about your week." He kissed her temple and tightened his hold on her. God he loved her luscious curves. Her softness against him fired every protective cell in his body.

"You know you don't need to worry, right? I was happy to see an old friend, but I would never jeopardize what is between us. You're the only one I have ever loved. Nobody has ever been able to replace you and nobody ever will. I love you, Joey."

Now didn't that just inflate a man's ego? Feeling twenty-feet tall was addictive.

"I'm not worried. I'm possessive and extremely jealous. Once I'm gone, you can and will find a good man. But here? Now? You're mine. If you have a problem with that, we should talk."

"I don't want anyone else, Joey. I don't think I ever have and I know I won't go looking for someone once you leave." She held up a hand and spoke before he could. "I'm not going to sugar coat the fact I hate what Morales and your past life are taking from me. But here and now? No, I don't have a problem as long as you promise not to kill anyone who isn't trying to kill me." Her small laugh was an apparent attempt to hide the sadness he could feel wrapping around her.

"You need to kiss me, little girl, and then we'll go talk to your friend."

"Oh, I can do that." And damned if she didn't lift up on her toes and nail him with one hell of a kiss. As he followed her into the office, he decided her tongue should be registered with Guardian as a potentially deadly asset. 'Cause damn, what she could do with it was killing him.

Joseph stopped at the large chair before he pulled her back to him and down on his lap. Ember shifted slightly resting on her hip. Her shy smile his direction made his cock perk up and take notice.

The doctor cleared his throat again. Joseph logged the annoying habit and studied the man as he prepared to talk to the woman he held in his lap. "Ember the file says you have had a hell of a week. Care to fill me in?"

He felt her release a deep sigh and sink back into his chest. Her head landed on his shoulder and she shook her head. "No, I really don't. What has happened in the past week is between Joey and me. I resent Gabriel's insistence in keeping this appointment and I resent Joey's coercing me into coming."

"Huh. Same old Red. Okay let's do this the hard way. How many people have you seen killed this week?" Jeremiah's voice was calm as he asked.

Ember cocked her head and then looked up at Joey. "Ahh… none. I didn't see anyone killed. I was in the vicinity."

"Really? What makes you think the men who Joey killed this week were going to harm you?"

Joseph tensed and sent a dagger-edged glare across the room at the doctor. Where the fuck was he going with this line of questioning?

"Dale, a friend of mine died first. He died because he discovered information that jeopardized a lot of criminals, information he'd passed along to me. The next two were going to try to kidnap and kill me. Joey stopped them, but they shot him in the process. The last was a paid assassin. He almost killed Chief. So yeah, I believe if they went after the men protecting me, I have reason to think the last three would have killed me. If not then, eventually."

"As a doctor the Hippocratic Oath is our creed, our foundation for everything we do. Fight for life at all costs. How are you dealing with the death that surrounds you?"

Joseph felt her tense and watched as she focused on the arm of the chair. She didn't speak for several minutes. He finally glanced at the doctor who was focused on Joseph's hand that softly circled at the base of Ember's spine. An unconscious gesture he hadn't noticed until this second and one he sure as hell wasn't inclined to stop.

Her strong, steady voice finally responded to the question. "If those men had been presented to me to try to save I would have done everything in my power to do so. I have no doubt about that. What has happened around me happens everywhere in the world. Most of the time I have one or two degrees of separation from the reasons behind the aggression. That separation allows me to play at being omnipotent and I admit I routinely passed judgment on the people who caused or inflicted the suffering I try to fix."

She lifted her eyes to Joseph and spoke to him, not to the doctor. "Joey did only what he had to do to keep me safe. I trust him to do the right thing." She turned back to the shrink. "I have absolutely no doubt what was done was needed. So to answer your question, I'm dealing. Life happens. Death happens. We can't stop it. We either accept it or we don't."

"That answer is a rationalization isn't it? Why won't you respond to the question?"

Joseph couldn't help the growl that emanated deep within him. What was the bastard doing? Her hand tightened on his arm immediately quieting his anger.

"Remi, I'm dealing with it in the best way I know."

The man cleared his throat and crossed his legs. "By romanticizing it? Really, that's the best way you know?"

"I'm not romanticizing anything."

"Sure you are. You have your knight in shining armor coming in to sweep you off your feet. This week is just a romantic diversion for you isn't it?"

"You have no idea what he's been through! What he has already sacrificed for me. Fuck!"

"What? I'm right, aren't I? You aren't looking at the issue. You've made it all cotton candy clouds and valentine hearts. How are you dealing with the deaths, Ember? Oh… wait… you're not dealing with them!"

Joseph wanted to grab the fucker's neck and squeeze until he never uttered a word again, but neither the doctor nor Ember appeared to recall Joseph was even in the room. Ember sat up, almost teetering off his lap, and spat at the man.

"You want the truth? Okay, here is the truth! I'm fucked up and I feel guilty! It's my fault they're dead! It's my fault because I called Joey! It's my fault I ran with the damn information. If I had given the information to his employers, I would be the only one dead. Chief and Joey wouldn't be hurt. Joey wouldn't be leaving me to go after that horrible man! None of this would have happened! It would only be me… only me. I'm a curse!"

Retching sobs tore through her as she crumbled onto the floor from his lap. Joseph slid out of his chair and pulled her into him rocking her gently as he stroked her hair. His eyes leveling an honest to God notice of pending death at the doctor. The man watched Ember with keen interest—never looking toward Joseph.

Joseph bent his mouth to her ear and whispered, "I live in a world you don't want to know about. The deaths that haunt you are not your fault. Morales caused this. Not you, not me. I won't let you shoulder his blame." She clung to him as the sobs continued. The pain, confusion and loss she held bottled up inside her, seemed to spill out in torrents

When the flood of emotion crested and ebbed, the doctor spoke. "You need to grieve, Red. What has happened and what is going to happen is not your fault. You can't take responsibility for drug dealers or assassins. You have feelings of guilt but the reality is none of these events was of your making. Joseph killed the men, but that guilt rests squarely on the person who sent them not on you and not your man. You've been placed in unusual circumstances and dealt with things most of us will never face. It's alright to grieve, to be mad, to feel confused and at times…responsible. It's alright to wonder what if. But the truth is none of the past week's events were your doing. None. To get through this, you're going to have to accept that. Oh and by the way… the man holding you… the one who would kill me in a heartbeat if I ever hurt you… he's an extraordinary man. For whatever time the two of you have, be thankful."

The doctor sat back and closed his notebook. "You're blessed, Ember, not cursed."

The doctor finally looked at Joseph. "I know you'll take good care of her, but a word to the wise? Don't let her bottle it up inside. She's afraid for you and that's normal. Tell her what you can, it will help."

Joseph nodded. He uncoiled off the floor rising to his full stature before he bent down to lift her in his arms. When he stood again, she rooted into his chest as if he could protect her from the world. God, he prayed he could. Throwing the doctor a glance, he nodded. "You're a fucking dick… but thanks."

The doctor let out a long breath. "Been called worse. I'll be here for her after you… leave."

CHAPTER FIFTEEN

WITH EVERY OUNCE OF WILLPOWER AND THE LAST shred of strength she possessed, Ember tried to balance in the saddle the way Keelee showed her. Use your feet to stand in the saddle. Lift so the saddle doesn't smack you in the butt when the obstinate animal pounds your brains out and dislocates your spine at a trot. Yeah, right. Em had saddle sores on top of bruises on top of chaffing. Of course, the physical woes were inevitable because that harbinger-from-hell she rode, made sure to jolt her six ways to Sunday and back again. They named the damn thing Charmin. What a freaking joke! There was nothing, absolutely nothing, soft about the damn animal.

The two men who went with them on the ride looked like they were born to live in the wild, wild, west. Dixon and Drake—twin Adonises. Was that even a word? Okay, maybe Perseus and Hercules; anyway they rode like it was second nature. The men also had enough guns strapped on to rob a stagecoach. Who would have thought smelly old cows could be so scary you needed to wear that many guns? Yeah, they were serious eye candy, but Lord above they never stopped talking. Never. The banter between the brothers fell seamlessly, as in without a breath, between the one-liners. Ember would be willing to place a bet those two were afraid of silence. Oh, and of course, they offered advice, too. Like that helped.

Rounding the small curve on the road to the barn, she discovered another level of humiliation. The intensity of her mortification knew no boundaries today. Joey and Adam casually sat atop the corral fence waiting for them. How was she going to get off the damn animal, let alone pretend she could walk? She heard Keelee's sharp intake of breath. "Damn it, why is he here?"

Ember didn't let go of the saddle horn, but she did manage a fleeting glance in Keelee's direction. In all actuality, she probably couldn't have let go because her hands were molded to the leather with a death grip. Somehow in her mind the stranglehold on the saddle equaled making sure the Tasmanian devil under her didn't jolt to the left or right without her noticing it.

Ember risked another glance towards her new friend and whispered so the two Greek gods riding behind them couldn't hear. "No walls, remember? This could be your chance to start your relationship over. If he doesn't remember the first time around, you have a blank slate. The future is yours to write. Besides, you said there's an attraction, right?"

Keelee threw a quick look over her shoulder making sure Gorgeous One and Gorgeous Two weren't in hearing range. Satisfied neither twin was listening she hissed back, "Crap Em, I shiver at the thought of that man. He could be my everything, but he's already told me he doesn't want me. Is it sick that I'm happy he has no idea he rejected me?"

"No. The heart wants what the heart wants. No walls, girlfriend. This could be your do-over."

Crossing the hundred yards to the two men sitting on the wooden corral rails seemed to take forever. Ember and Keelee finally stopped their horses where the two men waited. Thankfully, the Delicious Duo continued their ongoing conversation and walked their horses straight into the barn. The laughter they shared had nothing to do with her. Nothing at all. That was her story and she was damn well sticking to it. She was a board certified doctor. She had skills, mad skills, talents people envied! So what if one of them wasn't riding a mammal the size of a Volkswagen van? Joseph jumped down and grabbed the reins of the devil's spawn somebody had the audacity to call a horse. Ember let out a huge sigh of relief before seeing the mirth in Joey's face.

"Don't you dare laugh at me, Joseph Theodore King!"

"Laugh at you, little girl? Now would I do that?" His shoulder's shook as he looped the reins so they wouldn't fall.

"Okay, I admit this was a mistake. 'Just come with me,' she said. 'It'll be a fun time. You really don't need to know how to ride,' she said. Oh my God, I have never hurt so much in my life. Muscles I, as a doctor, didn't even know were part of the human anatomy hurt." Her voice turned whiney when she admitted, "I ache, Joey." Keelee's carefree laughter at her mocking didn't bolster Ember's deflated spirits.

Joey's low roll of laughter joined Keelee's. "I won't bring up the fact I told you maybe you should start with a shorter ride. You were out for over three hours." His smile as he leaned against her leg and looked up at her did nothing to help her bruised ego.

"Ember, you did really well for your first ride. You'll have to come out with me again. Believe me, it gets easier. You're sore now because you were trying to fight the natural balance of your body on top of the horse."

Keelee swung off her horse and looked damned graceful doing it. "What are you doing here Doctor Cassidy? Were you afraid I was going to allow serious bodily harm to come to our guest?"

Ember watched the doctor. His gaze locked on the tall sexy blond who was busy adjusting something under the stirrup of her saddle.

"No. Actually I was hoping I could speak with you if you have the time, Ms. Marshall."

"My name is Keelee. We don't stand on ceremony on the ranch side of the compound. But since you haven't been over this way before, you probably didn't know that. Give me a couple minutes to put up these two and I'm all yours."

Keelee turned her back on Adam and gave Ember a wide-eyed look over the back of her horse. She cleared her facial expression and turned to Joseph. "If you could get the good doctor off Charmin for me I'd appreciate it. I think you may have to pry her hand off the leather though. Lucky she didn't break the glass inside that saddle horn."

Ember released the leather immediately with a gasp. "You didn't tell me it was made of glass!"

Joseph, Keelee and Adam all laughed at her shocked exclamation. Oh, great...another level of humiliation hell.

"Oh ha, ha, ha! Sure, go ahead make fun of the city slicker." But Ember gratefully fell into Joseph's arms when his hands circled her waist pulling her off the miserable mountain of hoofs and hair. She luxuriated in the strength and hardness of his body as she slid down him before her feet hit the ground. Pushing into his hardness, she buried her face against his neck and linked her arms lightly around his waist.

"A hot shower and a full body massage should blot out some of the horrible memories of your first experience on the back of Beelzebub, here." Ember felt the rumble of his words throughout her body and couldn't help but notice the laughter it contained.

She kept tight against him but lifted, kissing his earlobe before she bit it gently. He groaned and tightened his embrace.

She sighed and shimmied her hips against the growing bulge in his jeans. "I know you're making fun of me but I don't care. I'll take you up on both the shower and massage as long as somewhere in the mix there is mind altering sex." At her whispered words, Joseph dropped his forehead to hers before he responded so only she could hear. "Oh, little girl, I guarantee it."

.

CHAPTER SIXTEEN

THE TRIP TO THE HOUSE AND JOURNEY UP the stairs hurt her poor chaffed thighs as much as walking on hot coals without shoes would hurt. Admittedly, having never walked barefoot on hot coals she couldn't be certain, but damn, the rub of her denim jeans against the tender skin of her inner thighs made every step a challenge. Joey set the shower taps and gently helped her out of her clothes. His almost constant laughter at her expense was rather smug on his part, but all things considered, Em knew she looked and acted comically. Just hearing the unusual sound of her lover's laughter made the pain easier to tolerate.

Joseph's hands guided her under the warm pulsing shower head. And thank God he did, because voluntary movement didn't seem a remote possibility. Her body groaned in appreciation. Okay, it wasn't an actual groan, but oh, if her abused glutes and hamstrings could make a noise—they would have. With her eyes closed and the hot water working against her tired muscles, she knew without a doubt heaven existed. When Joey's hands massaged her shoulders and pulled her back against his chest, she discovered she had a few more stops in between the near angelic delight of the shower and real heaven on earth. His hands lightly brushed down her shoulders to her arms and rested on her hips with fingers splayed across her midriff.

"Shower with a massage, little girl." He lowered his lips to her neck and sent rivers of sensation through her when he nipped her skin. His tongue soothed the sting of his bite.

"Turn and face the wall." Ember complied without hesitation. Joseph sensually lathered soap over her body. His strong hands worked every muscle down her neck, back, thighs and calves and turned her aching body into putty. Yep, as a doctor she had determined the formula for being turned to putty needed just three ingredients: Joseph, hot water, and soap. Alright, the last two elements were optional.

An aroma of citrus and vanilla wafted through the building clouds of steam surrounding them. When his strong fingers massaged the shampoo through her hair, she leaned back into him and smiled. His obvious arousal pressed against her very sore derriere. Without regard for her delicate condition, she pushed back into him and shifted her hips.

Joey chuckled and grabbed her hips, stilling her. "You little minx. Be good or I'll take you right now, just like this." He pushed forward placing his hard cock in between her cheeks letting her know exactly what he would do.

"And you're saying that like it would be a bad thing? Why should I be good if I like the reward for being bad?"

Joseph delivered a sharp slap to her abused bottom and Ember yelped in surprise. "You'll be good because I told you to behave." The sizzling demand flipped a switch deep within her. A little moan escaped her lips, but she held still. His hands blazed a trail of heat and strength as he worked her body. His ministrations induced a mind-melting laxness from head to foot.

After he rinsed her off, he turned her around. His eyes blazed with unconcealed passion. He dropped his lips to hers and licked the seam of her lips, coaxing them open and devouring her soft recesses. The demand of his possession reminded her she would indeed do what he wanted, when he wanted. Ember gave him everything he asked for and slumped limply against the tile wall when he finally pulled away.

"I'm not the type of man to wrap the stars in moonbeams and offer to give you the universe, but I'll carry this time we've shared with me forever… here." He placed his hand over his heart. Ember's breath caught in her throat. Could this man, the one who spoke of moonbeams and stars, be the same one who killed for a living? She felt a tear slip down her cheek knowing with a fatalistic certainty that he would be leaving soon.

"When are you leaving?"

"Don't cry, little girl. I'm flying out tomorrow."

"How long will it take? How long before…?" Ember shivered even under the hot fall of water.

"Realistically? Several months… perhaps longer. Gaining access to Morales won't be easy. I need you to promise you will stay here on the ranch. If you leave, one of the Alpha team members will be with you at all times."

Joseph turned off the water and reached for a fluffy bath sheet. He wrapped one around Ember and used a smaller towel to dry her hair. The flapping terry cloth muffled her reply. "What's an Alpha team?"

"Not what. Who. Chief, Doc, Dixon, and Drake. Until Doc and Chief are back in fighting form, one or both of the twins will be with you every time you leave the ranch. Understand?"

"Oh, please, make me suffer! Okay, okay… I promise to take one or both of the Delicious Duo with me wherever I go."

Joseph stopped his drying and pushed her hair out of her face. His eyebrow lifted. Its effect sinister. Joseph walked her against the wall with his body and growled. "Delicious Duo? Do I have reason to kill them?"

"No, no killing needed. I'm not into blonds, or hadn't you noticed the type of man who turns me on?" Em traced a bead of water in a meandering path as it trickled down his chest.

"Good. Didn't want to deal with the paperwork killing them would entail. Plus, I'd have to talk to your biker-shrink friend again."

He grabbed a towel from the rack and stepped back. She looked up at him and asked, "Will I ever see you again? Or just talk to you from time to time… when it's safe?"

She watched him dry off. His hard chiseled muscles flexed gloriously as he stretched his towel around his back.

"No. There can be no connection between us. I can't risk it." He dropped his towel and lifted his hand to the bath sheet he had tucked around her, pulling one edge. It fell to the floor.

"Never?" Her traitorous voice trembled.

"Little girl, if I could without jeopardizing you or getting myself killed, I would." He kissed the tip of her nose and smiled sadly. "Now, no more of our night spent talking about what can't be. Tell me, Doctor Harris, what would you recommend for this serious medical condition I appear to be suffering from?" He took her hand and placed it on his hard cock.

Ember swallowed the desperation she felt, determined not to spoil their last night. She stepped back and put her hand on her hip. "Honestly, Mr. King, I'm afraid for your wellbeing. If we don't relieve the pressure soon, you will expire from an extreme case of erectus maximus complicated by a terminal case of cobalt orb syndrome. I hesitate to speculate on how much paperwork an explanation of that cause of death might involve."

Joseph's laughter rang out and echoed in the bathroom. "Dr. Harris, your diagnosis is spot on. What is the prescribed course of action to reverse this life-threatening condition?"

Slowly moving up to him she placed her open hand on his heart and lifted her eyes looking at him through her lashes. Her voice trembled when she spoke. "I think I'll allow the patient to determine the method. You see, I trust him with my life."

"And I trust you with my heart, little girl. Don't worry. I'll protect you. But tonight is about us. Let me make love to you. My way."

Ember lifted to toes and brushed a kiss across his lips. "No. Our way, Joey. Our way."

He leaned down and trapped her mouth with firm pressure seconds before he lifted her into his arms. His kiss held her lips as he carried her to the bed. He devoured her mouth with a savage force that robbed her of all air. He released her mouth and she gasped, filling her lungs with sweet cool air. He rolled her so she straddled his hips. Her legs, back and glutes objected immediately. Ember's whimper didn't go unnoticed.

"Poor little girl. You didn't learn your lesson very well today so I'm giving you another. You're going to ride me tonight. But be warned, little one, I'm not a gentle old nag." Her back complained when he pulled her down and sucked a nipple into his mouth. His tongue flicked the hardening peak and then his teeth applied steady pressure as his hand found her other breast. His fingers mimicked his mouth's assault and Ember shivered seconds before she moaned and tried to pull away.

Joseph's free hand wrapped around her and pulled her down to him stopping her attempt to move. He spoke, clenched around her nipple. "Mine."

Ember braced herself with her hands grasping the sheets next to his shoulders. His assault continued. Teeth, tongue, suction and fingers assailed her nipples and the sensitive flesh of her breasts sending plumes of desire rolling straight to her sex. His relentless possession of her breasts heated and moistened her folds. Ember tried to grind herself against him. His hard cock strained just below her. She could feel the heat of his shaft but couldn't lower her body without causing intense pain to her breasts. A distant sound of frustration registered. It took Ember a moment to realize she was the source. Finally, Joseph stopped his attack on her now hypersensitive breasts.

He pulled her down to his chest. Painful rivulets of sensation streaked through her tender breasts as he held her to him. He kissed her hard. His tongue dominated hers as it tunneled into her. She willed her body into compliance, relishing his power and strength.

He released her and gazed up into her eyes. The depth of the emotion she saw floored her. It was as if he had lifted the walls around his feelings and let them flood out. Ember couldn't tear her eyes away from his.

"Lift up, baby girl."

She moaned as her overused thigh muscles spasmed in pain.

She felt him spread her with his hand. "So wet and so hot. It's time for your riding lesson." He centered his thick, long shaft under her. "Brace on my shoulders." When she did as he asked, he lifted his hands and pushed the riot of curls away from her face. "Lower yourself and don't stop until you reach the base of my cock. Understand?"

Her eyes went as big as saucers. Joseph gripped her ass with both hands and squeezed. "Answer me."

Ember tried to speak, but she couldn't make the words come out. Instead, she nodded.

"Say it, Em. Tell me you understand."

She cleared her throat before she spoke. "I heard you Joey, but… You're too big! I don't know if I can take you all at once. I don't know if I'm wet enough."

His hand lifted to her face and he forced her to look at him. His velvet smooth words mesmerized her. "You can and you will. Do it now. Make me proud, baby girl. Take me. All the way. Don't stop."

Em closed her eyes and lowered onto his shaft. Her body opened, but he was so large she cried out after taking only half of his shaft. He rubbed his hands over her thighs and encouraged her. His words flowed over her, bringing her concentration back to him. "Fuck, so good, baby girl. Keep going. Don't stop. You can take me."

Ember's entire body shook. His hand covered her mouth forcing her whimpers into her consciousness. "You're almost there. A couple more inches. So hot and tight for me. Yeah, that's it."

She felt his pubic bone hit her clit and stopped. Her body tried to reconcile the pain, pleasure and desire that tumbled through her. He removed his hand from her mouth and trailed fingers down her throat to her breast. Joey rolled both nipples in his rough, callused fingers. A nebula of conflicting sensory inputs tortured her already overtaxed body. He lowered his hand and pressed lightly on her clit. An explosion of sensation ripped through her. In an uncontrollable spasm, her climax blew. Her hips bucked in helpless reaction to the detonations of intense feeling. The forward and back movement while impaled on his cock triggered a second blast. Her body wept around him.

Somehow, she managed to stay braced against his shoulders. Opening her eyes, she gazed down at the man underneath her. His pupils had almost overtaken the color of his eyes. His chest had flushed dark red and his breath came in shallow pants. He waited until she drew a deep breath and then ordered, "Lift up, two or three inches." He closed his eyes as she rose slightly. His hands stopped her where he wanted her. He opened his eyes and the intensity of his gaze drilled through her.

"I'm going to take you now, baby girl. Don't move. Do you understand?"

Ember shivered. "Joey, oh God!"

"Shhh…just feel. Just feel." Joseph waited for her to brace on his shoulders then drove into her. He held her hips, his fingers biting into her soft buttocks as he pierced her deeply. He assaulted her with a fierce, determined invasion. There was no gentleness. This wasn't love making. He claimed her, possessed her, and she knew it. Her moans became cries as his rock hard shaft hammered through her, penetrating her recesses. Joseph owned her body and held her breaking heart in his hands.

"I need more, baby girl." He drove faster into her body. He was taking what he needed from her and she wanted to give everything to him. The sexual assault on her overwrought senses reached an unbearable limit.

"Joey, please, please!" She begged wildly. Her nails raked over his shoulders as she tried to anchor herself against his physical aggression.

"Em, are you ready to come?"

Her mind searched for a way to answer. He thrust harder. "Answer me!" He growled between his pounding thrusts.

"Yes, God, Yes!" Her cries seemed to release his control and unbelievably he forced himself into her harder and deeper. His own animalistic utterings rivaled her cries.

He growled, "You're mine." He caught her as her body exploded. Somehow through the fog of climax she sensed his orgasm racking his body as he spread his seed deep within her.

He lowered her down to him and rolled her gently to his side. Joseph grabbed the sheet and threw it over both of them while still buried deep within her. He wrapped his arms around her, holding her tightly as they recovered from the earth shattering orgasms. Her exhausted body melted into the intense hard warmth of the man next to her.

The low rumble of his voice reverberated through the room. "I love you. I always have and I always will."

CHAPTER SEVENTEEN

THE FEEL OF SUNSHINE FROM THE WINDOWS HEATING her skin woke her from the exhausted slumber she had succumbed to last night. Her body ached from the very physical and extremely emotional love making. Joseph had ravaged her body, melted her heart and seared his love into the deepest parts of her soul.

A strong, callused hand cupped her ass and squeezed the sore muscle. A groan escaped her as she pushed back into Joey's body.

"Good morning." She could feel the rumble of his voice running through his chest.

"G'morning." Ember pulled her hands up and rubbed her eyes, willing her brain to kick into gear.

"You're fuzzy when you wake up."

"You laughing at me? Coffee. Coffee now." Her mumbled reply did get a laugh.

"Nope, not right now. We need to have a discussion first." He pulled her onto her back and anchored his weight on his elbow looking down at her.

"You want talk? I need coffee first. No coffee—no talky." Ember closed her eyes and smiled at her little rhyme.

Joseph's hand caressed her stomach and landed on her breast. She cracked an eye open and looked up at him. His eyes locked with hers as he pinched the nipple. Her back arched and her body flared. She was tender from last night. His touch bordered on painful.

"You don't need to talk. You need to listen." He released her breast but kept his hand on her ribs. Almost as if he were pinning her down. "Are you awake enough to listen now?"

Ember nodded, her gaze never leaving his emotion-filled eyes.

"I have been up front with you, Ember. Before I get on that plane later today, I need to make sure you understand. When I leave—this is over."

If she could have, Ember would have bolted from the bed. His hand gripped her and held her down as if he had read her mind. She didn't want to hear this. She didn't want to face a reality without Joey in it.

"Look at me." At his commanding growl, she looked up into his eyes as he ordered.

"I am a violent and dangerous person with lethal enemies, enemies who would stop at nothing to hurt anyone even remotely important to me—assassins who would track me to the ends of the earth and kill me just to garner their nation's gratitude or reap monetary reward. The world I live in has no happily ever after. I chose this path a long time ago and I knew what the price to live this life would be. It has severed all but the most superficial ties to my family. It has prevented any relationship I may have wanted to build. And it has cost me a life with you."

Ember rolled into him and buried her head against his shoulder and neck. "We can go somewhere and hide. I trust you to take care of me. I'll wait until you work things out. Please, Joey. Please say there is a way this works out. A way this isn't goodbye forever."

His hand caressed her back softly. The small act of gentleness seemed so at odds with the harsh, demanding man stretched out beside her. His soft touch sliced her heart open and laid her soul bare to him.

"Little girl, if I could make this right, I would. There is nothing on this earth I want more. But I have to live in reality. You and I can never have more than this time. We'll never be together again."

Her resolve not to cry melted. She had tried so hard not to accept that fact. "You said you loved me. Why won't you fight for me?" The tears dripped from her face to his arm.

She felt his long exhale against her shoulder. His husky whisper filled with emotion he rarely showed. "I do. God, I love you so much. I'm not leaving because I don't love you, little one. I'm leaving because I love you more than life itself. I have to make this world safe for you. In order to do that I have to…go."

Ember shook her head and burrowed deeper against him. If she didn't believe it…it couldn't be true. Right? She didn't have to accept never seeing him again. Her world would be on hold until he came for her again. Because he would come back. He loved her.

"I'll wait for you Joey. You know I will. Until it is safe for you to come back to me." The words came between sobs.

He placed his hand under her chin and forced her away from her hiding place. "I won't be coming back, little one. After this passes, the best thing you can do is find a good man. Have some beautiful babies and live your life. Live it for me. Please."

Ember wrapped her arms around him and emptied all the stored up pain she had been suppressing. She didn't believe this was it. She couldn't.

"Joey, please. Just… please make love to me. One last time." Her body shook as the cries of anguish tore through her body. His hard body moved against her. For the last time.

CHAPTER EIGHTEEN

JOEY LOVED HER. THEY HAD MADE LOVE AND held each other tight knowing with the passing of time their world would shatter. And it came too soon for Ember. Joey put several shirts in his pack and walked back to the dresser. Her voice cracked "I promised myself I wouldn't do this, but I can't stop myself. I know you believe we can never be together. Isn't there a way? I mean nobody knows that you're that guy... Fury, right? If Fury just stopped working, vanished, wouldn't that be enough?"

She saw him straighten and give a long exhale of breath before he turned with several pair of jeans. "It wouldn't matter the name I choose to live under. Facial recognition programs, fingerprints, retinal scans, dental records... the intelligence community would demand some evidence to validate my death. Honestly, the only way to lose Fury is for me to die."

"Can you pretend to die?" Her voice sounded high and strained even to her own ears.

His brows pulled together furrowing before he spoke. "That's Hollywood clouding your mind. Look at it realistically. There are too many variables, too many things that could go wrong. No baby, girl, the safest thing for both of us is for me to walk away and for you to forget I exist."

The tightness gripping her chest cinched further. "It's not fair. How can I lose you now? Joey? Why can't we just go? Find a little corner of the world away from everyone and live together until we grow old and wrinkled?"

Joseph walked over to her and grabbed her around the waist lifting her to the middle of the bed. He rolled on top of her. His hard muscles and heavy weight pinned her down and his eyes drilled into hers. "Stop. With everything I am I promise, if it existed, I would find a way to come back to you. But you must face the reality of my life. What we are together can never survive because of what I am. Maybe this is karma kicking my ass, or fate bitch slapping me for the lives I've taken. I don't know. I'm sorry my past has ruined our future. This is it, baby girl, this is our goodbye."

This morning, the pain of her heart being ripped from her chest intensified with each step they took towards the runway. By the time they reached the tarmac of the ranch's runway she could barely keep it together. Be strong. Be strong for him. Don't let his last memory of you be this way. Let him see how much you love him.

In the bright glow of the morning sun, he kissed her hard and held her for the last time. "If there were any chance of a normal life for us, Ember, I'd marry you in a second. I love you. Be my good girl and promise me you'll take care of yourself even if that means one day finding someone else to love you."

She felt the tears run down her cheeks. Looking into his beautiful green-blue eyes, she spoke the truth in her heart. "No. There has never been anyone but you. There can never be anyone but you. I love you. Only you."

He placed a feather soft kiss on her forehead, lingering there, holding her just as softly. His whispered, "Goodbye, baby girl," echoed in the empty cavern that used to hold her heart.

He turned, picked up his backpack and walked away. His broad back remained ram-rod straight as he climbed the stairs to the waiting jet. He ducked through the door and boarded the plane. He never looked back.

Ember couldn't hold back the tears blurring her vision. The shiny black G6 taxied to the end of the long runway. Joey was onboard. When the plane took off, he was gone. Forever. Standing in the hot July sun, she shaded her eyes and watched as the aircraft held at the end of the runway. The ten days he had spent with her at the ranch seemed to evaporate like the jet trail following an aircraft. How could time slip by so quickly?

With a revving roar of jet engines, the G6 released its brakes and catapulted down the runway, lifting off the ground and up into the air. The reflection of the sun on the aircraft momentarily blinded her, a brilliant flash of light before the plane pulled higher into the cloudless blue sky.

"How you holding up?"

Ember looked over her shoulder. Adam and the Delicious Duo of Dixon and Drake stood behind her, her Guardian appointed protectors for the foreseeable future. Snuffling and wiping her cheeks she drew a deep stuttering breath. "I really don't know right now. I don't know what I'm going to do with myself now that Joey's gone."

Adam put an arm around her shoulder. "Well, Thing One and Thing Two have a plan, Dr. Harris. And unfortunately for you, you're the key to this ill-conceived and poorly thought out effort."

Ember sniffed and looked back at the twins. Both had what Frank Marshall called their shit-eating grins plastered across their faces.

Lifting an eyebrow she asked, "What are you up to?"

Dixon hit Drake and started, "Well now, Dr. Harris, we have this team member who's been a royal pain in our ass."

Drake chimed in, "He's this massive guy who used a boo-boo to get out of any and all physical training over the last what… well, damn, it's been about two years hasn't it Dixon?"

"Yep. See, we think he is malingering. Has a psychotic issue that is preventing his muscular development and thereby impeding his mental capacity."

Drake turned to his brother and put his hands on his hips. "Well, there you go again, pulling out the flipping forty dollar words. Why couldn't you just say Doc has been a lazy son of a bitch and not doing his self any favors by forgoing his physical training?"

"But I did say that! Exactly that!"

Doc laughed and pulled Ember back towards the house leaving the twins to catch up after they realized they were alone.

Doc's voice hit her from behind. "As senior medic on staff, my day consists of addressing the rehab of Guardian's personnel injured in the line of duty. But as Thing One and Thing Two explained poorly, as part of my own rehabilitation, I want to start working out again and I plan on continuing my appointments with Doctor Wheeler. In order for me to do that, Guardian will need to hire another doctor. I suggested to Gabriel that you do it since you're here anyway. What do you think about working with us for the foreseeable future?"

Ember glanced back to the vast sky and sighed. She felt… empty. "I think perhaps you're only doing this because of Joey."

"Ha! Not true! Look, I've been stuck in a clinical depression for a while now. I knew the symptoms, but I just couldn't bring myself to give a damn. Wheeler verbally knocked me on my ass the other day and gave me some mild anti-depressants. I honestly need the space and time away from the clinic to start to heal physically. Dixon and Drake will drag my ass through the PT but in order to participate I need to be able to be away. If you

196·KRIS MICHAELS

don't take the job, I'll put out for resumes. What do you think?"

Ember stopped and looked at Adam. "I think that is the most you've spoken to me since I've been here. You didn't stutter or pause once."

Adam blushed a brilliant red and a small smile spread across his face. "Yeah, the speech impediment may have been a stress-related issue. The harder I tried to speak the more stressed I became and the more problems I had. The more problems I had, the more stress I felt and it became a self-fulfilling prophecy."

"And since you refused to get help with the stress, you lived in a little hell of your own making."

"Until I started taking the anti-depressants." Doc nodded almost to himself and looked away. She got it. He was embarrassed.

"Hey, don't feel like you have the copy write to living in a hell you've created. I've lived in my own little corner of Hades for too many years. I made a change. Or I was going to before Morales forced this one on me." Ember smiled and shrugged before she turned back to the house. "Alright, Doctor Cassidy, I'll take the job. But not today. Today I'm going to throw myself a pity party and cry until I have no more tears, and then I'm going to get drunk. Right there." She pointed to the main ranch house. "Out on that porch swing with Keelee."

"Sounds like a plan Doctor Harris. I'll see you tomorrow, then?" He stopped at the crossroads between the Guardian complex and the ranch.

"How about you stop by tonight and have a drink with us?" Ember couldn't resist playing matchmaker. If she couldn't have a happily ever after, maybe Keelee could.

"Sorry, can't mix alcohol with the script I'm on right now."

"Have you seen Keelee lately?" Ember absentmindedly drew a circle in the gravel with the toe of her boot.

"No, not since we reintroduced ourselves. I think I want to work on me a little bit. I guess I hurt her pretty bad a couple years ago. I don't know how or why. Sometimes there is a wisp of a memory, but when I try to grasp it… nothing."

Ember put her hand on his forearm. "It will come back, Adam. And if it doesn't? Well then, I guess you need to make some new memories with her. Let's try for happy ones this time, okay?"

Adam smiled and his dimples made a glorious appearance. "Yeah, I think I'd like a happy memory or two."

CHAPTER NINETEEN

JOSEPH NOW KNEW EVERY HIDING PLACE IN CUIDAD Juarez, Mexico. The sprawling city of one point five million inhabitants situated a stone's throw from El Paso, Texas was where he stalked his prey. Morales was a dead man. The fool just didn't know it yet.

A metastasizing cancer fed by the warring drug cartels infested the urban sprawl of the border metropolis. The city had the highest murder rate in the world, a body count Joseph would personally add to. The Mexican government flooded the sprawling urban blight with military troops and federal police officers. Did they actually think the poorly armed and uneducated forces stood a chance? Joseph saw the result every day. The answer was a resounding no. The criminals ruled the streets and Morales reigned as the top cartel in the city. The bastard owned ninety-nine percent of all illegal smuggling operations out of the area.

It had taken five months of living as a shadow in abandoned houses in the Rivera Del Bravo district to track down Morales' lieutenants. The trail to the top started with crumbs. Crumbs found in retched, stinking, shit-holes of houses that pumped the drugs into the veins of the city. Joseph went to the small peddlers, bought the drugs and ingrained himself in the culture. He used his skills to track the street dealers to the houses.

The houses were nothing more than whore houses. Unfortunately, the whores were young, too young, and drugged beyond comprehension. There were too many houses to watch. Joseph picked one that appeared to have more business than most and watched. His job now was to gather intel.

He worked the business end of Morales' human trafficking and drug running. He forced himself to disengage from the sense of being human he'd reacquired with Ember. As the days passed, one bleeding into the other, Joseph felt himself slipping back into the persona that made his enemies look over their shoulders. His defenses once again in place, he focused on sifting through the filth, contamination and abominations that fed Morales' bottom line. In a few short weeks, he'd gathered enough intel to make killing anyone associated with the Morales Cartel a 'go' in his mind.

The intel given to him by his brother, Jared, stated there were four street-level lieutenants in Juarez. The four reported directly to the big guy. The bastards at the street level were cagey and scared. They'd not be easy to get close to. Joseph had witnessed more than one execution of dealers that weren't producing or taking an unauthorized cut.

He'd followed the hit squads with no success. They received phone calls and moved, no physical connection to the power structure of the cartel. The lead went nowhere. He started over, going back down to the houses. Watching, observing and waiting for his trail of crumbs to materialize.

With dogged determination, Joseph had located all four lieutenants after four months of living with and among the filth of the streets. Now, he ghosted between shadows and dark alley ways keeping track of the four officers. Three displayed the intelligence to vary their routes, change up their routines and keep him guessing on their schedules and meets. They wouldn't lead him to the boss. They were too disciplined.

The fourth? Well, he was a fucking idiot. Carlos De La Cruz, or SF, "Stupid Fuck" as Joseph thought of him, was Morales' brother-in-law. SF's sister was Morales' trophy wife. The wife got the beauty, but SF sure as hell didn't get the brains. The punk had the intelligence of a gnat. His cocksure attitude, lack of disciplined security team and distinct belief that his brother-in-law's reputation would protect his ass were the very reasons Joseph targeted SF. The mental moron had to be the weakest link in Morales' organization. No way the cartel could survive any more idiots like him. For the last three weeks, Joseph followed the original gangsta wannabe. SF had been traveling the exact same routes and pulling the same revenues from the same sources. The punk flashed his weapon, cash, and ignorance more than a rookie cop flashed his badge. It was a miracle he hadn't been killed by a rival cartel.

Joseph settled down in the alley, half a block up the street keeping surveillance on his best lead to Morales. SF had one more stop before heading to his hacienda for the night. The fucking stucco and tile prison where SF kept the young boys he used. Last night the sick bastard had partied poolside with his amigos. The fucker was doping kids. Kids! He still could hear the pleas and cries the night breeze had carried to the secluded position where he observed them. The bastards had shot up four young boys. SF and his posse used those innocents like seasoned whores right there by the pool. Damn he hated he couldn't slice the fucker into ribbons. Wasn't his M.O., but he could see how someone would be able to dissect the slimy son of a bitch. Joseph swore to himself he would get those boys out of there. Yeah, this sick bastard was going to be a pleasure to take out. God have mercy on your soul, SF, because I sure as hell won't.

Glancing down at his watch, Joseph shifted in the shadows. SF wasn't following his normal pattern. He should've left the restaurant by now. A pearl white Suburban pulled up behind SF's blinged-out black Escalade. A contingent of three heavily armed guards exited the new vehicle and cleared the area. The men were professionals, nothing like SF's crew. When the team seemed satisfied, they opened the rear door. There she was in all her Prada glory. Morales' wife and a little boy exited the SUV. SF came out of the building laughing and smiling like he didn't have a care in the world. The little boy's, "Tio Carlo!" carried the distance.

Eur-fucking-reka. That silicone enhanced woman was his direct link to Morales. Joseph watched the guards hurry the eye candy and boy into the establishment. Now that he had the woman, he no longer needed the moron. SF's minutes left on earth were running out.

THREE-AND-A-HALF HOURS LATER, AS SHADOWS LENGTHENED AND PEOPLE around the city were settling in for the evening, Joseph carefully pushed further along the roofline of a three-story hacienda behind the Morales family compound. He had tracked the wife's Suburban from the restaurant to an upscale shopping center and then on to the estate he now observed. A glance from the neighbor's rooftop confirmed the opulence surrounding the Morales family. Fuck, it rivaled some of the royal palaces he'd seen in Saudi Arabia.

Joseph mentally diagramed the security he could see. High-resolution cameras had been installed at each corner of the twelve-foot concrete wall surrounding the compound. The land immediately outside and adjacent to the complex had been cleared. No one was going to approach without being seen. Heavily armed guards patrolled the grounds. Four guards in the back and three—no four—in the front. They were just the ones that made themselves visible. He needed a more accurate accounting of the man's security. He hit the power switch on the burner phone he carried, typed the address of Morales's house and hit send. With that one action, the carefully crafted, researched and rehearsed plan launched.

The illicit trade of cocaine, marijuana, guns and human beings made Juan Morales a very wealthy man. Money bought expensive security and security allowed a person to assume they were untouchable. Never fucking assume. No one is untouchable, asshole.

Joseph settled down to wait and watch, hidden against the rise of the neighboring villa's rooftop. As he watched, a motorcade of three black SUVs entered the compound. The guards didn't deploy but casually sauntered out of the vehicles. Morales hopped out of the back passenger door on the left hand side of the middle vehicle and strode to the house. Position of travel, configuration of convoy, and number of guards confirmed. Yeah, that's right. Kiss the wife. Hug the kid. Enjoy, amigo. You're on borrowed time.

Soon the end would come. The end of Morales' reign of terror. The end of SF's sick abuse of innocent boys. Ember would be free to live a life unencumbered by the death and violence that surrounded him. That dull ache in his chest notched up and roundhouse kicked him as his subconscious geared up and beat the shit out of him one more time. The only way she walks away from death is if you walk toward it. His conviction grew stronger with each passing day. She was safe. Safe because he walked away from her and toward his end game. An earth without her on it wasn't even conceivable. He wouldn't—couldn't face that. The only way to save her was to finish this mission, a mission designed specifically to destroy not only Morales, but also the assassin Joseph had become—his suicide mission.

With a sigh, Joseph took out the battery and Sim card. Pitching them into the bushes below him, he leaned back and gazed over the pool into the house. He watched Morales come home from his long hard day at the office dealing death and peddling flesh. Yeah, have a drink, asshole.

Bingo, just as planned, the entire sector plunged into darkness. Joseph started the secondhand sweep of his watch. The generators in Morales' compound flared. Auxiliary power flickered and then lit up the compound. Thirty-three seconds. A total of fourteen heavily armed guards poured out of the house and took up positions at the front and rear entrances. Commands shouted from inside the house sent the guards to the outbuildings by the pool. Finally, the man who appeared to be the chief of security exited the house talking on a handheld radio. Two minutes later the entire grid powered back up. Recon complete.

Joseph nodded to himself. Amazing coincidence that one of Guardian's subsidiary companies controlled the entity that powered the Mexican state of Chihuahua. Nah, not really. David Xavier, the owner of all things Guardian, was one connected mother. An hour passed before Joseph carefully egressed from his rooftop perch under the protection of full darkness.

Time to return to SF's hellhole and liberate some kids. Motherfucker would never hurt another innocent. Granted, the stupid prick's death would have to look like an accident. No need to give Morales a reason to batten down the hatches, or worse yet, bolt altogether. Nope, a drunken fall down a flight of stairs would do the trick. Guaran-fucking-teed.

CHAPTER TWENTY

EMBER PICKED UP HER CARDS. SHE HELD THEM close and fanned them carefully so the Wonder Twins couldn't cheat. They swore they didn't, but somehow those two communicated without words. Ember discarded three cards and looked at Chief.

"Three."

The massive man dealt her the cards and turned his eyes to Drake.

When Drake rapped his knuckles on the table both Ember and Keelee groaned. "How? How do you have a pat hand? You have to be the luckiest person on the face of the Earth!" Ember laughed when Keelee gave a weak attempt at kicking the man. He dodged it easily.

Chief smiled that almost-smile of his and Ember called him on it. "Oh, no. I know that tell. Mike thinks he has the winning hand."

All eyes swiveled to the dealer. "And what makes you say that, Ember?" Chief's face had blanked, but she had definitely seen that smirk.

"Oh, hell no! Mike, I saw it. You have a tell. I saw the smirk. You thought everyone was watching Keelee beat up on Drake…"

"She didn't even touch me! Dixon, back me up here."

"Dude when are you going to figure it out? This woman is your better. She can out ride you, out rope you and out work you. Now you want me to get involved in a lie that would perpetrate a grievous malfeasance for which she could rightfully kick my ass? No thank you, sir."

Drake stood straight up and dropped his cards on the table. "Grievous malfeasance? Grievous fucking malfeasance? Damn it to hell Dixon, how many times do I have to tell you to put that thesaurus away? Why in the hell do you have to start with the ten dollar words? Speak English, will yah? 'Merican would be better. Grievous fucking malfeasance my rosy red ass."

Ember looked from brother to brother and smiled. They never shut up, but in the last five months, she had come to realize they only acted like this around people they trusted. Lucky her. When they escorted her into the city for medical supplies, they didn't speak. The macho 'don't fucking think about talking to this woman' attitude effectively prevented just about any contact with people outside the ranch.

Dixon smiled sheepishly and grabbed a sandwich off the platter on the corner of the table handing half of his to his brother. The weekly poker game had become a tradition. The twins, Keelee and Ember always played. Chief, Adam, and Frank rotated in occasionally.

"Sorry, Drake. Here, can't have you die of malnutrition. The ramifications of going without a meal could lead to untold manifestations and dilemmas of biblical proportions."

Drake took a huge bite of the ham sandwich and spoke around the food. "It's cool man, and my dilemmas won't perpetuate or propagate into phobias if you pour me some more of that whiskey."

"Deal 'cause, God only knows what type of phobias you would harbor…"

Ember grabbed a sandwich and looked at her cards. Two pair, eights, and twos. Dang it, it was going to cost her at least three dollars to see Chief's hand. The hand played around with Drake raising the pot. Make that four dollars.

"Why not? I'm definitely the most handsome and the most intelligent. Don't you think so, Ember?"

Ember shook her head slowly. "I'm sorry I tuned you out. After five months of living here, I've gotten used to turning off your volume. You bicker all the time."

"We don't bicker." The men spoke in unison.

Keelee and Ember both laughed before Keelee taunted them. "Yeah, you really do. Like two old women." Keelee dodged a flying poker chip that Dixon launched toward her.

Chief quietly added almost to himself. "Two brainless teenagers is more like it."

"I heard that Chief! Man, when did you start teaming up with these two? Have you three become BFFs?" Drake's response lifted over the women's laughter.

"Yeah, like Fury would allow that." Chief's head snapped up and his eyes cut to Dixon, the nonverbal reprimand whipped across the room silencing the twin's banter immediately.

"Ah, fuck. Sorry, Ember… I… I didn't think." Dixon put his hand over Ember's. The warmth of his skin on her suddenly shaking hand didn't lesson the verbal slap to the face.

"No… no, it's okay, Dixon. Joseph's gone. He's not coming back. When he's done with what he has to do, I'll be on my way. It's been great working and living here, but…" Her voice cracked and mentally she tried to slap a Band-Aid on the broken heart she still nursed.

She took a deep breath and threw five chips in the pot looking directly at Chief. "Anyway I'd be glad to have Chief as my BFF. Call. Let's see what you got!"

"If we don't train exactly the way we fight in the field we're doing our people a tremendous disservice." Chief's explanation hadn't changed nor had her opinion of the real-world tactics Guardian used to train its agents.

"Yeah, but at this rate there will be nobody left to put in the field!" Ember finished placing the personal security officer's newly wrapped and freshly relocated wrist in a sling. She picked up a prescription pad and wrote in the dosage. Before the young officer could voice his objection, she held up her hand. "Stop right now and listen to me closely. You will take these. It's an anti-inflammatory script, not pain meds, because God knows nobody employed by Guardian ever wants to take pain medication!"

She glared at the man on the exam table. "If you don't take them exactly as prescribed, I will not clear you for field duty. Bounce your head north and south, Mr…" She stopped to check his name on the chart again. "Maher… or you'll be pushing a desk for the next ninety days. Understand?"

The rakish looking man glared at her. The furrows deepened on Ember's forehead as the blush of anger rose from her chest to her face. "Oh, don't tell me you plan on arguing with me? You don't want to go there. I guarantee you won't win."

Ember turned her back on the men to try to collect the calm that had scattered to the four winds. Chief cuffed the man on the shoulder. "Nod your head up and down and get out of here, Brad. Before you say or do something to really piss her off. She lost a lot of money last night at poker and she's not in a good mood."

The massive personal security officer cleared his throat. "Got it, Doc. I'll take 'em."

She cast Chief a wink and smile before she turned and raised an eyebrow to the agent. "Good, follow-up with me in three days. Until then absolutely no physical or weapons training."

Ember turned around and watched the young man limp out of the clinic. The phone on her desk rang. Ember nodded towards it as she started to clean her workspace. "Would you get that? It's most likely for Adam. The only people I get calls from are you and Keelee. You're here and Keelee's out with the ranch hands breaking ice for the cattle."

"Yeah, cause I'm your secretary." Chief laughed and reached over and picked up the receiver. "Clinic."

His eyes bounced to Ember before he spoke. "This isn't within protocols."

Chief's voice and immediate look in her direction sent a premonition of uneasiness through her. Ember couldn't avoid the wave of fear that swept through her mind.

Chief looked down at the tile floor and nodded his head silently as he listened to whoever called. "Yeah, I got it. I don't like it, but I understand."

Chief took a deep breath. "Yeah, she's right here. Hold on."

He lifted off the desk and extended the phone to her. "Joseph."

Ember lunged at the receiver and slapped it to her ear. "Joey! Is it done? Are you safe? Where are you?" Her heart beat so loud she was sure he could hear it on the other end of the line.

His low, wicked laugh rolled over the connection. "No, little girl, I'm not done. Not yet. I'm safe for now. Things are going to happen fast from here on out. The op has reached the point of no return. I needed to hear your voice."

"Why? What's happening, Joey? You're scaring me."

"Em, I want you to focus. Will you do that for me, little one?" His voice softened as he spoke.

"I ahh… yeah. I will." She shivered when an unexplainable fear wrapped a choke hold around her neck.

"That's my good girl." Her insides clenched at his softly spoken words. Something was wrong. He wasn't supposed to make contact with her. He was supposed to walk away. Oh God, what's happening?

"Ember, I had to call to tell you that I thank God for the time we had together. You made me realize, what I am, is not who I wanted to be. You gave me the strength to do what I must in order to escape the chaos and death that surrounds me. I need you to know that I love you. I think I always have. I'm sorry for what I've put you through. Can you forgive me?"

"Joey there's nothing to forgive. I love you so much. What is going on? Why are you calling? You said you couldn't… Please… tell me the truth. I have… I need to know what's happening."

Overwhelming certainty shot through her. Nauseated and lightheaded she grabbed the desk. "Oh, God!" She cried holding the precious handset that connected Joey to her. "You don't think you're going to make it. Oh God, Joey, please…please tell me where you are. I'll get you help." The floor stopped her descent. Her legs wouldn't hold her.

"I'm sorry. I have to go. This is it."

Ember sobbed into the phone. "No!" The screamed response was wretched from somewhere deeper than her soul could fathom. "No! Please, God! Joey don't hang up. I love you! Please don't go." God, No! Please don't take him! She couldn't live knowing he was hurt or dying. Holy God, No!

"I'm sorry, little girl. Remember—I loved you." The line clicked and when it did Ember lost the tenuous grasp she had on her reality. She felt someone pick her up and hold her before merciful nothingness overwhelmed her.

Low voices softly heralded a returning consciousness. "Why, Adam? Why would he call after telling her he couldn't contact her again? She was just getting over his leaving five months ago."

"He left to keep her safe, Kee. I don't know why he called. Chief said Joseph didn't think he was going to make it through this one. Morales has an army surrounding him. If Joseph felt the odds were stacked against him? Hell, I don't know. Maybe talking to her gave him peace. I just don't know. I haven't walked in his shoes. I've always had a team to count on. He only has himself. Maybe that's why. Maybe she makes him feel… connected?"

"How can you do it? How does a man face death and walk into the danger?"

"I guess each one of us has our own reason. I walked toward it because as a team we were stronger, better… more capable. I can't imagine working alone. The pressure. Knowing nobody is there for you. Nobody is coming back for you? It must be a desolate feeling."

Desolate. That word resonated with Ember's soul right now. She was on her side facing away from Keelee and Adam. Tears fell unrestricted across her nose, over her cheek and onto the sheet. Joey knew no one was there for him and now she knew—deep down in the fabric of her DNA—she knew Joey would never be coming back. She couldn't hold back her quiet sobs any longer.

Ember heard the bedroom door close before she felt Keelee's hand on her shoulder. Em reached over clutching Keelee like she was a lifeline. Keelee lay down behind her wrapping her arms around Ember. But even the body heat of her new best friend couldn't stop the shivering. Cold, so damn cold and alone, even wrapped in caring arms.

"I got you Em. I'm here." Keelee's soft reassurances drifted through the anguish that had built within her.

In between involuntary sobs and shuddering breaths, she asked, "Have they heard anything? Is he gone?" She didn't recognize her own voice. Rough and raw from crying.

Keelee shook her head on the pillow. "No. Chief hasn't left the communications facility. Jacob called Gabriel, but he's out of the country—out of reach. Right now, everyone is praying that Joseph will be alright."

Ember pulled Keelee's arms tighter around her linking their hands. "Thank you, Kee. Thank you for staying with me." She fought back the tears ending with ragged stuttering breaths and hiccupped gasps of emotion.

"Hey, where would I be but right here? You're my friend and you're exhausted. Try to get some sleep. I promise I'll wake you if I hear anything… good or bad."

Ember stilled and quieted but couldn't shut her brain off. Even sleep wouldn't be an escape. Closing her eyes summoned his image. Dry-eyed, her heart lay in shreds, desolate.

Her whisper barely carried to Keelee. "I guess I never really believed he wouldn't come back. I thought, hoped—there would be a way we could be together. I just couldn't comprehend he wouldn't come back to me… but now I know he won't be back. Ever."

"You don't know that, Emmy. He's a King. By all accounts, they are resilient men."

"Even if he lives through this, Kee, he won't be back. He knew I still expected him to come to me. That call? It was the only closure he could give me. He… he told me he loved me. At least I have that."

Keelee hugged her and kissed the back of her head. "I'm so sorry, Em. What are you going to do?"

"When I go, you mean?"

"Yeah."

Her shoulders shrugged almost of their own volition. "I'll leave. This is a beautiful place and I have friends here, but…"

"Will you keep in touch?"

"Yeah, of course. I need to pack and get ready. Joey said things were going to happen fast. When word comes, I want to be able to be gone. There are too many memories here that I can't face right now. God, am I even making sense?"

"Yeah, you are. I'll help you. You can take my Jeep. It's an old four-wheel drive but very reliable. I never use it and God knows you'll need it if you leave now. The snow is wicked deep this year and the storms won't let up until March."

"I'll pay you for it."

Keelee laughed but without any humor. "Oh no, you won't. I don't need the money and you need the transportation. When you get tired of it or buy one you prefer, pay it forward. Give it to someone in need."

"Keelee?" Em tilted her head back and Keelee lifted up so they could see each other.

"Yeah?"

"Don't take this the wrong way but… I love you, girl."

Keelee smiled sadly before she put her head back on the pillow. "I love you too, Em. Now go to sleep. We'll pack in the morning."

"Not going to happen… sleep I mean."

"Then just lay here and rest."

"Okay."

Chapter Twenty-One

"King." Jason's deep voice carried over the line.

"Hey, lawyer dude. Got a pen and paper?" Joseph watched the traffic creep past the funeral home.

"Joseph? Yeah, hold on a sec." He could hear his brother's movements through the phone as he reached for something to write with. His deep voice muffled for a moment when he spoke, "I got your last email and completed the actions you requested. I worked it all through Gabriel offline as you instructed. He blessed the actions and release of information...which is unprecedented. Told me to tell you good luck."

"Thanks. Have the documents and the letters been sent to the ranch?"

"Yeah."

"Good. I need another favor. Take these coordinates down for me." Joseph rattled off longitude and latitude markers quickly. "I need you to fly to that airstrip and land in exactly sixty-four hours. If I'm not there—leave."

"What is going on? And why in the hell are you using a masked IP address to bounce your cell?"

"I could ask how you know I'm masking but I won't. The fact of the matter is, I'm done, Jason. I'm pulling out. As you've probably assumed, you've been coordinating my exit strategy. In order to leave it clean for Ember, no one in the community can have any doubt. Fury has to die.

"Dude, have you thought what this could do to Mom if it's not controlled right? Man, it could kill her." Joseph felt Jason's concern over the phone.

He knew it could play out badly. That's why he called in a favor. "Gabriel has her out of the country with his wife and kids. They'll be out of contact until this is over. She won't see the news. Once a positive identification is made and the press does their thing, he'll make sure she's taken care of."

"Are you sure your woman will do what you ask?"

"No, she's a stubborn little minx. Honestly, she could just tear up or burn the letter, but I got to dream man. I got to hope." Joseph cleared his throat and dropped the line of thought blocking out the emotion that threatened to overwhelm him. "Just be there, okay?"

"You got it. What type of range do we need?"

"Bring the G6. You won't be on the ground long enough to refuel."

"Roger that. See you in two-and-a-half days."

"God willing, but listen to me. If I'm not there, you don't wait. You get your ass out of Dodge and fast. Understand?"

"I'll wait as long as I can, but I'm not going to do anything stupid."

"Land. Look for me. If I'm not sprinting across that runway, you clear out." Joseph's growl contained almost as much gravel as Jason's voice.

"Alright. In case I don't see you again… I love you, Joseph. You're the head of the family even though you're not around much anymore. You've been more than a brother to me."

"I love you, too, kid. Keep kicking that addiction's ass for me. You're more than what you do, buddy. You always have been. I got to go."

Joseph hung up and disassembled the phone with practiced ease. Joseph looked up at the slice of sky he could see from his position hidden in the shadows of the foul-smelling alley. The December morning sun couldn't quite penetrate the overcast skies. It was a typical winter day in Juarez, Mexico. Traffic sped through the heart of the city. The busy drivers remained unaware of the pending drama about to unfurl. Armed guards patrolling the perimeter of the building down the street were the only indication of anything unusual. Hell, strike that. In Juarez, armed guards were common.

Two guards stopped their casual pacing and pulled up short. They glanced toward the door of the funeral parlor. A subtle indication the memorial service was letting out. SF had himself a nice little ceremony. Only Joseph knew the SF's neck had been broken before he plummeted down the steep tiled steps in his lush hacienda. All the cartel's hierarchy attended SF's funeral. Intense security had been focused away from the vehicles and onto the attendees. Just the distraction he needed.

Joseph put his helmet on and nudged his motorcycle off its stand. When the Morales family exited the funeral home, half of his entourage of guards went with the wife and kid and half left with the drug lord and his lieutenants. Joseph waited for the caravan carrying Morales and his minions to pass before he pulled into the heavy traffic. He followed at a discrete distance until the road narrowed just before his primary exit.

Joseph thumbed the small switch he held in his hand. The lead suburban's engine blew. Civilian drivers slammed on brakes and people swerved to avoid the fireball. Unsuspecting motorists struggled to understand what was happening. A second push of the switch detonated the trail vehicle's explosive charge. The SUV flipped end over end landing in the path of oncoming traffic. Horrific grinding of metal against concrete filled the sudden silence following the detonation. The third push of the button triggered a carefully constructed and weighted charge under Morales' armored vehicle. Not enough to kill, but enough to incapacitate. The doors of the vehicle flailed open as the stunned guards stumbled out. Joseph hit the gas and came level with the disabled vehicle. His Uzi sub-machine gun palmed smoothly and the guards fell with a pull of the trigger.

Joseph dismounted the bike and stalked towards Morales, who'd exited and hobbled away from the vehicle when the gunfire started. The dazed man swayed. His wild eyes scanned the dead men surrounding him in the middle of the road. Blood ran from his nose and ears. The percussion of the explosion had done its job. Disbelief and shock crossed the face of the self-proclaimed king of Juarez's drug trade.

Joseph stopped five feet in front of the son of a bitch and lifted the visor of his helmet as he leveled the Uzi. The drug lord's eyes latched onto Joseph. Joseph saw when the man's mind finally understood what was going on. Looking down the barrel of a sub-machine gun can do that to a person. That type of visual tends to make things real clear, real quick.

"You went after my woman, amigo. You had the balls to send an assassin to kill my woman! Did you think that Spaniard could take me out? That bastard murdered my woman." Joseph heard the approaching sirens and sneered under the helmet. He kept his gun leveled on the man backing away as he shouted, "I will have revenge for her death. But your woman and your child will pay, not you. You take from me. I take from you. Guardian doesn't control me anymore, motherfucker. The wrath of Fury will rain down on you."

The squeal of tires from responding forces, either Morales' or the Mexican government's, signaled the imminent need to move. He mounted his bike and slammed forward through the rubble. His primary escape route remained uncompromised. Joseph glanced at the review mirror as he leaned down over the powerful motorcycle nailing the throttle wide open. Morales still stood in the middle of the road staring after him. Now the scene was set, the players were identified and shit was about to hit the fan. Bonus? He was still alive. So far… so good.

∾

JOSEPH CAREFULLY PARKED THE MOTORCYCLE HE HAD USED during this afternoon's op where it could be seen if someone was looking for it. The bike was bait. A green tarp positioned over it partially hid it from view. The kid he paid a hundred dollars US should have delivered the message to Morales' minions by now. The only wild card to be played was whether or not Morales himself would come. The profile Jared's intelligence section had built on the man suggested he would, but that remained to be seen.

A month ago, he had rented out five rooms in a hovel that called itself a hotel. Their position was in the northern most wing of the rattrap. Since that time, he had cut holes through the paper-thin sheetrock linking five rooms into one. Luring the cartel to the room he was supposed to be in would take two items, a lamp, and a fan. The light to show occupancy and a remote controlled electric fan directly in front of the curtain draped window to draw the asshole's attention. A John Doe corpse he'd liberated from the hospital morgue in a neighboring city and held on ice in the bathtub for the last week was defrosting on the bed. Mr. Chilly was wearing the leathers he had worn this afternoon and had some unique dental work recently installed. The bed his frigid friend occupied was rigged to blow along with a five hundred gallon propane tank that sat one hundred feet from the building. Bullets had a tricky way of ricocheting now didn't they?

At the end of the farthest room, he waited, careful to avoid the gasoline soaked bedding. He almost didn't see the black SUV creep up without its lights on. A second and then a third vehicle pulled in. Joseph watched from his sheltered position as the men deployed and formed a semi-circle around the front of the building. The back of the building abutted a ten-foot chain link fence topped with razor wire. Joseph double-checked the monitors he installed to ensure Morales hadn't staged any men along his escape route. He put on his tux jacket and adjusted his bow tie. He checked the documentation in his pocket. The wallet that linked the dead body with the cover he used as Fury stayed with Mr. Chilly in the decoy room. It would be protected from fire by a piece of foil from the staged food that Mr. Chilly would never eat.

One of Morales' men pulled the tarp off the motorcycle and gave a wave to the men in front of the room. Joseph drew a deep breath when Morales stepped to the front of the lead SUV. What he wouldn't give to slice the bastard's neck now. Stick to the fucking plan. He sneered as he hit the remote that activated the fan in front of the window. The sudden movement of the curtains propelled the militants into action. In unison, a barrage of bullets flew into the room shattering the glass and riddling the pressed paper walls. As the men advanced on the room, Joseph keyed the remote detonating the outside propane tank. The concussion of the blast sent the men flying. Joseph keyed the switch again and the far room erupted in flames and then exploded.

He put the remotes in his pocket and lifted himself out the back window, through the cut fencing, and darted across the highway. He keyed the remote again. The series of explosions would prevent any sign of his egress. He ran across a service road and vaulted over a small retaining wall. After dropping soundlessly onto the green carpet of a highly manicured lawn, he took a second to assess the devastation behind him. Fucking perfect. One dead assassin. Lots of dead bad guys.

Now for the PR blitz Gabriel would put into motion. His exit was Guardian's coming out party. The organization was taking its rightful place at the forefront of the war against evil on an international scale. He wiped down the remotes and tossed them into a garbage container beside the gardener's shack. Joseph insured the small smoking area was vacant before he emerged from the recesses of the back buildings. Pulling out a cigarette case, he placed several used butts around his feet and lit up a fresh one. He stretched his legs out in front of him when he sat down on the bench. The speeches for the awards ceremony being held at the small elegant hotel rumbled on in the background. He would wait until they broke and then leave with the rest of the crowd, an unseen addition to the multitude. No sense drawing attention to himself. Blend in, move out and move on.

"Hey, mind if I join you?" The woman's sultry voice carried over to him from the far side of the building. A willowy blonde wrapped in something pink and shiny glided across the cobblestones to the bench where he sat.

He measured her against his vivid memory of Ember. The blonde may have been pretty, but she couldn't hold a candle to his flame-haired beauty. "No, please feel free." A flurry of sirens blasted down the busy road behind the back wall.

"Thanks, I needed a break. Can you believe how dry and long winded those guys are?"

Joseph drew deeply on his cigarette before he offered the woman a light. "Yeah. Which one do you think was the worst?"

"Pfft... Carlson of course, he always is a blowhard. What, like this is the fourth year in a row he has won for top sales? But seriously, Howard is just as bad. Good thing his wife gave him the cut it off sign this year."

Joseph chuckled. "Same stuff, different year, huh?"

He felt the woman's eyes on him and leaned back. Turning his head towards her, he returned the stare.

"I don't remember seeing you at one of these award ceremonies before. I'm Mindy Cochran."

"Yeah, I recognize you. Leo Fallen. I was at Cancun and Progresso the year before that. I don't know why Clexis can't pick decent cities to have these recognition events in." Another fire truck screamed past the back wall of the hotel. "God, the sirens never stop around here, do they?"

The woman took a long drag off her cigarette. "Yeah, Juarez is a hole but it's an excellent base for manufacturing and the sales of Clexis' data processors has doubled in the last year."

Joseph shook his head. "Tripled and the projections are for another twelve plants in two years so we could see a six hundred percent increase if we can get in on the ground floor."

The woman relaxed, the facts he had gleaned off the Internet seemed to calm any suspicion she may have harbored. She ground the butt out near the ones he'd littered on the grass. She leaned forward and looked at him over her shoulder. "Cancun was alright. I missed Progresso. Had the flu. Hey, how about we get the hell out of here? I found this nice quiet jazz bar not too far away."

Bingo. An express ticket out. Standing he offered her his arm. "How did you know I wanted to escape? Let's go."

The whisper of cloth from his movement was indistinguishable from the sound of the fire crackling in the massive fireplace. Each inch moved him nearer to his last kill. As always, his mind quieted. He ghosted forward silently and positioned himself for it, his focus on nothing but a man—the target. He became the shadow on the wall and the darkness between the flames. For the last time, Joseph's mind slid into

Fury's and became death. His grip on the hilt of his steel had been diminished by the viscosity of the blood that had erupted from the severed arteries of Morales' guards. His heart tattooed a steady rhythm against his chest, now alive with purpose—kill the monster that had threatened Ember. His senses soared, heightened by the adrenaline thrumming through his veins. Morales sat in a large leather chair in front of the fireplace. The asshole swirled golden liquor in a crystal snifter. Joseph's hand covered the man's mouth. His arm extended with a quick snap and the blade lodged on the throat of the seated man. A quick pull and slice would silence the man forever.

Fury whispered into his ear and he sensed the man's terror. He knew this fear intimately. The mechanics of the kill were the same tonight as they were when he killed his father's murderer almost twenty years ago. Each kill since had brought the same disembodied precision and the same sense of purpose. The weight of the knife—his knife, lay perfect in his palm. The razor sharp blade sliced through the drug lord's skin. Muscle, tendons, and arteries severed. Although the men he had killed in this way did not articulate a sound, their body's give to the blade made its own concert. The snap and sluice of the tendon and muscle told him exactly what his blade accomplished. His signature kill with the knife couldn't be left. No, this kill was brutal and the man was obliterated. His body dismembered. No link to Fury would be found. Tonight the kill was personal. Tonight it ended as it started twenty years ago. Making things right for those he loved. Fury flipped the cover from the remote and toggled the switch. Now it was over.

An explosion ripped through the exclusive neighborhood. Windows shattered in houses three blocks away. Car and house alarms sounded, activated by the concussion of the massive detonation. The sky filled with black smoke and orange flames.

CHAPTER TWENTY-TWO

THE VIP LOUNGE AT ATLANTA'S HARTSFIELD-JACKSON INTERNATIONAL AIRPORT bustled with a never-ending stream of weary travelers. The third floor, mezzanine-level lounge acted as a blue and grey shield cocooning Ember from the hustle and bustle of the busy international terminal. For the first time in months, she sat in front of a television. The mindless drone of looped news somehow soothed her tattered nerves. Pulling her new smart phone out of her purse, Ember punched in the telephone number for the ranch. It was early yet on the East Coast, so maybe Keelee wouldn't have left the ranch house yet.

"Marshall Ranch." Keelee's normally sweet voice seemed flat and stressed.

"Hey. girl. What's wrong?" Ember almost wished she was back at the ranch.

"Em? Hey… nothing… everything. You know, crazy shit happens here. We have a blizzard forecasted and Clint is being… Clint. Where are you?"

"Atlanta airport. Waiting for a plane."

Keelee let out a long sigh. "Thank God. You're going."

"Yeah. Have you… have they heard anything? I mean, is there any more information?" Ember's eyes flooded again.

Damn tears. She was so tired of crying, but her heart and her mind kept shredding her pitiful attempts to be strong.

"Kinda. But I don't really think it's anything you want to know about."

"If it concerns Joey, I want to know. Please, Keelee… I need to know. I have to have some kind of closure."

"Okay. Just wait for a minute. I'm going to get out of the kitchen so I won't get interrupted."

Ember heard Keelee opening and closing doors and moving through the huge ranch house. Finally, she came back on the line.

"Okay. This is just from what I've overheard and what I've been told, alright? I mean, it's not anything official."

"Kee, please…"

"Okay. Jacob flew to Mexico and identified Joseph, but the news coverage that has been going non-stop used a different name. His alias maybe? Anyway, the guys here? They're all acting weird. I guess it's losing one of your own or something. They just stopped talking. Stopped. Dixon and Drake haven't said a word since they found out Joseph didn't make it out of Mexico. But before that I overheard something about Morales taking all the credit for killing Joseph and you."

Ember shifted in her seat and looked at the people around her for the first time. Hearing the man's name brought back the insane fear of being found again.

"I know Chief called and told you that Morales is dead. Chief said the man's home exploded. The reports say the generator for the house got too hot during an extended power outage and blew up. Evidently, the propane tank that powered it wasn't buried and blew through the room where the bastard and the majority of his security team were located. Dixon said it was an accident. I'm thinking God had enough of the demon and took vengeance."

"Morales is really dead? I'm free?"

"Yeah, sweetie, he's gone. Joseph didn't kill him, but three days after he was murdered by that sick son of a bitch, the universe got even." Ember flinched as if she'd been slapped. She knew Joey was dead, but hearing it said out loud hurt. God it hurt so bad. Keelee was still talking and Ember forced herself to tune back in.

"…but Adam said Morales thought you were dead. Killed by that guy that went after you at Joseph's place. So he said as long as you use the cover Guardian gave you… you're safe. The training annex shut down here at the ranch for the holidays. The Kings and some of the guys that are close to the brothers are getting together, for some sort of ceremony for Joseph. They haven't asked me how to reach you or even if you'd want to go. I'm really upset about that. They knew what you meant to Joseph… well at least Adam, Chief and Jacob knew."

"I wasn't married to him, Kee. I was a one-and-done as far as they know." Ember closed her eyes and thought back to when Joey had first used that term. Back when she'd offered…No. Stop torturing yourself. "I understand that they need to grieve. But could you do me a favor? When they come back to the ranch, would you find out where he's buried? Probably back home in Mississippi. I can't call Mrs. King. I just can't deal with her suffering, too. Someday soon, I'll call. But, not yet. I'll go and say goodbye myself after I get done with…" Tears ran down her cheeks unchecked. She didn't care who saw or what she looked like.

"Em, do you want me to come with you? I'll get the first flight out of Rapid. I can leave the Koehler's to mind the ranch for a couple days."

"Where's Frank?"

"He, Dixon, Drake, Chief and Doc are gone. The guys left for the ceremony I just told you about. Dad is meeting a lady friend. Said she was celebrating something and was going to be needing some help. He wasn't inclined to say more and I wasn't about to ask him about it. If he is interested in someone, then I'm damn sure happy to stay here and tend the ranch. But I can leave if you need me."

Ember shook her head. "No, stay at home. You said there was a blizzard coming. You'd be worried to death the entire time you were gone. The Koehler's aren't going to look after the place like you will. Besides… this is something I need to do. Something I want to do. I miss you, Kee."

"Aww sweetie, we can talk every night and you know what? I'm done with giving my life to the ranch. Told dad he needed to get a ranch manager and a couple more full time hands. I'm ready to stop living in the past. How about you get settled somewhere and then I come out and you and I can have a vacation? I've never been farther than Denver."

"I know that was a hard decision and I'd like that, Kee. I'll call you in a couple days. Okay?"

"You better. Love you, Em."

"Love you too, Kee." Ember hung up the phone and wiped at the tears. God, please give me the strength. I need to do this for him… for me… for us.

Ember waited in a daze of agony until her flight was called. She managed to walk through the crowded terminal and handed the attendant her ticket. The hustle and bustle of the thousands of people coming and going didn't even register. Her body functioned. Her mind worked on some level. But her reason for living lay broken into a million pieces. While everyone else jostled about doing their everyday business, she carefully cradled what remained of her soul and tried to piece her life back together.

Once seated in first class, she turned to gaze out the window and focused beyond the tarmac. Joey was dead. She'd known it in her soul as soon as Chief held out the document pouch to her.

"It came with instructions to give it to you, today, if I didn't get a phone call by 5:00 pm. I think it may be from Joseph." The big man's soft words sent a tremor through her.

Ember sat down, her legs suddenly too weak to hold her up. Her eyes traveled from the packet to Chief. "Is it over?"

"Yeah, Ember. You're free to go. The call I received from Guardian this afternoon confirmed the mission was complete. Joseph left instructions. If I didn't get that call, he asked that I deliver this to you when it was… done."

"Joey?"

"I don't know. I haven't received any official confirmation."

"Official?"

Chief took three steps across the room and squatted down in front of her. His hand gently placed the large envelope on her lap. "Ember, he wouldn't have let me give this to you if he was alive. I know you plan on bolting out of here. Do me a favor? Read what is in here. Let me know what you want to do and I'll make sure it happens."

Ember raised her eyes from the yellow envelope on her lap to Chief's kind brown eyes. "What's in here?"

"I don't know. The letter I received thanked me for watching you and asked me to keep an eye on you if you stayed at the ranch. Obviously, he couldn't have known you've been packed and ready to go." Chief stood and put a large warm hand on her shoulder. "He loved you, Ember."

Hot tears rolled freely down her cheeks. She nodded but couldn't speak. The echo of his boots over the clinic floor as he left reminded her of the raw emptiness in her life.

Her fingers plucked at the corner of the envelope. She didn't want to open it. A humorless huff pushed from her lips. As if not opening it would change anything. Carefully, she pulled the tab and unsealed the contents.

JOSEPH · 229

A long envelope fell out followed by a dark blue folder and a small packet. The envelope had her name scrawled across the front. She recognized Joey's horrible handwriting. A small smile pulled at the edge of her mouth. With care, she opened the letter from the end not wanting to damage the handwriting. A keepsake of her lover.

She unfolded the letter, handwritten on a yellow legal pad. Tears pooled in her eyes blurring the writing. She swiped impatiently at her eyes and focused on his words.

Em,

I told you once I couldn't give you the moon and stars, but I find I want to try. In this envelope is a key to the house I own in Aruba. It overlooks the beach. Standing on the balcony at night, the stars are so bright and so brilliant that you feel you can almost touch heaven. I can't look at the night sky without thinking of you, of us, and of our love. Would you do me a favor, little one? Go to Aruba, to the home I dreamed we could share. I've taken several liberties, but I hope you will allow me to show you how much our love means to me. The packet contains the financial documentation giving you the home and access to a bank account. Please take both. Remember, little girl, though I cannot be with you, I still expect you to follow my directions. You have always made me so proud of you. I love you more than I could ever hope to express. Please go to Aruba, baby girl. See the stars from the balcony of our home and know I will always love you.

Joey

The letter lay in her hand as the plane took off on a four-hour flight to Aruba. She would go and look at the moon and stars and she would say her final goodbye. There were no more tears to shed, her mind and body numb with grief.

The flight attendant's announcement crackled overhead. Ember closed her eyes, blocking out the mundane announcements. One last thing to do before she could start to piece her life back together.

.

CHAPTER TWENTY-THREE

EMBER PAID THE CAB DRIVER AND THEN TURNED back to look at the impressive villa he'd dropped her at. Twice she clarified the mansion was the correct address. The red Spanish tile roof topped the white stucco finish of a facade bordered by perfectly manicured greenery. A grand stairway of granite led up to a double oak and glass door boasting ornate iron scrolls throughout the wall of windows on either side of the door. Ember put the key Joey had left her into the lock and sighed, closing her eyes momentarily when the tumbler turned. She pushed the door open. Joey's home sprawled in its reserved splendor in front of her. The character of the home was so like the man it brought instant tears to her eyes. The white marble floor flowed throughout the great room first floor. The furnishings of oversized couches covered in soft brown leather reminded her of the furniture in his Wyoming cabin. The fireplace mantel boasted a massive painting of a brilliant blue ocean hosting a gala of brightly colored boats. Splashes of the same bright colors were used as an accent in the formal dining room and in the obscenely large kitchen. The home's open concept allowed for an unobstructed view of the pounding surf from every room.

"Excuse me, Miss?"

Ember jumped and screamed. Her hand flew up to her chest. The small woman wearing a maid's uniform held up a hand. "I'm so sorry, Miss! Forgive me, please. We expected you later. Your flight must have come in early."

Ember sucked in a lungful of air. Her knees shook as adrenaline from the shock pounded through her system. "You're expecting me? I… I wasn't expecting you!"

The little woman smiled. Creases in her face bunched around her eyes and mouth. "Oh Miss, didn't Mr. King tell you?"

That statement knotted Ember's gut, pulling hard against her barely existent emotional control. "Ah…no. No, he didn't."

"That's okay. Mr. King gave us explicit instructions, Miss. I am Consuela, your maid, and cook. My husband, Jose, he is the gardener, handyman, and chauffeur. He is not here right now, but he will return soon."

"Wait. You work here? For me?" Ember had planned on staying long enough to see the stars and leave. She had booked a hotel for one night and had a purchased a return ticket for tomorrow. Joey had provided a one-way ticket in the packet Chief had given her.

"Why yes, of course, Miss. Please, follow me to your room. I have everything arranged just as Mr. King directed."

Ember fell behind the little woman and then stopped. "No, wait. I'm not staying here. I have reservations at a hotel in Oranjestad."

The tiny woman stopped and cocked her head at Ember. The smile on her face was nothing less than angelic. "You have had a long day, have you not? Why don't you take a nice relaxing bath? Everything is arranged just as Mr. King directed. Oranjestad? Too many tourists, too much noise and traffic. Not what is needed for you tonight."

Ember shook her head. "I don't think so. I came here to

look at the stars from the balcony. I'll leave after that."

Consuela looked at her and blinked rapidly as if what Ember said didn't compute. "Yes, Miss, the balcony is upstairs off the Master's bedroom. That's where I'm taking you."

"Oh. Alright, lead the way."

The older woman beamed at Ember. "Yes, Miss, please this way?"

Ember followed the diminutive woman up a wrought iron stairway to the second story. The woman led her down a protracted travertine hallway to the only door on the right-hand side. The maid smiled and curtsied. "Here you are, Miss. If you have a need of me, please dial two on the phone."

Ember's brow creased as she watched the elfin-like woman walk away. A tendril of distrust ignited into a small flame. Something didn't feel right. Tentatively, Ember opened the door and peeked into the bedroom. The entire beach side view of the second floor opened to the panoramic vista. A king sized bed faced the majestic seascape but was dwarfed by the vista of nature heralded through the vast expanse of open balcony. The sea breeze pushed white silk curtains to and fro gently. Gossamer canopy fabric stirred against the bulky wooden bed frame. Ember walked as if in a trance across the room and directly out onto the balcony. The expanse of royal blue ocean kissed soft puffs of white clouds and hypnotized with its beauty.

The sound of voices pulled her eyes away from the panorama. A white arch and seats in rows had been erected on the beach past the mansion's pool on the white sand beach. Ember held onto the banister and swung out looking to the right. A few men walked towards the far end of the estate. Another massive house stood next to Joseph's. Someone was planning a wedding. She closed her eyes, took a deep breath and willed the thoughts of her loss to the back of her mind.

She cautioned herself, "Tonight. Just make it through this evening."

The sea breeze swirled around her. A small whiff of a familiar scent popped her eyes open. She tensed immediately and then crumpled. It was his bedroom. Of course, it would smell like him. If she didn't turn around she wouldn't have to admit he wasn't really here. She could pretend, just for tonight.

"Oh, Joey. I miss you so damn much." Ember's words could barely carry the weight of her loss.

"I missed you too, baby birl."

Ember twisted violently at the shock of the spoken words. He stood at the edge of the bedroom. Grasping the balcony's top rail to keep on her feet, Ember couldn't move. She couldn't breathe. She couldn't think. "How? What?"

Joey walked out of the room and dropped to his knee. Holding a ring in his hand, he looked up at her and smiled. "We're free. Will you marry me?"

Her non-stop emotional roller coaster sent her on a final loop she couldn't keep up with. Black swirled before her eyes and the world shifted radically.

JOSEPH LURCHED FORWARD AND CAUGHT EMBER AS SHE fainted. He lifted her into his arms and carried her to their bed. Great fucking work, King, save her life, then shock her to death. Her freckles stood in sharp relief due to the pallor of her skin. The dark circles under her eyes tore at his gut. He'd wanted to go to her, to contact her, but they had to be sure neither he, nor she, was followed or targeted. Guardian had provided surveillance from the second she left the ranch. Fury's demise had shocked the international community and several deep probes had attempted to disprove his death. None had succeeded. He was free to be Joseph King. Whoever the hell that was.

He laid her down carefully and checked her pulse. It beat strong and true. Color slowly crept back into her features. He bolted into the bathroom and dampened a washcloth. Returning to the bed, he sat down beside her and gently stroked her face with the cool rag.

Ember woke in stages. The fluttering of her eyes under her eyelids and a quickening in her breathing signaled her return. A slight roll of her head and a deep breath preceded what he knew to be her mind finally engaging. He moved aside quickly when she bolted upright, almost colliding with him. He grabbed her arms and pulled her to him. "It's all right, little one. I'm here. I have you. We're safe."

Her body shook violently in his arms. Her hands lifted and she cautiously touched his shoulders. A muffled sob against his chest preceded her vicelike grip around his neck. Pulling her long legs across his lap, he stroked her hair and rocked her while she cried.

Ember pulled away from him. She knelt on the bed and touched his face. "You're alive? You're really alive?"

Joseph nodded right before a punch caught his chin and twisted his head violently.

"You Prick! You're alive! You sadistic son of a bitch! You're alive and you didn't tell me! I thought you were dead! How dare you? Of all the vile, demented….bullshit things to do! The whole world thinks you're dead!" She pushed away from him as she spit the accusations.

Okay, you deserved that one King. Joseph slowly brought his face back around to the front of his body. He moved his chin carefully. Damn, she packs a punch.

She doubled up again and reared back. "How could you!"

He blocked her next attempt at smacking him into next week. Joseph grabbed both her hands pulling them together, holding her immobile. He put his face directly in front of hers and forced her to look at him. "Em, think about what you just said. The entire world thinks Fury is dead. Fury. Is. Dead."

"No, you're not! You're right here! You're alive and I'm so damn mad at you!" Her struggle to free herself from his grasp continued.

He grabbed her chin with his free hand and held it in what had to be a painful grip. "Ember Lyn Harris, damn it, shut up for two seconds and listen to me! The assassin, Fury, is dead. I'm not him any longer." His shouted words shocked her into stillness.

He watched as the realization of what he said sunk in. Ember shrieked and launched from her knees forward pinning him beneath her body raining kisses down on his face. Laughing at her, he pulled her down to him and rolled over trapping her against the bed.

"So how about it?"

Ember stroked the chin she had punched moments before. Her eyes locked with his and the depth of her emotion hit him harder than her doubled up fist ever could.

"How about what?" Her cheeks were flushed. When she licked her lips and pulled the bottom one in between her teeth, his hips punched forward automatically.

"Will you marry me tonight?"

"Tonight?" He loved it when her voice squeaked with surprise like that.

"Tonight. The whole family is here. You actually flew in with Jasmine and Jade. They said you didn't seem to notice them."

"I did? They're here? All of them?"

"Not here. They are staying at a resort in Orjanstad. I thought we might need our privacy." Joseph dropped his eyes to her mouth. He slowly pressed his lips against hers and licked his way inside her delicious mouth. The fresh, clean taste and scent of his woman combined to wreck his carefully prepared agenda. With the last of his resolve, he lifted away.

"It was a test of sorts. If their travel incited any chatter in the community, I wouldn't have been able to reveal myself to you. There was zero interest. We are free, baby girl. Now are you going to make me ask you again?"

Her eyebrow arched ever so slightly. "Maybe. I'm still mad at you."

He lowered again and pressed into his kiss driving his tongue into her, forcing her surrender. When she mewled, he ran his hand down her side tucking it under her ass squeezing the soft globe. "You can be mad at me. Mad sex with you would be awesome, but you still have to marry me."

Her swift intake of breath and hips grinding against his cock notched his need up into the stratosphere. "You want me, Ember?"

He watched the flush of red overtake her chest, neck, and face. His grip tightened and he pulled her closer grinding into her. Her breathless "Yes" drifted to him.

"Tell me you'll marry me, and I'll make love to you." He nipped the creamy white skin exposed at her neckline.

"That's blackmail!" Her accusation lost all credibility when she ground against his cock and groaned.

"True." Joseph rolled her on top of him. He grabbed both cheeks bringing her legs as far as her tight skirt would allow on either side of him and pumped up against her core. "Give me my ransom, wench."

Ember threw her head back and laughed. The happiness in her expression and the sound of joy in her laughter made all the sacrifices of the last six months worth the price.

"Alright, I'll pay your ransom. Tonight. I'll marry you."

Joseph pitched to the right and dumped her onto the bed lurching towards the balcony. "Joey! What the...? Where are you going?"

He stopped and bent down picking up her engagement ring where it had dropped when he caught her. The three-and-a-half carat, marquise-cut diamond winked at him in last rays of the setting sun. He smiled at the woman sprawled across the bed. "Don't worry, little one, I'm never leaving you again. But I will require you to display my ownership." He held her gaze with his as he stalked back ready to brand her as his possession. "Since I'm technically out of the assassination business, I had to figure out how to ensure every male on the planet knew you were mine." Slipping the ring on her finger, he kissed it before he slid his arm around her waist and lifted her from the bed.

Joseph walked to the center of the room and let her feet touch the floor. Stepping away from her, he held up a hand when she made a move to follow. "No." He backed away until his legs touched a big, wing-backed chair. He sat down and made a motion with his hand indicating she should turn around in a circle. Ember's blush spread instant and deep, but she complied. Her white button down was tucked into one of those skirts that fit her like a second skin all the way down to where it flared at her knees. Her stiletto heels had that little strap around the ankle. Fuck me now… oh hell yeah, the shoes are staying.

"Take off your clothes, Em. Slowly."

"But Joey…"

He cut her off before she could finish. "No. Do exactly as I say, little one. Take it off. Slowly. The shoes stay on." Damn he loved those spiky heels. Fucking sexy.

Ember looked down at her feet and back at him. He saw the minute understanding hit her. And damn it all if she didn't turn the tables on him. Her hand caressed the line of buttons on her shirt traveling up and down between her breasts before she pulled it out of the waistband of her tight black skirt. She slid her gaze to him when she licked her lips and unbuttoned the small pearl buttons one at a time, deliberately prolonging the process.

Ember let the material of her shirt float off her shoulders while still keeping her arms in the sleeves. Her hands moved around her waistline and then back up to her white lace bra. She ran her hands over her breasts and gasped when she pinched the nipples of both. Joseph's cock raged against the material of his slacks. Fuuuck. When did he lose control? Her skirt whispered to the floor and lay draped over her shoes. Those fuck-me-now shoes added just a little something to her already perfect ass. Damned if he'd ever let her out of the house wearing them.

She stepped out of the material and dropped her arms allowing the shirt to flutter to the floor. Ember's fingers traced the top of her white lace panties. Joseph shifted uncomfortably in the chair.

"Stop. I want you to put your hands behind your back." She didn't hesitate to pull her arms behind her. Her breasts pushed forward and her breathing sped up.

"That's it. Now spread your legs." She sidestepped a couple inches.

"Uh huh, baby girl. Expose yourself to me. Give me access." Joseph lifted from the chair and nearly groaned at the pain of his erection.

Several small steps split her legs, openly displaying her lace-covered sex. Her pupils were blown wide. "Did you enjoy your tease? Just remember little girls who play with fire usually get burned." Joseph lowered his lips to her neck and was rewarded with a shiver.

He licked her skin and growled his appreciation, "Fuck, I missed you."

"Joey, please let me touch you. It's been so long." Her breath fanned his hot skin.

"Soon, little one. Right now, I'm marking you. Staking my claim. Collecting my ransom. Make me proud of you, little girl. Hold still." In between each statement he licked, kissed and nipped down her chest to the top of her bra. Lifting her breasts out of the cups, he held one in each hand and used his thumbs to tease those rose colored nubs. Joseph lost himself feasting on her luscious soft skin. She pulled away from him when the sensations became too much. His growl and bite on her nipple froze her backward retreat. He knew how much to push her before the pain overtook the pleasure and he'd be damned if anything was going to stop him from placing her right on that razor sharp edge.

Her small plea and moan followed him further down her body until he ended on his knees in front of her sex. He hooked a finger around the tiny wisp of lace and yanked. The fabric rent and fell from one leg, exposing her weeping sex. The heady smell of her arousal drove into his brain compelling him to delve into her sweetness. His arms snaked through her legs allowing him to capture her ass in his hands. Her body sandwiched between his mouth and hands he dove into her folds forgoing any pretense of gentleness.

Her cry echoed in his ears as his lips and tongue pulled her clit into his mouth. His tongue lapped at her center, alternating between suckling her clit and tongue-fucking her sex. Her body tensed and her hands dropped to his shoulders as she convulsed around the ferocious mating of his mouth to her sex. He inhaled her essence when she shattered around him and in his aggression, Joseph bit down on the swollen bud of her sex sending another wave of cream onto his waiting tongue.

He allowed her body to fold down against his and took her mouth still crazed in his need. In the work of a second, he had her back on the bed and his clothes on the floor. Her beautiful porcelain skin held his vivid red love bites from her nipples to her sex. Oh, fuck yeah she belonged to him!

Lifting her leg, he placed her heeled foot on his hip and pushed forward spreading her open. He locked his stare on her as he centered at her core. "Mine." The word snapped from him a split second before he struck forward impaling himself deep within her. His mouth covered hers, trapping her cries. Oh, fuck, those sounds. The small gasps and cries he controlled added layers of euphoric lust to his need. He had to move. The white-hot magma pooling at the base of his spine screamed for release and he was damn well going to take it. The pull of her body when he retreated, coupled with the resistance when he slammed forward, catapulted him towards his finish. He lost any rational thought. His only need—to make this woman his, drove him relentlessly. Her body tightened under him and her nails raked his scarred back sending a delicious stream of pain through him. His orgasm ripped down his spine and burst from him. He shattered, driving his cock as deep inside of her as he physically could go. He released a guttural roar when a second wave crashed through him.

Joseph's arms shook with the effort it took to keep from falling on top of her. Both of them panted desperately for air. He lowered his head to her shoulder and kissed her soft skin just under the collarbone. "I love you."

Her soft chuckle under him brought his head up. Her satisfied smile, flushed relaxed face and closed eyes, defined sexual contentment. Absolutely beautiful and mine.

She slid her hand down his back. His muscles reacted to her caress trembling in the wake of her light touch.

"I love you too, Joey. Promise me you'll keep us safe and together. Forever."

He pushed the mass of red curls off her face and kissed her freckled nose. "I have every intention of doing just that, little girl."

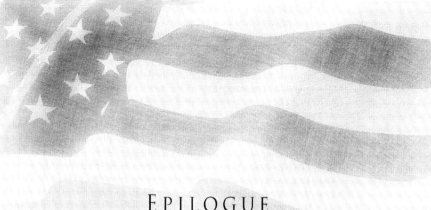

EPILOGUE

ADAM SAT BESIDE THE POOL AND WATCHED THE family celebrate Joseph and Ember's wedding. Leave it to the assassin to A: be alive when everyone thought he had bought it and B: to have a surprise wedding and not a funeral. On the beach. At midnight. In Aruba. Seemed the family knew he was alive, but all being in the business, no one had leaked a damn thing. If the community didn't think Fury was dead, Joseph wouldn't be able to resume his life. The body that charred in the flames of the explosion in Mexico had fooled everyone. Thanks to a couple donated teeth from Joseph, some really impressive dental work and planted x-rays, the local coroner and at least three independent examiners for various governmental agencies had confirmed the assassin Fury was dead.

He smiled at Ember's joyful laugh. Keelee would've loved to have been here for this. If he'd known, he would have used a pry bar to get her off that damn ranch. His mind wandered back to South Dakota. He wondered what Keelee was doing right now. Looking at his watch, he laughed quietly. It's two in the morning. She's sleeping you fool.

A motion to his left brought his head around so he could see with his good eye. Jacob hit his shoulder and smiled handing him a fresh glass of whiskey. "How the hell you been, Doc?"

"Getting better, Skipper. Got the speech problem fixed. Working on the memory."

"Chief tells me you been working out with the teams we're running through the training facility."

"Yeah, feeling better than I have in a long time."

"Glad to hear it. Have you remembered anything?" Jacob stretched his legs out on the pool chair.

"I have nightmares of the mission. Everything else? Impressions really. Kind of like a ghost of a memory but not enough to say, 'Yeah, I remember that.'"

Adam cast a look toward Jacob's wife. Tori and Keelee could be mistaken as twins, not just sisters. Except Tori almost always looked like she had just walked off a fashion runway. Adam preferred the simple beauty Keelee possessed.

As if aware of eyes on her, Tori turned and looked at both men, her baby bump very prominent. Adam chuckled, "Oh and, by the way, congratulations on child number two, dad. When is she due?"

Jacob's eyes devoured his wife as he spoke. "Not for four more months. Twins this time. Two more boys."

Adam laughed. "Serves you right Skipper. Three boys? Damn."

"Yeah, I'm one virile son of a bitch, ain't I?" Pride dripped from his boasting statement.

"That you are, Skipper. That you are. What are you naming them?"

"Keeping the T's going. Talon will be a big brother for Trace and Tanner."

"Damn solid names, Skip." Adam chuckled and sipped his drink. The King tradition of naming all the children starting with a particular letter of the alphabet amused him.

Across the pool, Joseph pulled Ember from the laughing crowd of family and into his arms. Music filled the air as he spun the woman away from the crowd and pulled his wife into him looking at her as if she were the only other person in the world.

"I never thought I would see the day." Jacob's voice filled with emotion.

"They both deserve some happiness. What is he going to do now?"

Jacob lifted a finger and motioned toward his brothers, Justin and Jason, who sat on the other side of the pool visiting. "He's funding two new businesses for Justin. After that? Who knows with him? He has enough money to live this way for the rest of his life."

Adam nodded. "Yeah, thanks to Gabriel, money has never been a worry for any of us."

"Really? Are you telling me I need to adjust my pay scale?" Gabriel's voice came from behind the two men.

Doc twisted looking back before he lifted off his chair and shook Gabriel's hand. Jacob stood too and offered his hand.

"No, sir. I'm pretty sure nobody here would be happy with me if I suggested that."

"Damn, it's good to hear you talking without that hesitation anymore." Gabriel slapped him on the shoulder and gripped it in a warm hold.

"Thank you, sir. I appreciate you hiring Ember so I could work on my health. I've bulked back up and my cardio is probably better than it ever has been."

"Not saying much there, dude. You could never outrun me or the wonder twins over there." Jacob's taunt brought a wave of laughter.

Adam looked over at the twins who were talking to Jasmine and Jade. "True, Skipper, but you were usually chasing them because they pissed you off."

"Yeah, and if they keep hitting on my sisters, they may be running again." Jacob's growl earned a laugh from Gabriel.

"What about your memory?" Gabriel nodded at Jason, who walked up to the group.

"A work in progress." Doc moved over allowing Jason into the conversation.

A wicked scar on Jason's lower neck slashed a violent purple against his skin. Doc extended a handshake. "How are you doing? I'm sorry I missed you at Talon's christening. I wasn't quite ready to take on a crowd."

Jason dropped his hand and looked at his shoes for a moment before his eyes rose directly to Adam's. "I'm ultimately the reason for your injuries. If my team hadn't been ambushed and captured, you never would have had to go through any of this. I know it doesn't mean shit, but if there was anything I could do to change what happened, the pain you endured…just know I would do it." Jason's voice had changed, no longer the smooth baritone of all the King men. His voice had deepened and carried a gravel none of the other brothers possessed. The fucking garrote tied around his neck while he was held captive was probably to blame.

"You didn't cause my injuries. The fuckers who beat the shit out of me caused them. I'm not looking to point a finger of blame. Never have been. If you are trying to shoulder it, then you need to drop that burden, man. The fact is, we work in a dangerous world. We all know the risks and we go into every mission with our eyes wide open. I'm in a good place."

Jason stared at Doc as if trying to determine if Doc was being up front with him. Finally, he nodded. "Good enough."

"Well damned glad you two had your moment. Now that the past is firmly in the past what do you two have planned? I got Jacob's and Jared's life scheduled for the next twenty-five years, but you two are wild cards. I don't like wild cards." Gabriel's question caused a momentary pause as the two men looked at each other.

Jason chuckled and clapped his brother Jacob on the shoulder hard enough to send him two steps forward. All the Kings were brutes, but Jason was so fucking bulked with muscles he could compete for Mr. Universe. Doc knew the hours of dedicated training it took to get that big. A hell of a lot more time than he was willing to devote.

"I'm hanging in Mississippi. I have a good practice now. I'm working contracts for some new talent in Nashville. I have a small clientele list, to include you and your family. Couple that with playing flying taxi for select personnel and that is enough to keep me busy, but not enough to stress me out. Too much." Jason winked at Gabriel and drew a deep breath before adding, "And I'm focusing on staying sober."

Doc got it. Hell, he'd bet they all got it. The man had been through the ringer. His prescription pain medication addiction had almost cost him everything. Yeah, staying in control of what happens in your life… well damn, didn't they all strive for that?

Jason lifted his soda can and pointed to Doc. "What about you?"

"I'm sure as hell not fit for the field. I'll probably head back to the ranch after the holidays. There is no one in training now. No need for me to be hanging around up there. Figure I'll find a beach and get a tan until training starts back up."

Jacob turned on his heel and gawked at him. "Excuse me? What the fuck do you call Keelee? That girl, son… is a reason."

A surge of pissed-off pumped through him. "I don't call her a reason to go back. She has a boyfriend. A rancher."

Jacob threw back his head and laughed drawing everyone's attention. "Doc, pull your head out of your ass. She's only dating

Clint because no one else is paying her any attention. Frank told me he thinks the moron is after the ranch, and she knows it. You know you're my best friend, but damn it, man, you're blind in both fucking eyes, not just the one with a patch over it."

Joseph, Ember, and Tori walked up as Jacob ranted.

"That's true you know, Adam." Ember's soft voice soothed some of the sting from Jacob's retort.

Tori agreed before she added, "My sister has been gone on you since the two of you stayed at the line cabin. You hurt her. I don't know what you said. She'd never tell me. Only that you didn't want her."

"But she was sick! For God's sake, I told her we couldn't. How the hell was I supposed to…"

Doc staggered and sat down hard on the chair dropping the glass in his hand. It shattered, but nobody noticed. Nobody moved. He held his hands in front of him both shook uncontrollably. Memories collided violently filling the void that had followed him relentlessly. He knew… everything. He remembered it all, the mission, the ranch, the move of the cattle down to lower pastures.

He lifted his eyes to Ember and whispered, "Oh, fuck. I remember. She was so weak and sick. I couldn't take advantage of her. Then I… oh God…"

~ The End~

About the Author

USA Today and Amazon Bestselling Author, Kris Michaels is the alter ego of a happily married wife and mother. She writes romance, usually with characters from military and law enforcement backgrounds.

Kris was born and raised in South Dakota. She graduated many years ago from a high school class consisting of 13 students (yes that is thirteen, eleven girls and two boys… lucky boys). She joined the military, met her husband, and traveled the world. Today she lives on the Gulf Coast and writes full time.

Kris is an avid people watcher and dreamer. The stories she writes are crafted around the hopes and dreams of a true romantic. She believes love is essential, people are beautiful, and everyone deserves a happy ending.

When she isn't writing Kris enjoys a full life revolving around family, friends, laughing, whiskey, and cold red wine. (Yes cold… don't judge.)

Email: krismichaelsauthor@gmail.com
Website: www.krismichaelsauthor.com

Manufactured by Amazon.ca
Bolton, ON